Books by Karen Salamone-Jourdan

Gabriel's Gate

Redemption

Acknowledgments

First, my love and gratitude to my family, Kelly, Katie and Nancy, for their unending patience with me.

Second, to my editor and friend, Pam Nankin, for her invaluable assistance and encouragement.

Third, to my faithful readers. It's you whom I write for, and your love and support mean everything to me.

And last but not least, to my publisher with True Beginnings Publishing and Selina in particular. You're a gem, Selina, and you never disappoint.

House On Ransom Road

Karen Salamone-Jourdan

Published by True Beginnings Publishing.

Ordering Information:
To order additional copies of this book, please visit Amazon, or:
https://www.createspace.com/5627701

ISBN-13: 978-0692494738
ISBN-10: 0692494731

*To mom and dad
I love you and miss you.*

Prologue

He waited. Basking in his success. Such a simple thing, really. A little tweak here, a little tweak there, a few nails, and the house would go up in all that beautiful fire. Just took some ingenuity and a little luck.

He would wait though. The old man and his witch of a wife were resourceful. He would make sure they stayed put while the flames licked all around them.

Soon, very soon, he would have control of this farm and all that lovely money. Maybe, he would build his own house on the ashes. That would be fitting.

He had put up with a lot to get this far and this family owed him. Oh yeah, he thought, they owed him big time.

Of course, there was always a fly in the ointment. This particular fly would be the old couple's only daughter. He had had to put up with a lot from that little bitch, too. In the long run, now that is plan was in motion, it would all be worth it.

Through their daughter, all the property, the horses and all of that glorious money would come to him.

Years in the planning, brilliant in the execution, his plan is foolproof.

Thinking of the daughter, his face became grim.

She is weak, he mused. She depended on him. That was good. Eventually, though, she would have to go, and her two useless daughters with her.

Eventually, they would join the old man and his witchy wife.

He could hear the couple screaming at the top of their lungs.

"Good,"he muttered. Keep sucking in that smoke. Speed things along a little."

He knew, staying here, he risked all of his plans, but it could not be helped. One little slip and everything could go up in smoke, so to speak. A grim laugh escaped his lips at his own macabre joke.

The delay was justified in short order. A chair came bounding out of the master bedroom window. Smoke followed. The old man's face popped out of the broken window, followed by his panicked wife's face.

He congratulated himself for sharp thinking. He brought his gun, just in case. Casually, he removed the gun from his back holster and fired two warning shots and the couple darted back into their smoke-filled bedroom.

"You son-of-a-bitch,"the old man screamed down daring to peer out again.

"It's gonna take you that much longer to die, you old bastard. Die you will, though!"

It struck him that if he left now, there would be a slim chance they could survive. The old man proved himself resourceful. No, better to wait and hope help did not come too soon.

If they survived, prison would be on his horizon. He did not think he would do well in prison. Prison would not suit his tastes; therefore, prison simply was not an option.

For a split second, he considered running into the burning building and finishing the job. As fast as the thought came into his mind, he discarded it. What if he did not get out in time? No, better to just wait and see.

A thunderous explosion almost knocked him off his feet as the flames found the gas lines and worked their merry way to the source. There was no way the couple would have survived that blast. Just no way in hell.

Time to go. He had waited almost too long.

Taking one last satisfied look at the inferno, he climbed into his vehicle, rolled down his window, and listened. No screams emanated over the roar of the flames.

This part of the plan was over. Now, he had to get back to his present flavor of the month and ensure his alibi was still intact.

If the twit had awaken during the time he was gone, it could make things awkward, to say the least.

Laughing, more than pleased with himself, he put his Jeep in gear and headed down the old hunting trail and into the woods.

He knew the trail would take him straight out to the highway. How ironic, he thought, the old man never figured his hunting trail could be used for a purpose such as this.

He took one final look through his rear-view mirror and laughed again.

It was more than satisfaction coursing through him, watching the house burn. It was the knowledge he would soon come into a pile of money. Money he earned, putting up with the whole damn family for all these years.

He would need to think of something equally spectacular to rid himself of their whiney, miserable daughter and her two brats, but it would come.

For the time being, he was satisfied. Mission accomplished, he thought as he turned onto the main highway and deadheaded it back to his mistress' apartment.

Oh yeah, mission accomplished.

One

August in Wisconsin can be capricious at best. One day can be cool with a hint of fall in the air and the next could be hotter than hell. Toss in high humidity and the hot days were miserable.

Of course, the day Jillian Tolivar decided to drive to Molton, Wisconsin just *had* to be hot and humid.

The air hung heavy, like a wet wool blanket. She knew she could not have picked a lousier day to make the two hour drive, and just in case she forgot, her two daughters, ten-year-old Breana and six-year-old Megan had no problem reminding her. Then, of course, to add to the problem, the air conditioner in her aging SUV decided that today of all days, it would quit working, adding to the discomfort of the trip.

The only one happy was Charlie, their three year old Shih Tzu. Any day he could go for a ride was a good day and his little doggie heart was thrilled.

"*Moooom*,"Megan wailed, Bree's touching me!"

"Am not," came the quick reply followed by a muffled slap. Megan began to cry, pitifully.

Jill was not amused. She happened to glimpse into the back seat with the help of her rear view mirror. Megan slapped herself after giving her sister an evil grin.

Jill pulled the car to the side of the road, flipped on the four-ways, and turned to glare at her younger daughter.

"That will be about enough, young lady! Bree did not slap you! You slapped yourself! Now, if you two can find it in your hearts to behave, we'll stop for ice cream on the way home. If there is any more problems coming from either of you, not only will there be no ice cream, you will also lose your one hour of television and/or video games. You will lose them for an entire week. Do you understand me?"

The girls nodded, they could tell she was serious. Her eyes flashed sparks and experience taught them whenever that happened, she was not kidding around.

"Fine, now let's try to get along. We could play a game the rest of the way to Molton."

"What sort of game?" Bree wanted to know.

"We are going to see who can sit the quietest for the longest. We'll pretend we are in a forest and an evil witch is searching for us," she paused. "But she'll need a name. What shall her name be?"

"Diana!" both girls blurted out. Jill stifled a grin. Diana happened to be the name of her ex-husband's latest flame and the girls hated her.

"We can't call her that. It's not nice," Jill said.

"Diana's not nice, either," Bree told her.

Jill saw the dangerous look come back into her eldest daughter's eyes and sighed. If she wanted a little peace and quiet, she would have to go along.

"Okay, Diana it is. Now remember, not a peep. She will be looking for us. Oh! Besides having to keep quiet, you have to count all of the brown cows we see. The brown cows we count will keep us safe and hidden from her."

She dug into her purse and found two notebooks and a couple of pens.

"Use this to keep track. When we get to Molton, we'll see who counted the most. Bree, you can count them on our side of the car and Megan, you count them on her side of the car. Okay?"

Occupied with the impromptu game, the girls were quiet.

Opening the windows in the rear for a little more air, she moved back into traffic, carefully checking that the lane was clear. She had precious cargo with her.

Jill organized her thoughts. She and the girls had been looking at houses for weeks. Her divorce was final, and Judge Pamela Napier had given her everything she wanted.

Noah, her ex-husband, had gone too far. The pictures taken at the hospital had helped to put her in the driver's seat.

Jill remembered, although she would rather have forgotten, how Noah reacted when Judge Marcus Brentwood read her parents' will.

She was still reeling from the double loss, and Noah had stuck close to her. It didn't fool her. Jill was fully aware just why Noah had been attentive. He couldn't wait to get his hands on the money he was sure would be coming his way. He had been wrong.

Finding out the provisions in the will made him lose control. The money would be held in trust for the girls. Jill would get nothing.

She knew about the provision and knew the reasons for it. Jill, had in fact, had been in complete agreement. Noah would not benefit from her parents' deaths.

He beat her that night, breaking her arm, cracking ribs and injuring her hip. The physical damage healed and thanks to expert counseling, the psychological wounds would heal over time.

Jill learned some valuable lessons during her recovery. The most important lesson was never give up.

Noah was a lying, cheating, womanizing, manipulator, she thought, and those were his good points.

He hadn't won, though. She beat him and that made Jill feel great about herself.

Jillian knew she had many blessings. She had Judge Marcus Brentwood and his chic wife, Lavinia in her corner. She also had their son, Devin and his beautiful wife, Trudy as well.

Then, there was Ben Lightfoot, her dad's foreman, right hand man and another close friend. She hoped with all of her heart that Ben would come to her once she found her place. She would need his help.

Once she began her hunt for the perfect property, she tried to contact him. She had an e-mail address and a post office box. She fired off messages to both, but Ben had yet to respond.

Bree, kicking the back of her seat, brought her mind back to the present.

"Mom! How much further is it?" Bree wanted to know.

"Almost there. Do you feel the air, Bree? It's so much cooler here than in the city. Just five more minutes. Now, please stop kicking my seat. Don't forget. If you and Megan can behave yourselves, we'll stop for ice cream."

The anticipation of ice cream appeased Bree, for the time being. Not wanting to push her luck, Jill pressed the accelerator just a tad harder.

Entering the city limits of Molton, she reached for the directions the real estate agent had provided.

As Jill made the first turn, a sheriff's car swung in behind her, flashing his red and blues.

"Now what!" she whispered as she pulled over.

Through her side mirror, she watched a very large sheriff emerge from his car and saunter up to her window.

He was a mountain of a man. Going at least six feet five inches, he carried the wide shoulders very well on his obviously well-toned body.

His thick and neatly trimmed auburn hair had threads of silver shot through it and sharp gray eyes took in her vehicle, herself, the girls, and Charlie with one fast sweep.

"License, registration and proof of insurance," he said in a voice like thunder.

In the back seat, Megan squeaked while Bree scrunched down in her seat. Charlie commenced to bark. Jill rolled her eyes. Wonderful, she thought, simply wonderful.

Jill searched her purse and came up empty. Frantic, she searched the floor and again searched her purse before remembering. Just that morning, she had changed purses. She forgot her wallet.

Her face red, she turned to the sheriff.

"I… um… I changed purses this morning. I forgot my wallet." Her face burned in embarrassment. "I do have my registration and insurance card, though!" She quickly handed him the documents, trying not to squirm under his hard eye.

Pretty little thing, Sheriff Jake Logan thought. Cute kids and dog, too. He took his time, studying the gamin face infused with a very attractive blush. He liked the direct stare from cool green eyes and the stubborn set of her full mouth. Added to all that, her pert nose made a very attractive package.

"Do you know why I pulled you over?"

"I have no idea." Jill told him, watching him closely. "I don't think I was speeding," She added and then bit her lip. She wanted to ask him if he didn't have anything better to do, but decided to just keep quiet. No point in making things worse, and getting a ticket would not be beneficial, she thought.

"Your left tail light is not functioning. Also, that dog should be in a carrier for his own protection." His lips twitched when he caught sight of

Charlie sitting with his head cocked, the dog's eyes pinned to his face.

"Good to see your girls are using their seat-belts, though."

Jill's temper sparked but she bit her lip. Bree and Megan exchanged glances. They knew mom was mad. They wondered what would happen if mom yelled at the policeman. They hoped he wouldn't take mom to jail. If that happened, there wouldn't be ice cream.

He leaned against the SUV, taking his time, just looking at her and Jill's temper went up another notch.

Apparently, he didn't have anything better to do than annoy her. He was going to make her late to boot.

"Look! I have an appointment! Just give me the damn ticket! I'll have the stupid light fixed when I get home!"

"Where are you headed?" Jake asked as if he had all the time in the world. He watched with more than a little amusement as Jill's eyes shot daggers at him.

"Ransom Road!" she spit out. Jill noticed the surprised look flash across his face before he composed it again.

Well, well, well, he thought. It's possible he and the little firebrand could be neighbors and wouldn't that just be a kick in the pants.

"I'm not gonna give you a ticket. A verbal warning should be enough." He gave her a wide smile. "Maybe you can get hubby to fix it for you."

"I'm divorced," she snapped, making him grin even wider.

He pointed up the road. "You're on the right track. Just follow this road another quarter a mile. Can't miss it."

He sauntered back to his cruiser and waited for her to pull out. Yep. Pretty as a picture. He wondered if he would see her again.

Jill drove off in the direction the sheriff pointed out to her, absolutely seething. She'd be late and she hated being late!

She drove a little faster than normal on unfamiliar roads, watchful of small side roads. After all, she had her family with her, but if that odious man hadn't stopped her, they'd be at their destination by now.

Thanks to his off-handed directions and her scribbled notes, not to mention her increased speed, she arrived in no time at all.

Coming over the rise the house came into view and it took her breath away, her anger with it.

A wide circular driveway took her to the front of the house. It sat like a beautiful woman, slightly shop-worn, but still attractive. Wide concrete steps led to a broad covered verandah that boasted tall white columns and held the upper balcony. French doors on the second floor opened to the graceful gallery on the second floor. Double doors, leading to the foyer stood open and an attractive blonde stood in front of them, beaming a welcoming smile.

"Am I late?" Jill called out. "I'm late! I'm so sorry. The local sheriff felt a need to pull me over for a broken tail light and *he* made me late!"

"Ahhh, that would be Jake Logan. What a hunk o'man he is, and you aren't late at all."

Jill refrained from saying what she really thought about Jake Logan. Better to be quiet than make a fuss, she thought. Obviously, Jake is a friend.

"You must be Mary Lee." Jillian held out a hand to the woman.

"Yes, I am. Did you have any problems finding the place?"

"Oh no. Your directions were excellent."

Jill turned to her daughters. "Why don't you walk Charlie around a little. Be sure to clean up after him," she smirked at Bree's face.

"We want to see, too," Megan began and Jill cut her off.

"You'll have plenty of time to see the house."

The girls gave a sigh in unison and walked off with Charlie on his leash.

"Cute girls," Mary Lee told her. "You're lucky. I've got two boys and they are a handful."

Jill laughed. "Let me tell you, girls are a handful, too."

Mary Lee led the way into the house and gestured to the beautiful wide staircase that divided the foyer.

"This house was built in the eighteen hundreds, just prior to the Civil War. Harold Ransom built this place for his wife, Maudie, and their ten kids." Mary Lee smiled when Jill gasped.

"Ten kids! I couldn't imagine having that many." Jill said.

"Shortly after the house was finished, Harold went off to war and was killed in the Battle of Shiloh. Maudie kept the household running and managed to keep the wolf from the door by farming. At that time, there was over a thousand acres and she and her kids farmed every acre. The house passed down to descendants until the last one died in nineteen fifty-six. Gray and Alberta Peterson purchased it at auction. They were newlyweds and planned to begin a family right away. Sadly, Gray was drafted, off to Vietnam he went, was killed, and Alberta lived here until just recently."

Jill took in the blonde's appearance. Petite and pretty as a picture, Mary Lee owned her sparkling blue eyes, pert nose, and rosebud mouth. Dimples winked as she spoke, and her creamy skin glowed with excellent health. Jill liked her. She even liked the gray canvas mules, checked gray capris, and soft linen shirt in the same hue.

"How do you know all of this? You don't look like an historian," Jill said.

Mary Lee grinned. "If you buy this place, you won't get a regular deed. You'll get what's called an abstract. It's all in there. Pretty interesting reading."

Bree and Megan's voices alerted Jill that her daughters were about to catch up with them and she lowered her voice.

"Has Mrs. Peterson passed on as well?"

Mary Lee shook her head, making her blonde curls bounce.

"No. She went on and received a degree in business, worked at the bank here in town until two years ago, when she retired. She invested wisely and even managed to have the wiring, furnace, and roof updated. The stables out back need some work, but nothing major."

"Where is she? Where is Mrs. Peterson?" Jill asked and saw the change in Mary Lee.

"Her niece railroaded her into a nursing home, convinced a judge that Alberta was incapable of handling her own affairs, and became trustee of Alberta's estate. Rumor has it she's blown through almost all of Alberta's money and priced this place for a fast sell. This is the formal living room, also known as the front parlor." Mary Lee walked in ahead of Jillian. Turning, she watched Jill's reaction.

Jaw dropping was Jill's first thought. The twelve-foot ceilings, the beautiful hardwood floors, the large, white marble fireplace, and windows that reached almost to the ceiling and down to the floor left Jill speechless.

She could envision just how she would furnish this room. Formal, but not too formal. Elegant but cozy. Jill was practically salivating.

"It's a really beautiful room, isn't it?" Mary Lee asked.

Jill could only nod. Bree and Megan stared and even Charlie seemed to be on his best behavior, standing between the girls and panting.

"Let's go see the library, shall we?" Of all the rooms in the house, the library had been Mary Lee's favorite, having spent time in there as a child while Alberta Peterson tutored her in math.

Mary Lee swept open the double doors and ushered the family into the room. Here, floor to ceiling bookcases lined the walls. Charming French doors opened up to the portico and gave a lovely view of somewhat neglected gardens.

Here too, were the long wide windows placed between bookcases to let in the sunshine.

Across the foyer, Jill found a formal dining room. Every room was graced with those beautiful windows and French doors leading to the verandah.

The more she saw of the house, the better she liked it.

"Shall we go to the second floor?" Mary Lee asked and Jill nodded enthusiastically. Oh, she could not wait to see the second floor.

At the top of the stairs, the house split into two wings. Mary Lee led them into the wing on the right and opened more double doors.

"This is the master suite. I'll let it speak for itself."

Jill entered and came to a complete standstill, unable to believe her eyes.

She stood in the middle of an inviting sitting room. She stood and stared at the long windows and French doors leading to the upper balcony. Stepping out, she saw a set of discreet stairs leading down to the ground.

Awed, Jill moved back into the sitting room and into the master bedroom. This room also had a fireplace.

"Does every room have a fireplace?" she asked. Mary Lee nodded.

"Gorgeous, aren't they? They were all converted to burn either wood or gas. City gas and water has come out this far out of town.

Jill moved through the bedroom and found a full bathroom complete with a roomy tub and full shower. Everything she could possibly want.

Mary Lee led her into the room next to the master suite and Jill realized this was a mirror of the previous room.

Three more suites, smaller than the master but just as beautiful, made up the rest of the wing. She liked that each of the suites had their own bathrooms.

More cleaning, she thought. She would need help to keep up the house.

Good Lord, she thought, I'm thinking about employees. The thought made her stomach hurt, but in a good way.

"Let's look at the other wing, shall we?" Mary Lee suggested and Jill gave her an enthusiastic nod.

Jillian turned to close the doors to the bedroom and paused. A puzzled look flitted across her face.

"Do you smell that?" she asked Mary Lee.

"Smell what?"

"Cigarette smoke. It smells like cigarette smoke."

Mary Lee sniffed and then shook her head. "Maybe someone drove past while we were in there and the smoke wafted in, but I don't smell anything."

Jill shrugged. "Could just be my imagination."

Going through the remaining wing, Jill noted the rooms were smaller on this end, but they would suit. An idea began to form as she wandered the house. It could work, but she would need to talk to Judge Brentwood and his wife, Lavinia; her father's best friends, and the only remaining family she had left.

Leaving the house, they entered the stables. Jill was happy to see four stalls on each side of the large building. At the end was a room that would be perfect for tack.

The second building was wide open and would work for another stable. Here, she could put in an insemination room and a couple of birthing stalls and there would still be room for more stalls.

Two storage sheds would house the equipment she would need for grass cutting, snow removal, and gardening equipment. She would need help in that area as well.

A little set back was an old barn. It too would need work, but the foundation was good. She could find a use for that as well.

A path just beyond the empty pole buildings entered a heavily wooded spot.

"Where does that path lead?" Jill asked.

"Alberta used that as a riding trail. She was fond of horses and had a couple of real beauties in her younger days. That path meanders around and comes out there." Mary Lee pointed to another smaller path.

"Perfect!" Jill said with a wide grin. "Absolutely perfect."

Jill looked around again, noting the peeling paint on the columns and the dull paint on the inside of some of the rooms.

"The house needs a little work. The gardens as well and I'm going to need one stall outfitted with a steel gate and reinforced. Do you know who I could get to help me with this?" Jill sighed. "I'm also going to need a housekeeper, so I'd need a recommendation on that, as well. She wouldn't have to live here if she didn't want to, but she should be close by."

"Let me show you two more rooms. I didn't show them to you before, but since you've raised some interesting points, I think you may find a use for them after all. As for a housekeeper of sorts, Helen Logan may be interested. She helped Mrs. Peterson out now and again. I'll give you her number. She lives up the road, so probably wouldn't need to live in."

They reentered the house through the back door and walked into a huge eat-in kitchen. Off the room, Mary Lee flung open two doors and gestured for Jill and the girls to follow her.

Both rooms were inviting and warm and Jill could envision them with comfortable furniture and personal touches.

"How soon could we close?"

Mary Lee dimpled and shrugged one shoulder. "How soon can you get financing?"

Jill shook her head. "No financing. This would be a cash deal."

She had the pleasure of watching Mary Lee's eyes go wide. "Seriously?"

"Seriously."

Mary Lee did some rapid calculations. "I ran a title search when I listed it. I'll run another to be sure the house is still clear of any liens. That should only take a few days. We probably could close by the middle of August. If you're serious, I'll tell Steffi that time is of the essence. You'll want to get your girls signed up for school and be settled before hand."

Jillian looked around. The house, the outbuildings, and the land would be perfect for everything she wanted.

She looked at her daughters and saw the silent pleas in their eyes.

"Yes Mary Lee. Let's do this."

The offer was written while they sat on the grand staircase and Mary Lee promised to get it to Steffi right away.

Jill gathered up her girls and turned to shake hands.

The smell of cigarette smoke wafted through the foyer and Jill looked over at Mary Lee. The other woman had a puzzled look on her face as she surged to her feet.

Charlie, waiting patiently on his leash cocked his head and stared up the staircase.

Mary Lee bolted up the stairs, with Jill hot on her heels after giving the girls a terse order to stay where they were, close to the back door.

The two women ran from room to room, searching closets, bathrooms, sitting rooms and sleeping areas but found nothing.

"I know you smelled it, too," Jill told Mary Lee. She nodded.

"I'm going to have Zach, my husband, come in and go through the house. Make sure there's nothing amiss with wiring and such. I can't think of any other reason for smelling smoke."

"Is he any good?" Jill asked and Mary Lee's dimples flashed. "Well, since he's my husband, I would say yes. Don't take my word for it, though. Ask around town. People will tell you he's the best contractor around here."

"Your word is good enough for me. Will he be able to do the work?"

"Oh yeah. He and his crew will do an excellent job for you. I promise you."

Jill situated the girls in the car and Charlie in his carrier after a great deal of resistance on his part, and then sat and looked at the house. She wanted it more than she ever thought possible.

Breeding horses and the added bonus of therapy horses and riding camps during the summer to help defray the costs.

It was also hard to realize her future depended on the whim of one person. Jill hoped the woman would accept her offer.

Under the circumstances, she felt offering the asking price was the only way to go. The house was priced below market value, so it seemed only fair to offer the full amount.

Now, she would have to wait.

Sighing, she put her car in gear and pulled out behind Mary Lee's bright red SUV.

"Mom?" Bree's voice came from the back seat. She and Megan had been subdued since viewing the house.

"Yes sweetie?"

"Do you think we're gonna get it?"

"I hope so, honey. You liked the house?"

Bree nodded enthusiastically before realizing her mother would not see.

"I loved the house and Megan and me can share that room next to the one you would have. Maybe, if we make friends we can have sleepovers and stuff."

"Honey, you, and Megan are going to make lots of friends and yes, you can have sleepovers. It'll be fun."

"Mommy," Megan began then hesitated, took a deep breath and dove in, revealing what was on her little mind. "Mommy, will dad find us here?"

Jill pulled over and stopped her SUV. "Sweetie, dad *could* find us here, but he has to stay away. The judge said so. It will be fine, Megan. Don't worry, okay?"

Megan nodded and Jill sighed. She would make sure everything would be fine. She had Marcus Brentwood to help her make sure everything would be fine.

Heading into Milwaukee, Jill pulled into the first Dairy Queen she could find, and ordered burgers, then three double deckers, and a single for Charlie. Everyone deserved the treat.

Once home, she settled the girls and then checked her e-mail. There was one from her bosses; Steve and Garrett Boyle of Renaissance Games informing her that her latest game, *Battle Cry-USA* was set to go live in a few weeks and pre-sales were through the roof. Fans were clamoring for an expansion and Steve and Garrett were thrilled she had the first expansion; *Battle Cry-Europe* was ready to go. It would be ready for release right after the first of the year and she should probably be working on *Battle Cry -Asia*.

Jill had been working on it, but the thought that a game she had developed from conception to implementation was so popular was heady.

Maybe, she thought, ridding herself of Noah had been a positive thing and just maybe she should have followed her parents' advice and divorced him long before this. It would have saved a lot of pain, she thought.

Her mind traveled back to the day her parents' will revealed that everything would be put in a trust for the girls. Noah would not have access to any of the money. That brought on the beating that almost killed her.

Now, she was glad Marcus had withheld the addendum. If or when she divorced Noah, the money would revert back to Jill, but Noah didn't know that and, because of that, Jill could fulfill her dreams.

Well, hindsight is always twenty-twenty.

Her only regret was that the land her parents owned, along with the horses, had been sold but, then again, this gave Jillian the opportunity to start fresh. She would not waste it.

She could hear the girls whispering in their room as she stood and looked around. Her furnishings, while quite nice, would not come near filling that house and making it a home. Well, she had Aunt Lavinia for that. The woman's taste was impeccable. It would be fun, furnishing that house, making it hers. She hadn't had much fun in her life. It may be selfish, but dammit, if anyone deserved a little fun it was her and her girls, she decided.

Mary Lee Connor delivered the offer to Steffi Brandt, stressing that time was of the essence and then left and joined her husband, Zach, at Mike's Diner.

It was a welcoming little place and prided itself on serving comfort food. The very best Molton had to offer.

Mary Lee couldn't suppress a grin when Jake Logan strolled in and took a seat at the Connor's table.

Mary Lee, Zach, and Jake had been friends since childhood, separated only when Jake entered the Army. To Zach's relief, Jake had not changed much. A little more mature, maybe, then again… maybe not so much.

They all had been there for each other. When Zach married Mary Lee, Jake stood as best man. When Jake's short marriage fell apart, Zach and Mary Lee were there for him. And when Jake's dad died, Zach had traveled to Florida with Jake to bring Jake's mother, Helen, back to Wisconsin.

Gosh, had it been just three years, Mary Lee wondered. It seemed that Helen had been back for ages. More, it seemed as though she had never left.

But, they had been there for each other through thick and thin, so with the comfort of a long-time friendship, Mary Lee felt free to poke at Jake a little.

"I should be mad at you, Jake Logan," she said. "You could have cost me a sale."

Jake grinned back. "Tail light was burned out. Couldn't just let that fly, Mary Lee. I'm sure she can get some guy to fix it for her." Jake studied the menu until the rest of Mary Lee's statement filtered through his brain.

"She write an offer?"

"As the matter of fact. I just gave it to Steffi. We'll see what happens."

Zach leaned back and grinned at his wife. "I saw her going through town. Pretty little thing. Better not let Steffi know there's competition for our illustrious sheriff, here."

Jake shook his head. "Steffi and I are just friends and the snippy little city girl isn't my type, so put those thoughts right out of your head, Mary Lee. I know you." Eyes narrowed, he zeroed in on his best friend's wife. "Don't even think about playing match-maker. I'm happy just the way I am."

"Jake, how dense can you possibly be? The whole town knows Steffi Brandt has set her cap for you and her hooks for your money. She'd have your mother in the room at Shady Pines right next to Alberta Peterson if she ever succeeded." She shook a finger at Jake. "As for setting you up with anyone, I wouldn't think of doing that."

"Uh-huh! How about that fiasco with your sister? She's gorgeous, but it would be almost incestuous, Mary Lee. What were you thinking?"

"That you needed a buffer between you and Steffi." Mary Lee said, blue eyes shooting sparks. Jake grinned.

"Like I said, Steffi and I are friends." He broke off as their orders were delivered. Taking a bite out of her burger, Mary Lee pinned him with her eyes.

"And I still think you're dense, but whatever," she said.

Steffi Brandt breezed in the door. Dressed in a backless white summer dress, wide red belt, and red open-toes shoes, she was the epitome of the fashionable woman. Rubies circled her wrist, flashed in her ears and a thin chain of the same gem circled her graceful throat.

"Oh-oh," Zack muttered under his breath, "Here comes the lady in question even as we speak."

Mary Lee sat back and wiped her mouth as Steffi joined them uninvited.

Steffi tossed back her glorious spill of ginger hair and fixed her shrewd, cold, and calculating hazel eyes on Mary Lee.

"Mary Lee, this is a very interesting offer. Cash? Is she rich?"

"I wouldn't know. I know she is offering you the full asking price and she's offering cash."

Steffi sat back and reaching over, grabbed Jake's coke, took a sip.

"Can we get a little more?" she asked and Mary Lee gave a cold shrug.

"She's offering the price you set. You are, of course, free to write a counter-offer, but as the saying goes, a bird in the hand…"

Steffi sat, tapping a bright red nail on the table. Then, to everyone's shock, she brought out the neatly folded offer from her very stylish red hobo bag, grabbed a pen out of Jake's shirt pocket, and signed the offer.

"Let's get this done with, Mary Lee," she ordered and then turned to Jake. "Will I see you tonight?" she cooed. Her warm, sexy smile turned frosty when he shook his head.

"I've got a man out sick, Steffi. I'm working tonight."

Steffi got to her feet and stormed out while Zach speared his friend with a wide grin.

"Yup. Just friends," Zach said, and Jake frowned at him before grabbing his hat and tossing some bills on the table.

"I'll catch up with you later," he said as he followed Steffi out the door.

"If Steffi ever gets a good look at Jillian Tolivar, there's going to be hell to pay and in spite of what dear ol' Jake says, I would say Jill Tolivar is exactly his type. Smart, warm, caring and a horse lover." She cocked her head and met Zach smile for smile. "And speaking of which, she's going to hire you to do some work on the house and barns. Looks like Ms. Tolivar is going to keep us in hotdogs and beans for a while."

She took a careful glance over the contract, ensuring all was as it should be. "In the meantime, I have a call to make. This is going to make Jill's day. I'm glad. I like her. I like her very much."

Jill answered on the second ring, sounding a little out of breath.

"Is this a bad time, Jill?"

"No, just getting the girls settled down for the night." Jill's stomach tightened, waiting to hear what Mary Lee had to say.

"Ahh… Well, I have news and I didn't want to wait."

Jill took a deep breath. "Good news or bad news?"

Mary Lee laughed. "Welcome to Molton, Jill. You have the house!"

Two

Jill was busy packing. Closing would be in less than two weeks. Everything moving along quickly and efficiently.

Jill and Lavinia had done the whole shopping thing, buying some beautiful furnishing for the house, along with window treatments. Mary Lee Connor had been sweet enough to send her window, door measurements, and let her know that Zach and his crew were hard at it. They would, of course, work on the house first.

A brisk knock at the door interrupted her packing. Icy tendrils reached in and grabbed her gut. She lived in constant fear that Noah would show up. By now, he knew she and the girls would be leaving Milwaukee. More, he knew by now that she had money.

Jill didn't know how he found out these things, but he always did.

The knock came again, more insistent. Jill held her breath as she looked out the peephole. That breath rushed out in one relieved gush.

"Uncle Marc! What are you doing here so late? Where's Aunt Lavinia?"

"I'm sorry to come by so late, but this couldn't wait. Lavinia wanted to come with me, but she's feeling a little under the weather."

"What's wrong?" She took one of his beautiful hands in her small one.

"Would you care to give an old man a cup of tea?"

He's stalling, Jill thought. Whatever it is, he doesn't want to tell me.

"Sit down. Just let me move some of these boxes and you sit on the sofa. Tea's coming right up."

She set the kettle on the stove, measured out leaves and fetched two teacups and saucers. She added a plate of cookies and waited, her stomach in knots.

She waited until the water boiled and poured it over the leaves, into a teapot, letting it steep. Grabbing a strainer, she poured the steeped tea, put the cups on the tray, and carried the whole thing into the living room. It occurred to her that maybe she was stalling as well.

Jill handed him a cup and waited while he doctored it.

"Uncle Marc. Something is upsetting you. I wish you'd tell me what it is."

Judge Brentwood sighed. He wished he could spare her this.

"Jillian, they found some evidence that is… let's say disturbing. It appears the door to the bedroom had been nailed shut." He paused, letting that sink in.

Jill's face blanched. "The fire really had been deliberately set?"

Marc nodded. "I'm afraid so." He sipped his tea, watching her closely. Watched as his words sunk in.

"You are saying my parents were murdered, Uncle Marc!" Her head was reeling and she went paler yet as the realization hit home. "That would make me their prime suspect."

Marc nodded. "You were on the top of their list, Jill. The police figured your inheritance would be your motive. After I explained about the codicil, they took another look and removed you from their list. You loved your parents, were close with them and you didn't stand to gain anything. In fact, you stood to lose a great deal. No, they don't think you had anything to do with it."

"Then who?" Jill went very still, her eyes wide as she grasped the truth of it.

"Noah! They think Noah did this!"

Marc reached over and squeezed her hand. "He had motive, means, and opportunity. His reaction after the reading of the will and his assault on you all adds up. He's prime suspect. They're checking his alibi; see if it holds up." Marcus grew quiet again.

There was much he did not tell her. He did not tell her about the bullets found in the wood that had made up the side of the house. Bullets that belonged to a .357 Smith & Wesson. A gun that Noah not only owned, but also was very proud of.

He did not tell her that the gas line from the propane tank to the house had been tampered with.

He also did not tell her they were looking at her father's foreman, Ben Lightfoot as well, although Ben didn't stand to gain much. No, their prime suspect was Noah.

While she digested this, tried to wrap her mind around it, the girls, followed by Charlie wandered into the room.

"Uncle Marc! Did you bring us treats?" Megan asked. Jill felt her face burn.

"Uncle Marc doesn't have to bring you treats every time he comes to visit," she admonished.

Charlie wedged himself between Judge Brentwood and the girls, nosing at Marc's pockets. He was looking for treats, too.

"Charlie! Stop that!" Jill reached for his collar, but Marcus stopped her.

"No. I didn't bring treats this time. I'll bring double next." He played with Charlie's ears and then leaned back.

"Mom?" Bree's eyes were sharp on her mother's face. "Are you sick? You look sorta funny."

Jill closed her eyes and tried to calm herself. "I'm not sick, honey. Just tired I think."

Megan leaned against Marcus's knee, put her little hands on his cheek, and turned his face towards her. "We've been helping mom pack. She said we have to pack all of our toys, Uncle Marc. That's hard work!"

He pecked the little girl on her cheek and ran his hand down Bree's hair. Both girls favored their mother. Not much of Noah in either one of them. To Marcus's way of thinking, that was a good thing.

"Packing is hard work, but unpacking will be fun. Sort of like opening presents at Christmas time or for your birthday," he told them.

Bree nodded her face solemnly. "Mom is working hardest of all, Uncle Marc. Maybe next time, you could bring *her* a treat, too. She likes Twinkies best," Bree whispered.

"I remember," Marcus said with a wink. "She loved them when she was little, like you."

Marcus got to his feet and walked over to Jill. She looked so pale it broke his heart.

"Try not to dwell on this. You're getting ready to begin a new phase of your life. Try to concentrate on that. Let the cops do their job."

Jill nodded. She stood and hugged him hard. "I'll try. Can you keep me posted?"

"Sure. When I know something, you'll know."

"Thanks, Uncle Marc," she began and he shushed her.

"Walk me to the door. There's something else we need to discuss."

Curious and more than a little afraid, she complied.

"Jillian, your restraining order is for this county. We're going to have to file in Molton County. Do you want me to do that?"

"I hadn't thought of that. Yes, please." She wanted all of her bases covered as far as Noah was concerned.

"Consider it done." He patted her cheek and went out the door.

Jill ran her hands through her hair and contemplated the moving boxes around her. Trying to concentrate on the job at hand, she did a mental inventory.

A moving truck was hired to take her current furniture and all the boxes. Devin would drive that. Electronics would go into her SUV and she would drive that with Lavinia driving their Escalade packed with anything not in the moving truck and her own SUV. Trudy, Devin's wife, would drive their own vehicle.

She thought she had it covered.

Furniture she purchased would be delivered by the store the day after the move, giving her little time to unpack and set the house to rights before the next wave began.

While she contemplated this, the fact her parents had been murdered nagged at her. Murdered and Noah was the prime suspect. She wondered if her life would ever level out.

She hadn't heard from Ben, either. Another worry to add to the pile weighing her down. She had e-mailed him, telling him of the house and her plans. That was weeks ago and still no reply. She sent a letter to his P.O. Box and nothing from that source, either.

If she didn't hear from him soon, she'd make other arrangements. In the meantime, she had to deal with the fact her parents had been murdered and her ex-husband was the prime suspect.

Jillian stayed busy. Boxes to be packed and labeled, school records to be collected, and a search for a good doctor for herself and the girls.

They had their last counseling session and Dr. Robbins said they were ready. He wished them well and sent them on their way.

She was in constant communication with Mary Lee and over the weeks since viewing the house, and they had become friends.

Everything was coming together, but the thought of how her parents had died and the fact that Noah was a prime suspect still nagged at her. She wasn't sleeping well and couldn't concentrate on her work. So, she stayed busy with other tasks.

The days flowed into weeks and, finally, all was ready. In the morning, she would pick up the truck. This would be the last night in their apartment.

"Mom?" Bree sidled up to her. "Are you still excited?"

"Oh yes, sweetie! We're starting a new adventure! Tomorrow Uncle Marcus, and Devin and Aunt Lavinia will be coming and we'll load up the big truck... then we will be on our way. Are you excited?"

Bree nodded. Megan joined her mother and sister and leaned against Jill. "I'm excited, too, mom. So is Charlie."

Jill glanced over to where Charlie lay sleeping, all four paws in the air and laughed. "Yeah, I can see how excited he is."

She sighed and hugged her girls close. "Time to get ready for bed. We have a busy day ahead of us and we have to get an early start. We have to be in Molton by noon to sign the rest of the papers and get our keys to our new home."

"Tomorrow we get to sleep in our new house, right mom?" Bree asked. She looked relieved as Jill nodded.

"The rest of our new furniture won't be there until the day after, but we'll have our beds and we can all camp out in my room if you like. You know, just until you get comfy in our new house."

With the girls snuggled in for the night, Jill felt at loose ends. She supposed she could work, but all of her materials, including her computer, were all packed.

She thought about hauling some stuff out to her SUV, and then thought better of it. It's late, she told herself, and it's not a good idea to leave the girls alone.

Jill looked around, rubbing her hands against her arms. This place had been her refuge. She would always be grateful to the Brentwoods for letting them stay in this apartment they owned, while she recovered from her injuries. Injuries she received from the man she promised to love and cherish, but he never cherished her. She doubted he ever loved her. Noah certainly had not shown love or cherishing to the girls, for that matter. He cared only for himself and her paychecks.

Oh, she remembered that night after they returned from the Brentwoods' home, after Marcus read the will.

Noah had been furious. He accused her of all sorts of things. Screamed at her that all of his plans went up in smoke because of her and her parents.

"You knew, didn't you!" His voice had been so deadly and so quiet. For once, Jill stood firm. "Yes, I knew."

She never saw the first blow coming, but she sure as hell felt it. She remembered screaming for the girls to get out of the condo Noah had insisted they buy.

Jill felt the blows rain down on her but watched as her daughters, her two great loves, ran out the door.

Only when Noah broke her arm did blackness overtake her. He would probably kill her, she had thought, but the girls were safe. He wouldn't touch them.

Somehow, Marcus and Lavinia came to her rescue. They had the girls and they were safe. They offered her a place to stay, to heal. Grateful, she had taken them up on it.

Still, when it came time to move on with her life, she found refuge in this sweet and roomy apartment Marcus and Lavinia offered her. It wasn't hers, but it was a sort of gathering place. A fresh start.

The house in Molton would be another fresh start, but this time, the walls around them would be their own.

Jill settled down in her bed, willing herself to put the past where it belonged. Not so easy, she thought. It was the not knowing if Noah had been responsible for her parents' deaths. That was hard to take.

Tears flooded her throat and spilled out. Clenching her pillow, she sobbed quietly, not wanting to upset the girls. Now that she was about to embark on the next page of the life of Jillian, she missed her mom and dad terribly.

She felt a small nudge under her elbow and turned. Charlie stood on her bed looking at her with his beautiful brown eyes. She clutched him to her and let the tears come… wetting his fur. He didn't mind.

She drifted off to sleep, still clutching the little dog, hoping with everything she had that she'd made the right decisions.

Jill slept until the sunlight streamed into her eyes. She had forgotten to close her blinds.

Checking her watch, she saw it was just after five-thirty in the morning. Although her eyes felt gritty from her cry fest the night before, her mind was already racing.

"Way to go, Jill. You packed your coffee pot last night. Not too smart a move," she told herself. Well, she decided, at least she had the shower.

No sooner had she emerged from the warm spray, she heard a knock on her door. She pulled on clothes and hurried to the door.

"Good morning, sunshine!" Devin Brentwood, Marcus and Lavinia's son, chirped. "Did we wake you?"

Pointing to her damp curls, she cocked her head. "Do I look like I just woke up to you?" she snarled.

Good-natured and the closest thing Jill had to a sibling, he flashed his irrepressible smile. "Good thing I thought ahead." He held out a cup of steaming coffee from Kwik Trip. "Figured you'd pack everything, so Trudy and I stopped and got you this."

Jill almost fell on the cup. "Bless you, Devin! Bless you!" She took a careful sip as she led Devin and Trudy into her apartment.

A very pregnant Trudy looked around, and Jill pointed to an armchair. "Sit. Don't even think about lifting anything. You've got a big enough load to carry," she ordered. "You look beautiful. How do you do that at what, six oh five in the morning?"

Trudy laughed. "Clean living, kiddo. Clean living," she said.

Jill rolled her eyes and took another sip.

"One more sip and my brain will be awake," she told no one in particular as she headed to wake up the girls.

She anticipated Bree and Megan giving her a hard time, but they were up and dressed before Jill knew it.

"Looks like I'm not the only one looking forward to this move," she told them as she ruffled Megan's hair. "Come on and let's see what we can rustle up for breakfast."

Jill located a couple of Pop-Tarts and tossed them into the microwave. Not exactly a healthy alternative, but it would suffice until they stopped for breakfast after Marcus and Lavinia arrived.

"C'mon," Devin said. "Time's wasting. Let's start carrying stuff down and get it loaded. The two of us can handle the boxes and the smaller furniture until dad and mom get here."

They picked up boxes and prepared to carry them down to the truck. "These can go in grandma's attic," Jill said, referring to the space in the moving truck on top of the cab. "These will fit just fine. We can put the beds on last so they come off first and can get set up right away."

Trudy would be on door duty.

Jill grabbed two boxes and hefted them up for better purchase as Trudy opened the door for her. Standing on the other side were Lavinia and Marcus, wide smiles on their faces.

"Mornin'," Lavinia sang out. "Put those down. We will have breakfast and then get to moving on full stomachs."

They ate in record time and while Megan ran herd on Charlie, everyone else hauled boxes and small pieces of furniture.

Things went smoothly and, soon, all that was left was Jill's sofa and two dressers. Marcus and Devin wrestled those down while Jill turned in her keys and thanked the manager for her kindness to them and explained a cleaning crew would be coming in to clean the apartment, getting it ready for the next tenant.

"Oh, honey, you don't have to do that," the manager said, patting Jill's arm. "You and your girls were model tenants, and I didn't even know Charlie was here. You go on now, enjoy your new home. I wish you the very best of luck."

Jill and Devin walked back into the apartment to fetch Trudy, and Jill felt a tinge of sadness mixed in with excitement. This would be the last time she would step into this place. The next step would be into her unknown future.

Trudy leaned against the small kitchen counter as she slipped her cell phone into her purse.

"Doctor's office left a courtesy call, like I could forget my appointment on Monday." She shook her head and sighed. "Sometimes it's kind of nice, these reminders, and sometimes, not so much."

She looked at Devin and Jill, her eyes bright and a wide smile on her face.

"All set?" she asked and Jill nodded. "Then let's get this show on the road!"

Trudy waddled out the door ahead of Devin and Jill, who exchanged amused looks.

"You heard her! Let's get this show on the road!" Devin said with a grin.

They pulled into Molton an hour early, and Jill's first stop was Mary Lee's home/office. Devin pulled in behind her, and Lavinia and Trudy took up the last remaining parking spots and then got out and let the girls and Charlie out of Jill's SUV.

"I'll let them stretch their legs for a little. If all is ready, go ahead and sign the papers and get this done, then we can have lunch. I imagine these girls are famished." Lavinia glanced over to her daughter-in-law and grinned. "I imagine Trudy could use a break as well."

Mary Lee answered her door, her cell phone pressed to her ear. She waved Jill in while continuing her conversations.

"Yes, Steffi. They are here. We can do this now if you are available."

Mary Lee rolled her eyes as she finished her conversation.

"She should be here momentarily. This is Saturday. The bank is open until noon." Mary Lee explained, her voice dry and cynical.

Jill cocked her head as she looked at Mary Lee. The real estate woman looked cool and chic in a blue cotton shirt and jeans, her feet encased in light blue flats.

"You really don't like her much, do you?" Jill said and Mary Lee's eyes danced with devilment.

"Nope. Steffi is spoiled and suffers from a terminal case of entitlement. She blew through the money her parents left her and, if rumors are true, she's gone through most of Alberta Peterson's money as well… and we'll keep that between us!"

"Lips are sealed," Jill promised as the woman in question swept in the door.

Jill and Steffi took one look at each other and it was a case of immediate dislike.

Jill saw a well-dressed high maintenance woman. Her spill of auburn hair fell in gorgeous waves falling down around her shoulders. Steffi's summer dress of cool light green linen showed off her more obvious assets and Jill noticed the emeralds set in gold, flashing at the woman's throat, wrist, fingers, and ears.

In Jill's mind, Steffi was over-dressed and ostentatious.

Steffi saw a small woman with the look of a sexy pixie. She resented Jill's healthy glow and the gamin face that required little in the way of cosmetics.

She took in Jill's jeans, checked chambray shirt, and soft moccasins. She also noticed the woman's fingers were bare and her lip curled derisively.

If Steffi did not need the money so damn bad, she would call off the deal, but money was money and Steffi needed a great deal of it if she wanted to keep her bothersome aunt in that very expensive nursing home and out of her hair.

"Let's get this done," Steffi ordered. She had things to do, like get to the bank, and she wanted to hunt down Jake Logan and possibly get something rolling. This house sale was a stopgap measure. The real prize would be Jake and his lovely money.

The ever-efficient Mary Lee took them through the contracts, quickly and thoroughly. She could not wait to get Steffi out of her general vicinity, and she had plans for later in the day.

Steffi snatched up her check and breezed out the door without so much as a thank you, nice meeting you or a go to hell.

Jillian and Mary Lee looked at each other, and Jill shook her head. "And isn't she pleasant," Mary Lee said, snidely making Jill laugh.

"We're going to lunch and then heading out to the house," she informed Mary Lee. "I had arranged for the rest of the furniture and appliances to be delivered tomorrow, but a phone call this morning reminded me that tomorrow was Sunday. My stuff will be here later this afternoon, so we have a lot of unloading to do."

"Go on over to Mike's Diner. I'll join you in just a little bit, and lunch is on me."

Jill gasped. "There are a lot of us. I can't let you pay for all of us."

Mary Lee giggled. "You just made me a lot of money. I can afford it. Go on over. I'll see you in a little bit." Mary Lee patted Jill's shoulder as she ushered her out into the bright sunshine.

Jill walked up to her little group and quickly brought them all up to date, and then jumped in her vehicle and led the way to Mike's Diner.

Mary Lee joined them with a tall handsome man in tow. Jill's first thought was that they made such a beautiful couple.

Introductions made and food ordered, they chatted about Jill's plans.

"Breeding and a riding camp *and* therapy horses? That is going to be a really tall order," Zach commented.

Jill nodded. "I know it but it can be done. It will take hard work and planning. I know how to do both."

Zach sat back and studied her with his gorgeous brown eyes while he sipped his coffee.

"We can get those stalls up in no time," he told her, "but winter comes fast up here, and you have a lot of fence to string as well. You won't be able to put all of your plans in motion until spring."

Jill nodded. "That's what I thought, too."

Marcus cleared his throat. "Jill is a planner, no doubt. She has been goal -orientated since kidhood." He looked at his wife and then added. "Lavinia and I will be coming up on a regular basis, so we can give her a hand with some of it, too."

"I have some ideas on that too, Judge," Zach said, and Marcus waved a hand.

"Let's just leave it at Marcus, shall we?"

Zach grinned. He really liked the old guy and his very attractive wife. The son was great, but the daughter-in-law was a quiet sort. He imagined she was just fine, too.

"With all of us in her corner, Jill can't lose," Mary Lee decreed.

Jill's smile was radiant as she snatched up the bill the waitress laid on the table.

"I'm getting this, Mary Lee," She decreed and then looked at her daughters.

"Come on, girls. Let's go home."

Three

Jake Logan watched the small caravan leave Mike's Diner and head toward Ransom Road. He was particularly interested in one vehicle and, as it passed him, he grinned.

He waited until a very large furniture truck bearing the name of a high-end Milwaukee store caught up with the little caravan and then pulled in behind them. He looked forward to seeing the little spitfire's reactions.

"Momma?" Megan said. "I think the furniture people are behind us."

Jill checked her rear-view mirror and felt excitement mixed with apprehension surge through her. Everything was happening so fast. Jill didn't know what to think.

Better not to think, she decided. Just go with the flow. Something she had never been good at.

Putting on a brave face, she smiled at her daughters.

"I think you're right, baby. Isn't that awesome?"

Jill began thinking ahead. She only had a few minutes now to get her thoughts organized.

"Megan. When we get to the house, you take Charlie out and walk him around a little. We can't let him run, yet, because he may get lost." She paused. Provisions would need to be made for Trudy. The poor woman could not be expected to sit in Devin's truck all day.

"Bree. As soon as Devin opens up the truck, can you hop up and find a chair for Trudy?"

Bree nodded. "What if I can only find a kitchen chair, mom?"

Jill shrugged. "I guess that will have to do, then."

Jill's mind raced. Either she or Lavinia could direct the men delivering her new furniture into the proper rooms while she saw to putting beds together. Other bedroom furniture would have to wait, and the kitchen would have to be put together quickly. She needed to make a run to the grocery store, as well. Maybe she could get Trudy to go. That would make the very pregnant woman feel like she had a part in helping. It was something to ask Devin about. She would also have to see about doing something for dinner, as well.

Most women would feel a little over-whelmed. Jill took it all in stride, until she saw the sheriff's car pull in behind the furniture truck.

"Now what does he want," she grumbled under her breath and walked back to meet him.

It annoyed her that she had to step back to look up into his eyes. It annoyed her further that he was so damn appealing.

"Can I help you," she asked in the coldest tone she could muster, taking in his craggy good looks and powerful build which smacked her right in her hormones, and that did not just annoy-it pissed her off.

"I see you didn't get it fixed," he said smirking down at her. It tickled him to see the confusion play on her face.

"What? I didn't get what fixed?" For the life of her, she could not figure out what he was talking about.

"Your rear light. Still burned out."

Jill ran a hand through her curls and watched gratefully as Marcus strolled up to them.

"I forgot," she told him in a flat voice.

"Problem?" Marcus asked, and Jill silently blessed him for his timely arrival.

"Not really, Judge Brentwood. Last time she was through here, the left taillight was burned out. I noticed as she drove through town, it still was." He tossed Jill a cool smile, which she did not return.

"Oh for Heaven's sake! I forgot! Write me the blasted ticket, and I'll get the damn thing fixed first thing Monday!"

Jake shook his head. "I'm not going to write you a ticket. I'm off duty. If I write you a ticket, I have to go *on* duty and I'd rather not."

He stood with his thumbs hooked in his front pockets. Jill thought it was also annoying that he looked so good standing there. Under different circumstances, she might even find him appealing. Experience taught her not to trust her hormonal reaction.

"I can see to it she gets it fixed, Sheriff," Marcus injected. He saw the mutinous look in Jill's eyes and hastened to defuse the situation.

"Jillian, the men from Hanson's Furniture store are waiting for you. Devin began to unload our truck, and we need to get Trudy settled before she has that baby in your driveway."

As planned, Jill hustled away after sparing one fuming look in Jake's general direction.

"It's good to see you again, your honor." Jake held out his hand, and Marcus took it.

"You remember me?"

"Oh yeah. I was the arresting officer on a few cases that you presided over," Jake explained and Marcus nodded.

"You were on the job down in Milwaukee. Thought I recognized you." He looked Jake up and down. "You're a little hard to forget," the good judge added with a wry grin.

Jake shrugged. "Your rulings were good ones, sir."

Marcus waved a hand. "Call me Marcus. And while you are here, I have some business to discuss with you. I would have come up or called on Monday to talk to you. Saved me a trip."

"What's up?" Christ, Jake thought, he just knew the woman was going to be trouble.

"Jillian's ex-husband is a violent man. We have a protection order in place down in the city, but we are applying for one in this county. He beat her, Sheriff. He beat her badly enough to put her in a hospital for weeks. Her daughters saw it all. If not for them, he would have killed her."

Jake's lips tightened. Nothing made him angrier than a man who beat women and kids.

"I'm going to need particulars on this. She just had to pick a house that's more than a little isolated." Jake shook his head.

"Jill won't let Noah dictate her life any longer. She is fiercely independent. Raising her daughters to be the same way."

Marcus handed the burly sheriff Noah's particulars.

"If he changes anything like the car or whatever, we'll know. His parents are cooperating." The judge hesitated.

"Something else?"

"Yeah. Jill lost her parents back in November in a house fire. The fire was deliberately set after their bedroom door was secured so they could not get out. The cops found bullets embedded in the wood of the house, as well. We can only assume they tried to get out through a window and whoever set the fire shot at them to keep them in place."

Jake looked down the drive to where Jill was giving orders to the deliverymen.

"She needs a break, that's for damn sure."

"I couldn't agree more, Sheriff. Keep an eye on our girl. Lavinia and I will be grateful."

"Yeah. No problem. I've got a couple of things to tend to, then I'll drop by again."

Jill raced from room to room, seeing to the placement of furniture. She was pleased with the colors of the rooms.

The cheerful yellow in the kitchen would show off her new stainless appliances to perfection and snowy curtains on the windows would give it charm.

The front parlor, the sweet color of a good champagne was too perfect. The gold sheers she chose for these windows would give the room a gentle glow and drapes, a deeper hue of gold, would pop against the subtle color of the walls.

Her room was a soft lavender, and the white eyelet curtains are a perfect foil for the restful color.

She dashed into the girls' room and hugged herself. The icy pink walls were perfect.

Each room had their own soft colors, and it thrilled her. Her vision for these rooms was coming to life. Her vision, not Noah's or the very expensive interior designer he brought in to do their condo, years ago. Her vision and hers alone.

A glint of chrome had her dashing to the window. She saw the sheriff's cruiser heading down the driveway and her shoulders relaxed. I have enough do to without putting up with that overbearing jerk, she thought as she raced back down the stairs.

Throwing open the back of her truck, she began to haul out boxes filled with electronics. She planned on getting the kitchen together, heading off to the store, making some dinner, and then tonight she would set up her space in that beautiful library.

Her thoughts racing, she did not notice Mary Lee arrive until the woman called her name.

"Jill! Hi! Where would you like me to set this up?"

Mary Lee gestured to a huge roasting pan currently hoisted by Mary Lee's very handsome and amiable husband.

Coming up behind Jill and Zach were two very appealing boys carrying a rather large cooler.

"These are my boys, eleven-year-old Sam and seven-year-old Cody."

Jill grinned at them. "Nice to meet you. These are my girls, Bree and Megan."

Zach, struggling with the large roasting pan, sighed. "Now that the intros are done, can we set this somewhere?" He shot a look at his wife. "Mary Lee cooked enough barbeque for an army, not to mention all the sides she made, and this thing is getting heavy."

Jill ran her hand through her short curls and thought quickly.

"We can put that on the counter right next to the sink. There's a plug. The rest we can put in the refrigerator." They brought that in first and it should be cool enough. I hope, she thought.

Trudy saw the little troop coming into the kitchen and slid her cell phone into her pocket. She quickly made room on the counters and grabbed the bags dangling from Mary Lee's hands.

"I can take care of that for you," Trudy said with a wide smile. She glanced at Jill. "It's not heavy," she said with a laugh.

The deliverymen from Hanson's Furniture finished unloading, presented her with the invoices to sign, and made their escape.

Jill stood in the middle of the rubble and ran her hands through her hair, temporarily overwhelmed.

There were empty cartons piled in almost every corner, filled boxes waiting to be opened, and beds that needed to be put together. She wasn't sure where to start.

Everyone clustered in the kitchen, awaiting her orders, but before she could open her mouth, she was sidetracked again.

"Where are your keys?" Jake asked. She had been so preoccupied, she had not seen the sheriff return.

"What do you want with my keys?"

"I'm going to fix your light. After that's done, I'll be coming in here and seeing what needs to be done next." He saw the narrowed eyes and the tight lips and grinned.

"We're gonna be neighbors. That's what neighbors do. Welcome to Molton." He snagged her keys from the kitchen table, where Jill and laid them, and took off out the back door before she could gather her wits.

Jill moved to follow him but Trudy called her back.

"If you tell me which cabinets are for which dishes, I can clean the cardboard dust off of them and begin to put your kitchen together, Jill. It would give me something to do."

They worked like fiends for a couple of hours. Jill made up beds, happy in the knowledge her girls would sleep in their own beds tonight.

Toys began to fill the shelves in their room, and Devin set up their television and video game system so they would have something to do before bed.

Beds were also set up in her own bedroom and in what she considered the family guest rooms. Trudy would have a comfortable bed to sleep in, if comfort could be found as far along as she was.

Jill, her arms full with files, entered her library and stopped. A beautiful antique desk stood in the middle of the room and two comfortable leather chairs flanked each side.

The mahogany desk gleamed in the afternoon sunlight.

Judge Brentwood and Lavinia came up behind her.

"This is our housewarming present to you. It's not exactly like your dad's, but it's pretty close."

She dropped the box of files and threw her arms around the elderly couple.

"I can't thank you enough for this and for everything you have done." Tears glimmered in her eyes, and she willed them back. This was not the time for tears.

Jake and Zach were busy putting the computer's components together and then, when they were done, plugged it in.

"Oh, this is amazing. Thank you! Thank you all so much!" Her annoyance with Jake momentarily forgotten as she rushed to her desk and pushed the ON button.

The clicks and whirrs made her smile. Forget coffee pots and dishes. Wherever her computer functioned was home.

She hugged herself and let the tears fall.

Jake watched her closely. This was no show. She was genuinely touched, and he smiled slightly.

A spitfire with a soft heart, he thought. He thought it was rather nice to see.

"Mom? Can we eat? We're *starving*," Bree announced. Jill hugged her tightly.

"Yes, we can eat. Get Megan and get washed up." She looked over her daughter's head at the two boys standing in the doorway. "You two get cleaned up, too. We're eating in a few minutes."

While Mary Lee and Lavinia put dinner together, Marcus and Jake put her dining room table together and set chairs around it.

Trudy brought platters of buns, a fruit tray, and a cheese tray and placed them on the table. Paper plates emerged from one of Mary Lee's bags, along with plastic utensils.

Everyone sat around the table and, for the first few minutes, chatter was at a minimum.

Once the original hunger pangs were satiated, conversation turned to Jill's plans.

"I'm going to run a riding camp, if all goes well, all summer long. I'll also offer therapy horses, and I plan on breeding quarter horses. I learned from the best." She looked at Marcus. "I still haven't heard from Ben, but if he doesn't contact me soon, I'll make other arrangements."

"Ben always did march to his own drummer, sweetie," Lavinia said. "But, I have a feeling he'll contact you soon. You don't think he would miss out on this if he could help it, do you?"

Jill shook her head. "No, but if he has another job that he's happy in, I certainly don't expect him to pull up stakes just to help me. Anyway, while Ben is careful, that hundred thousand from mom and dad won't last him forever, so we'll just wait and see."

Lavinia and Mary Lee cleaned up the dinner things and then Mary Lee called her brood together, preparing to leave.

"We'll stop by tomorrow, see if you need anymore help." She turned to Judge Brentwood and Lavinia and held out her hand. "It was really nice meeting you..." Her beaming smile encompassed the group. "It was wonderful meeting all of you."

Marcus and Lavinia each shook her hand. "It was good to meet you and your beautiful family," Lavinia said.

"See you, Jake," Mary Lee called as she sailed out the door.

Devin glanced at his watch. "Good God! It's after ten! C'mon Trudy, let's get you tucked in."

Marcus turned to Jill. "Lavinia and I have to leave tomorrow. We're planning to come up next weekend, though, and you'll be hearing from me about that other matter. I won't leave you hanging, Jill. When I know something, I'll tell you."

Jill nodded. The 'other matter' would be the deaths of her parents. It was always in the back of her mind.

She couldn't help but think of the terrible way they died, and it still nagged at her. Noah was a prime suspect.

Trudy's gentle voice broke through the gloom that threatened to envelope her.

"Hon, you wouldn't happen to have access to a couple of towels, would you? If I had been thinking I would have packed some."

Jill patted Trudy's arm. "As the matter of fact, I do. I'll get them for you."

Jake prepared to slip out the door until Jill's voice called him back.

"Sheriff Logan, I'd like to thank you."

Jake grinned. She didn't look particularly grateful. She looked like she had swallowed something disgusting.

"No problem. Like I said, we're neighbors. This is what neighbors do, at least in Molton." He gave her a good hard look. "I should warn you. My mother will most likely find her way over before too long. She's neighborly, too." He smirked and then strode out the door, leaving Jill wondering about her new neighbors.

More than a little confused, Jill ran up the stairs and found the box she needed. She pulled out several thick towels and handed four to Trudy.

She peeked into the bedroom she earmarked for the couple to make sure it was inviting. Her mood lifted somewhat. Lavinia had seen to the subtle touches. Devin and Trudy would be cozy in here and, hopefully, get a good night's rest.

Pausing in the sitting room, she noted some of the furnishings were not where she would have placed them, but they would do for now and she could rearrange them at her leisure. For now, the rooms were clean and cozy. She couldn't ask for more than that.

Grabbing more towels and face cloths, she laid some in the suite she thought of as Marcus and Lavinia's rooms and then dashed across the hall to the girls' room.

For the time being, Jill thought it a rather good idea for the girls to share this suite until they were comfortable in their new surroundings.

"I brought…"Her words died on her lips. Both girls were tucked into their beds, having found their pajamas, and were sound asleep.

Charlie had curled into a ball on Bree's bed. He raised his head and then dropped it back on his paws. He was exhausted, too.

"Please," she whispered, "let us be happy here."

She leaned over, kissed Bree's head, and then did the same to Megan. She gently rubbed Charlie's ears before walking out of the room, through the adjoining door, and into her own.

Not ready to settle yet, she gathered up discarded boxes and carried them to the kitchen. In short order, she had them broken down and remembered the really neat fire-pit just before the tree line; she decided to carry all the empty boxes out and dump them. Maybe, if the weather held, she and the girls could have a dandy campfire. They could begin making their own good memories to take the place of all the bad.

Jill stepped out the backdoor, her arms filled with empty boxes, and came to an abrupt halt.

The man stood just free of the trees, staring at the house, staring at her.

Jill couldn't make out his features, but she could see rage in his stance, the way his hands were clenched in fists and, even at a distance, she could see the fury on his shadowy face.

Her arms went numb and her knees turned to jelly.

Jill dropped the boxes and stepped back inside, intent on finding a weapon, but when she turned to secure the door behind her, she saw he was gone.

Jill went from room to room, securing all the doors. For a moment, she considered rousing Devin and Marcus and then decided against it.

She would confide in Jake Logan, no matter how much it galled her, but only if she saw the strange man again.

Feeling better, Jill went up to her own room, grabbed a fast shower, and climbed into a pair of cotton sleeping pants and t-shirt.

Climbing into bed, she was asleep before her head hit the pillow.

Four

Jake rolled into his drive and climbed wearily from his car. Even though it was his day off, it had been a long one. Parts of it, though, had been entertaining. He was especially fond of the times he lit Jill's fire. No shrinking violet there, he thought. He didn't know why that pleased him. It just did, and he was too tired to think about it.

What he wanted now was a little ESPN and a little peace and quiet although, seeing his mother move about in the kitchen, he just knew that wasn't going to happen. He could almost do a count-down on his mother. It wouldn't be long before she'd be strolling in with a zillion questions. He wasn't disappointed and smothered a grin.

"Did you eat?"

"Yeah. Mary Lee made her famous barbeque and took it over to the new neighbor's." He wished he could have bit his tongue off.

"Is that where you've been? What's she like? Is she pretty? Oh never mind, I'll find out for myself!"

Jake sighed. Better to answer her, he thought, than have her hound him hairless.

"That's where I've been. She's divorced, has two kids who are appealing as hell in spite of their ornery mother and she's planning on turning the place into a riding camp among other things."

There, he thought, hopefully that would keep his mother off his back for a while.

He was wrong.

"I think I'll bake a pie and take it over first thing in the morning."

"Ma..." Jake said and then snapped his mouth shut. It would do him very little good to try to discourage his mother.

"Never mind. You're gonna do what you're gonna do." He stalked into the living room and flipped on ESPN. He hoped his mother would leave him alone.

His hopes died as she followed him into the room.

"You know Jake, you are always comparing the women you meet with your ex-wife. Not all women are like Rhonda. She was a real piece of work. Greed, lazy and a natural-born liar are her trademarks. Now you've got another one, just like her, after your hide. I would hate to see you alone, but I'd hate it more if you teamed up with that nasty Steffi Brandt."

"Ma, Rhonda is part of my past. I'd like to leave her there. As far as seeing Steffi... we've gone out a few times, but there's nothing there, so don't worry. We're friends."

Helen Logan snorted at her son. "If you believe that, you're just stupid. I'm gonna go make that pie and check out our new neighbor."

"Ma! What on earth would I do with another woman in my life?" He walked over and kissed the top of her head. "I have you to drive me nuts. Now, I'm going to sit here, watch some sports, and then head off to bed. Zach elected me to give him a hand over at the new neighbor's."

Helen patted his cheek and headed for the kitchen. As she rolled out her pie dough, a small smile played around her lips.

She thought tomorrow would be rather interesting.

The storm woke Jill. She reached for her phone and flipped it on, checking the time. Great! Three in the damn morning!

Thunder rolled and lightening sizzled outside her window. The storm was thrilling and Jill smiled in the dark before practical matters entered her sleep-bogged mind. She decided it would be wise to check the house; make sure all was secure.

Climbing out of bed, she snagged her robe from the back of a chair and, securing the belt, made her way into her sitting room.

Her cell phone buzzed and she checked the display, a grimace of distaste flashing across her face.

"What do you want and how did you get this number?" she barked into the phone.

"Heard you got yourself a real nice house and some big plans," Noah slurred. "You owe me, Jillian. You owe me big. You give me twenty grand, and I'll forget your number and the fact you have my daughters."

Jill laughed into the phone. "Threats, Noah? I don't owe you a blessed thing, and if you actually believe I'm going to give you money on the hope you forget about us, then you are delusional."

"Your pal, the judge, made damn sure I didn't get a dime, Jillian. I went through a lot to get that money. Earned every penny and you're gonna give it to me." Jill caught the danger in his voice. Her breath clogged in her lungs.

"You *earned* it?" Her own voice became deadly quiet. Had Noah started that fire? *Was* he responsible?

Noah said nothing for several seconds, and she thought she lost the call until his laughter rang harshly in her ear.

"I earned it putting up with you and those two squalling brats. You sucked as a wife, Jillian. Always whining about money. You hoarded it. Never wanted me to have any fun. Oh yeah, Jillian. You owe me, and I'll be around to collect. Don't disappoint me."

"Sure, you do that, Noah, and I'll have your ass tossed in the slammer so fast your head will spin! Get this and remember it! I don't owe you anything! I'm not afraid of you! Don't call here again! Don't contact the girls! Just stay away or you will greatly wish you had!"

He was still sputtering as she terminated the call.

She realized that her words were true. She didn't fear him.

Sighing, she got to her feet, intending to check on her daughters. The storm raging outside was nothing compared to the storm raging within her. Worrying her thumbnail, she walked into her daughters' room, wanting to be sure the storm didn't disturb them. Charlie raised his head, gave a half-hearted thump with his tail, and snuggled back on his paws.

Jill was relieved to see the girls sound asleep, Bree snuggled into her blankets in her usual curled up position and Megan sprawled all over her bed. Jill tucked the blankets around Megan and wandered back to her room in search of some aspirin. That call from Noah upset her more than she cared to admit.

She would, of course, tell Marcus about the phone call, but it worried her. How did he know these things?

She found some aspirin and dry-swallowed them, and then snuggled into her bed. The storm thrilled her. It was cozy in her nest of pillows with the plump quilt cradling her. The knowledge that her own walls surrounded her thrilled her even more than the storm.

The rain beat tiny fists against the windows while thunder rolled and lightening sizzled. The wind tore at the doors with such ferocity, Jill raised her head and looked, expecting to see them blow open.

Lightning flashed, and she bolted upright in bed. Her stomach clenched and fear raced up her spine with clammy hoofs. Standing at her doors was the figure of a man. A slightly-built man. Every inch of the man threw out rage. In the glare of lightening, she could see his hands clenched at his sides, his legs spread wide and his feet planted as if to do battle.

"Not Noah," she whispered. "Too short, too slight to be Noah." She didn't know why that calmed her, but it did.

She bolted from her bed, racing toward the door, wanting to check the bolt, but in the next lightening flash, she could see the man was gone.

Terrified now, she ran into her daughters' room and checked the doors. She did the same, checking on her guests. Marcus and Devin, alerted by her running feet, emerged from their rooms. Jill, almost colliding into them, let out a small scream.

"My God! You two scared the life out of me!"

Marcus looked bemused. "May we ask why you're tearing from room to room like a crazy woman?"

Jill took their hands and led them further down the hall, not wanting to risk the children hearing her.

"I was almost asleep," she whispered. "It sounded like the wind was going to tear the doors off leading from the verandah into my room. I raised my head and, in the lightening, I could see a man standing at the door." Jill took a deep breath, searching for calm. She didn't think she was making much sense in her current state.

"It wasn't Noah. He called. Noah called earlier. I was going to tell you in the morning. This wasn't Noah. He was too short, too slight."

Marcus and Devin exchanged glances. Jill wasn't exactly a fanciful woman.

"I didn't imagine this. He was standing out there! I know what I saw!"

Marcus patted her shoulder. "I believe you, sweetie. Calm down. We'll discuss this in the morning. Vinia and I will be staying over until Monday. I mean to get to the courthouse and file the necessary papers. I am curious about one thing. How did Noah get this number? Would one of the girls have given it to him?"

Jill shook her head. "They won't speak to him. I'd know. Bree may not tell me, but Megan would spill the beans."

Marcus sighed. "I'll get his number from you tomorrow. I'll have someone run his number and find out who he's been talking to." He hugged Jill tight. "We'll get to the bottom of this but, for tonight, let's try to get a little more sleep."

Devin patted her cheek on his way back to his room. "Try not to worry, kiddo. Dad will get to the bottom of this, but I think you should consider getting an alarm system in here. Just to be on the safe side. Ya know?"

Jill waited until the two men returned to their rooms and then did a last sweep through the house.

Knowing everything was secure, Jill returned to her room and fell into a fitful sleep dreaming of Noah chasing her and the girls, a large blade flashing.

Five

Jill woke to sunshine flowing through her windows and the steady drip of rainwater off the eaves. She tossed back the covers and went to the window. She whipped open her doors and stood out on the verandah. Closing her eyes, she breathed in the fresh, clean air and let the sun warm her face.

Hearing the girls, she dashed back into her room, bounced into the shower, and emerged feeling energized. Pushing her fears from the night before into the background, she looked forward to the day.

Jill ran down the back stairs and dashed into the kitchen. Coffee, mingled with the smell of cooking bacon, greeted her.

Lavinia stood at the stove, flipping bacon and preparing to scramble eggs, while Trudy made toast and set the table.

"Good morning," Jill sang out. "How did everyone sleep?"

"That thrilling storm woke me, but other than that, I slept like a baby," Lavinia told her.

"Hmmmm. I don't sleep much, and the storm woke me, as well, but fell back asleep shortly after," Trudy said.

Jill dashed to the back door and flung it open. "Just breathe in all that fresh air! The breeze smells like it was washed clean."

She turned and beamed at the two women who smiled back. "You sure don't get air like that in the city," Lavinia commented.

"Where are my girls? Are those lazy bed-a-bugs still asleep?" Jill asked.

Vinia shook her head as she put the bacon aside to drain. "They've been up for some time. They took Charlie out and then ran back up to their room."

Jill spun on her heel and ran up the stairs. She found Megan and Bree opening boxes and exclaiming over the contents as if it was Christmas morning.

"Did you girls brush your teeth and wash your faces?"

Megan nodded enthusiastically. "We did! Charlie had to go out, and we thought we'd unpack and surprise you."

Jill gathered her girls into her arms and hugged them tight. She closed her eyes, laid her cheek on Bree's soft hair, and then did the same to Megan.

Here are my treasures, she thought. The money she earned would give them a good financial foundation, but her two girls were all the treasure she needed.

"Let's go on down. Aunt Vinia has been busy making us breakfast. Let's not disappoint her."

Charlie's head swiveled around at the word 'breakfast' and bombed out of the room and down the stairs, hell bent for leather to get to his dish.

Bree and Megan followed behind, laughing themselves silly… and it was music to Jill's heart.

She was laughing, herself, as she followed her girls into the kitchen. A wide and foolish grin crossed her face as she watched Bree fill Charlie's food and water bowls.

"I was up and about early," Lavinia said. "So, I dashed into town and picked up a few things for breakfast."

"Well, that explains the bacon and eggs miracle this morning," Jill said.

"I also ran into Mary Lee. She said to tell you they'll be out later this morning to lend a hand. Lovely woman and I think you've made a good friend, Jill. I'll feel better about leaving you here. You're not as alone as I first feared." Lavinia dished up bacon, eggs and toast. "She also mentioned she would be bringing food out, as well."

Marcus and Devin wandered into the kitchen and took seats at the table.

Lavinia, after years of marriage, silently handed her husband a mug of fresh coffee. Marcus didn't do well with morning conversation until he had a few hits of caffeine.

"We'll be heading back today," Devin said. "Trudy has her doctor appointment tomorrow morning and I have to get back to work, but if all goes okay, we'll be back up this weekend."

Trudy opened her mouth and then closed it again.

"Problem, Trudy?" Vinia asked. Trudy shook her head.

"I don't know if I'll be back up." She shot her husband a look. "It's getting pretty close now." She rubbed her belly. "But, we'll see how it all goes."

"I have a court date up here," Marcus growled in his I'm barely awake voice. "I have to file the restraining order in this county. The paperwork is all in order, so there shouldn't be a problem. After court, your mother and I will be heading back to Milwaukee, as well."

Marcus took another hit of life-affirming coffee. "I spent this morning speaking with the judge up here. Lucky for me, he's an old friend so he could fit me in on the docket since everything is pretty cut and dried." He turned to look at Jill. "What are your plans for today, Jill?"

Jill grinned. "My plan is to get these boxes organized and finish getting the kitchen and bathrooms in order. Zach and Mary Lee will be coming over to help, and I plan on going through the barns with him and getting a sense of how many stalls we can build, space for birthing stalls and I think a couple of reinforced stalls for stallions. After that, I plan to send yet another e-mail to Ben Lightfoot, although I'm beginning to think he won't be joining me, sad to say, so I'll need to start looking at employees. This evening, I'm hoping to work on the expansion pack for the *Battle Cry* series." She shook her head in disbelief.

"*Battle Cry - USA* has gone through the roof, and I'll be receiving another hefty check next quarter." She smiled fondly at Marcus. "If you hadn't negotiated a percentage of the sales, I would just be getting royalty checks, so thanks, Uncle Marcus."

He reached over and patted her hand. "Honey, from what I've seen of Steve and Garrett Boyle, your employers would have offered you a percentage anyway." He grinned. "But, you're welcome."

It was an unspoken agreement. The adults would not speak of the previous night's occurrences until the girls were safely away. No sense in alarming them was the universal opinion.

"Mom? I'm stuffed. Can I go?" Megan asked.

"Sure! I'll be up in a little while and we can start unpacking more of your boxes."

Megan held up a little hand. "No, mom. Me and Bree wanna do it. Right Bree?" Bree nodded. "We want to do it ourselves."

"Okay. You girls go ahead. I'll be up to check on you a little later but, first, I think Charlie would really like it if you took him outside and let him run around a little. Stay in the yard, though, and out of the woods." She would have to set boundaries for all three, but for now, it could wait.

They waited until the girls were out of earshot.

Lavinia got to her feet and snatched up the coffee pot, topping off everyone's cups.

"What exactly did Noah say?" Marcus wanted to know. Jill went through the distasteful conversation with her ex-husband. Devin took notes.

"For someone who's not supposed to know anything about you, the bastard has an awful lot of information about you and what you're doing. Thoughts?"

Marcus sipped, his eyes narrowed as he thought things through.

"Obviously, someone is feeding him information. We'll have to find out who and why. Right now, I'm leaning toward his mother. Mothers always have that soft spot for their kids, no matter how rotten said kid is."

Trudy let out a soft, "Oof!" and quickly put her hand over her round belly. "Sorry." She laughed. "I'm sorry, but this little one is bouncing around like a Jumping Bean." She looked around the table. "If you all don't mind, I'm going to run up and start putting our stuff together. This isn't any of my business, anyway." She gave Devin a look before heading up the stairs. He sighed and then got to his feet. "I'd better give her a hand."

Jill began to clear the breakfast dishes, but Lavinia stopped her with a hand on her arm.

"Just sit, Jill. I'll take care of this, but let's finish this discussion. Time is a premium and we don't know how long we have until the horde descends."

The conversation turned to the man Jill saw on the verandah.

"Tell me about the man you saw, Jill," Marcus suggested.

"I saw him the first time earlier in the evening. You all had gone up to bed, and I thought I could take the cardboard out to that burning pit. I saw him standing there and decided not to chance it. I came back in, though, looking for something to defend myself with in case he, you know, came after me, but when I turned around, he was gone."

Jill took a healthy drink of her coffee, more to settle herself than for the caffeine.

"Then, during the storm after that call from Asshole, I wanted to just wander around, make sure everything was secure, and I did that, but when I went back to my room in search of some aspirin, I thought how windy it was. I settled back and began to drift off, but it sounded like my doors were coming off the hinges. I sat up and that's when I saw him again."

"Good Lord, Jillian!" Lavinia wrapped her arms around the young woman and held on tight "Why didn't you come and get us?"

"Uncle Marcus and Devin heard me tearing from room to room, looking to see if this guy managed to get into the house. He didn't, so we all went to bed."

"Noah?" Lavinia wanted to know. Jillian shook her head. "No. This man is smaller, slighter. I don't know who it is, but it's not Noah."

"Oh, Jillian," Lavinia began, worry flitting across her handsome features. "Maybe this isn't such a good idea, after all. I hate the thought of leaving you here on your own."

Jill hugged the older woman. "We're going to be fine. I'll have an alarm system put in. We'll be safe."

Marcus came around the table and enveloped them both in a massive group hug.

"I'll put a buzz in the sheriff's ear. Probably just a local kid looking to put a scare in you." Jill nodded. She had come to the same conclusion, herself, but seeing the worry lingering on Lavinia's face, she wished she had never brought up the subject.

Further discussion was no longer possible as Mary Lee and her brood hustled through the kitchen door. Once again, she was laden with a roaster while her boys hauled in bags.

Mary Lee had pulled her golden curls back into a no-nonsense ponytail, and her bold blue eyes lingered on the coffee maker.

"Don't make me beg for a cup of that," she said to the room in general. "I only had time for one cup. My brain doesn't come close to functioning without at least two!"

Lavinia chuckled as she filled a mug and passed it to the attractive real estate agent.

"What have you brought us to feast on this time?" Marcus gestured toward the roaster.

"Stuffed turkey, grilled veggies, and I forgot something for dessert. I can always run in, this afternoon, and pick something up."

"I've got that covered!" A cheerful voice rang out from the kitchen door. "Mary Lee! You get over here and give me a hand, would you please?"

Mary Lee rushed over and opened the door. She relieved the very attractive elderly woman of one of the pies Helen was currently balancing in her hands.

"Jill, meet Helen Logan. This is Jake's mom," Mary Lee said by way of introduction.

While Mary Lee handled all of the introductions, Jill stood in the middle of her kitchen, wondering why the woman was here.

Mary Lee, sensing Jill's disquiet, rubbed her hand down Jill's arm and then led her to a chair.

"Now, I know you have oodles to do, and I'm not going to get in the way, but I thought you and your family would enjoy some home-baked goods, and this gives me the opportunity to meet my new neighbor."

"Oh. Well, that's very nice of you," Jill said in a faint voice.

Helen's eyes gleamed with a wicked sense of humor.

"Oh, don't be silly. Right now, you're wondering what I'm doing here and what I may want. So, to relieve your mind, I'm here because we're going to be neighbors and this is what neighbors do." Remembering that Jake had used almost the exact same words didn't exactly calm Jill's nerves.

"And I don't want a thing, except to meet my new neighbor and offer to help her any way I can."

Mary Lee poured Helen a cup of coffee and sat across from Jill. Mary Lee thought Jill seemed a little overwhelmed.

Trudy took that moment to wander into the kitchen, and Helen's eyes brightened at the sight of the very pregnant woman.

"Well now, aren't you gorgeous!" Helen exclaimed. Trudy blushed and gave the elderly woman a shy smile.

"When are you due?"

Trudy gave a small shrug. "Any day now."

"Well, you sit down here and take a load off. That's quite a bundle you're carting around with you. How are you feeling?"

"Oh, fine. A little tired."

"I remember when I carried Jake. I didn't think I'd ever get eight straight again. After he arrived, I didn't," Helen said with a laugh. "Now that he's grown, I still don't. So, get all the sleep you can, now," she advised.

The sound of Zach's diesel alerted them to his arrival and Marcus, outgunned, bolted from the kitchen, out the back door and almost ran to Zach's truck. "The kitchen is full of women. Help me."

Jake and Zach's boys emerged from the truck.

"Yeah, I see my mother's here, too." He gave a mighty sigh. "Well, come on, Judge. Let's measure out those stalls until all that estrogen disburses."

Jill spied them heading for the barns, and her lips tightened. This was *her* place and, by Heaven, she'd tell these men where she wanted things and what size her stalls would be.

She had a very definite plan in mind and no bossy, uber male was going to tell her different.

Putting her own plans on hold for the time being, she made a beeline for her barns, fully intent on putting that bossy Jake Logan in his place.

Four women watched in amusement. Jill bolted up to Jake's vehicle. She began to speak rapidly, throwing her arms wide and Helen grinned.

"Now that's interesting to see. I hate that we're missing it."

"Don't worry about a thing," Lavinia told the other women. "I'll get it out of Jill and report back." She looked at Helen, liked what she saw, and decided to go with instinct.

"Jill has had a terrible time this past year. First, she lost both of her parents in a house fire just after last Thanksgiving. A week later, her now ex-husband beat her bad enough to put her in a hospital for almost a month. She's not about to let anyone else run her show anymore."

Helen shook her head. "Men who beat women should have their arms and legs broken, in my opinion. It's good she still has fight in her. Most women wouldn't."

"Helen, I'm going to ask a huge favor of you." Lavinia sighed and looked out the window. "I'm going to ask you to keep an eye on our girl. She tends to overdo, pushing herself until she's ready to drop." Lavinia grabbed a piece of paper, tore off a corner, and scribbled some numbers on it.

"These are all of our numbers. If Jill is in some kind of trouble, call us. She won't ask for help and she'll try to tough it out on her own."

Helen took the paper and shoved it in her pocket and Lavinia took a deep breath. Her gut told her she could count on Helen Logan.

At that moment, Bree and Megan bounced into the kitchen, followed by Charlie. He took one look, gave out a single bark, and then scrambled up in Helen's lap.

Helen's eyes twinkled as she took in the two small girls and their precious pet.

"Now, who is this?" she asked. Lavinia introduced the girls to the sweet lady holding Charlie on her lap while she stroked his ears.

"I want to know what you think you're doing." Jill was fuming.

"I think it's obvious. I'm going to give Zach a hand. Christ, woman, what is your problem?" Jake shook his head.

"My problem is, this is *my* place, and I want things done *my* way. I don't need or want some man coming in here and telling me what to do and how to do it!" Been there, done that, she thought.

"Who the hell is telling you what to do? I'm helping a buddy and also helping a neighbor."

Jake stood, just watching her with his expressive and patient eyes. He knew a little about her history. He figured her for a fighter. So, he waited.

"Look, I'm sorry." Jill spit the words out, causing Jake to grin. She sure as hell didn't sound sorry.

"Let's try this. You tell us what you have in mind, we'll get the thing measured out and, afterwards, you can give me a cup of coffee and maybe a sandwich before using me as a pack mule."

Zack watched Jill get fired up again and rolled his eyes. "Let's not fight, kids. We've got a lot to do and a short time to get it all done, and if we don't make some headway, my wife is going to come down on me like a ton of bricks. Please, spare me."

Jill slid a look at Zach and her lips twitched. He tried to look pathetic. It came off amusing.

She stamped down her temper and explained her plans for her stables. Jake nodded. "It's a good plan. You're going to have two re-enforced stalls?"

"Yeah, why?" He could just tell she was ready to take the leap down his throat again.

"Because I have a stallion who's more than a little headstrong. My stalls are okay for what they are, but I'm thinking I'd like to rent one from you."

"Are you kidding? Why would you do that? Why not just build one to hold him?"

Jake sighed. "I could build one, that's a fact, but I don't have the time to do that and the cold weather will be here before you know it. So, let me rent one from you until you need it."

Jill bit her lip. She knew she was acting like a fool but, dammit, the man appealed to her and she didn't want those kinds of entanglements right now. She was still getting her feet under her. Throw in her mistrust of her own judgment and it was quite a quandary.

On the other hand, the extra money would help defray her start-up costs. Not by much, but it would be a start.

"We can talk about it after the stalls are built. If you think one of them would work, we'll discuss rent at that time."

Jake nodded. It was a start.

He liked her plans. The stalls would be roomy, which was always a plus, and her plan for a birthing stall was right on target. Plenty of room for mom and baby plus the humans who would be needed to give mom a hand.

Obviously, the woman knew what she was about. Jake liked that sort of competency

The sound of a vehicle gliding up the drive had eyes turning in that direction. Jill didn't recognize the small, sporty, candy-apple red car and she tensed. Marcus strode to her side while Zach swore under his breath.

"Who is that, Zach?" Marcus asked.

"Steffi Brandt." His tone was flat, his features rigid. "You can bet money that wherever Steffi shows up, trouble's right behind her."

Jill sighed. She was at the end of her patience. All of these visitors, while most were welcome, took time away from her plans for the day.

"I suppose I should see what she wants," Jill muttered. Zach shook his head. He slid a glance in Jake's direction. "You can bet she isn't here to see you, Jill," he said and strode off in the opposite direction.

"I'll see what she wants, Jill. You go about whatever it is you want to get done," Marcus offered, but Jill shook her head.

"If she's here to get a look at me, I'll give her one."

Jill was done running.

Six

Steffi Brandt was trouble. The only child of wealthy parents, she had been spoiled and pampered for most of her life.

She attended the best schools and lived abroad for a time while she dabbled in painting. She had no talent for it, nor the discipline to learn anything, but off to Paris she had gone to "study" after the death of her father and then her mother a couple of years later. Steffi went through her inheritance like water. Lucky for her, her father's only relative, dear old Aunt Alberta, had invested wisely. A widow whose husband bit the big one in Vietnam, Alberta gathered a small fortune through very wise investments.

Luckily for Steffi, they bought the house before poor Uncle Gray left for far off shores. It was the first thing Alberta paid off.

The poor old thing lived off her wages as the owner of Alberta's Flower Pot, a trendy florist shop she opened and ran until she retired.

Steffi knew there was money, and she waited until the time was right, visiting the old dear often, laying the groundwork for what would come next.

Dear old Aunt Alberta played right into Steffi's hands, and Steffi managed to tuck the elderly woman away in a nursing home and had herself appointed legal guardian.

Beautiful and entitled, she had no use for anyone with nothing to offer her, which meant if one didn't have a great deal of money, she wouldn't be bothered.

The only bump in her road was Jake.

Jake Logan was everything she wanted and believed she had coming to her. He was ever so virile, which appealed to her as a woman. He had a position in the community, which she felt she should share. And he had a great deal of money, which Steffi needed.

She tended to go through a great deal of money but, after all, it took a lot of the green stuff to keep up appearances, and the money from the sale of her aunt's home would last a short time. Today, Steffi decided, would be the day she began her campaign for the ruggedly sexy sheriff, but she heard rumblings.

She heard he was spending time with Jill Tolivar, and that didn't set well with Steffi. Steffi didn't like it when people got in her way. Jillian Tolivar was currently standing in her way.

She strolled into Mike's Diner, looking for her target, stunning in a pale blue sundress. Gems flashed in her ears and around her wrist. The gold ankle bracelet she slipped on to draw attention to the strappy sandals she wore glinted in the sun.

"Morning, Mike, have you seen Jake?" she asked the owner of Mike's Diner.

"Nope. Haven't seen him all morning." Mike shrugged. He didn't like Steffi and didn't bother to hide it.

"Come on, Mike. You know everything that goes on in this town. I know he isn't working, and he's not at his place. He's not answering his cell, either."

"Sorry, Steffi. No idea." Mike turned back to his grill and began to clean it vigorously.

She caught the smirk Mike's wife tossed at her husband, and she *knew*. He had to be at the Tolivar woman's house.

Only one way to make sure, Steffi thought as she turned on her heel and left the diner in a huff. It never entered her mind that she had just made a complete fool of herself.

In Steffi's mind, every man wanted her and every woman wanted to *be* her.

She climbed into her little red BMW and pointed it out of town. She would find out just what in the hell was going on and put a stop to it... fast.

Marcus watched while Devin hauled a duffel bag from the house and tossed it into his truck. He and Trudy would be making their way back to Milwaukee shortly and he wanted a word with them before they left, but he had other, more pressing things on his mind.

He caught Jake's eye and gestured toward the barn with a jerk of his head.

Marcus waited to be sure they would not be overheard.

"A couple of things I need to run by you." Marcus did a quick look around before continuing. "Early this morning, Jillian received a phone call from her ex-husband. Since there is a No Contact Order in place, I'll be investigating to find out just how he's finding out all of the information he seems to have concerning her and the children. My wife and I will be staying over until tomorrow when I'll be filing the necessary paperwork for a no contact in this county."

Jake's eyes hardened. "Did he ever harm the girls?"

Marcus shook his head. "No. Jillian always protected those kids. The last time he went after her, she made damn sure those kids got out of the condo they were living in and safely into a neighbor's. It was the neighbor who called the cops."

Jake nodded. He knew it was unprofessional, but he'd like to get his hands on the ex-husband and teach him some manners.

"What's the other thing?" Jake thought it better to change the subject somewhat.

"Last night, or rather early this morning, Jillian said she saw someone standing at her door. The one leading into her bedroom."

"The ex?"

Marcus shook his head.

"No. She said this guy was of a smaller build. She couldn't make out his features, but she said he was there." Marcus slid a glance at the huge man standing next to him. "Before you ask, Jillian is steeped in science. She doesn't have a fanciful bone in her body. If she said someone was out there... then, someone was out there."

"Okay. I'll look into it... see what I can find out."

Jake took two steps in Jill's direction, intending to get more information on the intruder, when Steffi pulled into the driveway. Cursing under his breath, he changed direction and went off in search of Zach.

Helen Logan watched as Steffi emerged from her car. Her lips tightened and she cursed softly, drawing Lavinia's attention.

"Problem?"

Helen gestured out the window. "That barracuda is circling, and she's got her beady little eyes on my son."

Lavinia grinned. "Care to fill me in?"

Helen snorted. "I'll give you the short version. Steffi is a spoiled brat who somehow managed to seize control of Alberta's estate and assets. She tucked the woman into a nursing home, proceeded to go through every cent Alberta managed to save and ended up selling this house to Jillian to cover her own ass. She plowed through the money left to her by her parents and, now, Alberta's as well. Everyone in town knows what she is."

"And other than a money grubbing witch, what is she?" Lavinia asked.

"She's the town bicycle. Most everyone has had a ride with the exception of a few of the men here who were smart enough to stay clear of her claws."

Lavinia snorted. "Wow! That's some accomplishment."

"Yeah, and now she's got her sights set on Jake. He made a bad mistake once before. That's his story," she added, seeing the avid interest in Lavinia's eyes.

Lavinia nodded as she watched Jill walk over to the other woman. Neither Jill nor Steffi looked happy to see each other. She wished she could be out there to hear the exchange.

"Well, well, well. You certainly don't look like the lady of the manor." Steffi studied Jill, taking in well-worn work boots, well-worn jeans, and a plain black t-shirt.

Jill studied Steffi in return. The woman's purring voice put Jill's nerves on edge.

"No? Well when there's work to be done, you dress for it if you're smart."

Steffi stiffened. She really didn't like this woman with the cute gamin face and the air of someone who knows what she wants and knows how to go about getting it. She glanced over to where Bree and Megan were playing with Sam and Cody.

"Those are yours, I presume?" She pointed to the kids and Charlie.

"Of course they're mine, and they're called children." Jill's tone was icy.

"Well, tell them to keep their grimy paws off my car, will you dear?" Steffi sauntered away, leaving Jill sputtering in fury.

Zach spied Steffi slithering into the barn before Jake did and muttered an "oh-oh" under his breath.

Jake heard and lifted his eyes from the measuring tape. His eyes glinted coldly as he watched Steffi sashay toward him.

"I've been looking for you. Don't you have better things to do on your day off?"

"I'm helping a friend and a new neighbor. I find that important."

Steffi laughed as she tossed back that beautiful mass of red hair.

"Well, maybe we can think of a way to reward you for your good deeds. How about I pick up a bottle of wine and we take a ride up to Sunset Point and watch the stars come out?" She ran a finger around the collar of his blue work shirt.

"Thanks, Steffi, but we're gonna be tied up here for most of the afternoon and evening." Sunset Point, Jake thought. Really? We're a little old for that nonsense, he thought. Wisely, he kept his thoughts to himself. No need to create a scene. He did wonder, though, if just maybe his mother and Mary Lee were correct. Damn, he hoped not. Steffi was a friend; he'd hate to lose that because she had other ideas in her pretty head.

Zach didn't bother to hide his smirk. That irritated Jake, too.

Steffi ran a hand down his arm, calling for his undivided attention.

"Yes, well maybe the little twit shouldn't have bought such a big place if she can't handle it alone. Besides, work has to end eventually. I'll be waiting."

Jake tensed at the insult directed toward Jill. Steffi saw the change in his demeanor and shrugged it off as she sauntered away.

Zach and Jake looked at each other and then Zach rolled his eyes. If anyone had zero twit factor, it was Jillian Tolivar.

"Steffi called that one wrong," Zach said and went back to his measuring.

Jillian ran her hands through her short curls. Time was wasting and she decided Steffi wasn't worth one more minute.

On that thought, she turned on her heel and headed for the house. A conversation between Sam, Mary Lee's twelve-year-old son, and Bree brought her up short.

"How come your dad doesn't live with you?" Sam wanted to know.

"We divorced him. He isn't allowed around us."

"How come?"

"He hit her. Last Thanksgiving time, he put her in the hospital. We went to live with Uncle Marcus and Aunt Lavinia until mom was better."

"Oh, wow!"

"Does your dad ever hit your mom?" Bree wanted to know. Sam shook his head.

"Nope."

"I'm afraid of my dad. He tried to hurt me and Megan, too, but we got away. We got to some neighbors and they called the police. Mom would always make sure he hit her and not us but, sometimes, it didn't always work."

Bree's eyes sparkled with unshed tears. Because this was important, Sam looked away.

"I'll protect you, too. You're my friend, and I'll make sure he doesn't come here and hit you or your mom again. She's nice. You and Megan are nice, too… for girls."

Jill stood with her hand on her heart. She needed to find Mary Lee and tell her what she heard, but she wondered… could that boy be any sweeter? Jill didn't think so.

Heading toward the house, a racing engine caught her attention. She watched as Steffi sped down the driveway and turned onto Ransom Road.'

"Bitch didn't even look for the kids!" she muttered to herself, followed by the thought, thank God she's gone.

A movement caught her attention. On a corner of her yard, facing the road, stood the man she had seen the night before. He watched as Steffi sped down the road, and he was angry.

His rage was evident in his stance. His hands were drawn up in fists and, even from this distance, Jill could see his feet were planted wide, his shoulders tense.

Jill opened her mouth to call out, turned away for a second to find Marcus and when she turned back, he was gone.

She rushed around the house in search of Marcus, Zach, or even Jake. Anyone would do.

She found the three men together. Speaking rapidly, she told them what she saw.

Jake listened intently, asked a pointed question now and again, and took mental notes.

"You see him again, you call me. This doesn't sound like anyone local, but obviously, he knows his way around the property." He gave her a hard stare. "I mean it, Jillian. You see him again, you call me. I don't care what time it is. Understood?"

Thank God, she thought. Thank God, he believes me.

Jill nodded and made her way toward her house, wondering if she would ever have any peace.

Seven

Trudy and Devin stood next to their vehicle, waiting.

"We're heading out" Devin told Jill.

She rushed over to hug Trudy and then Devin.

"I want to hear as soon as that baby gets here." Jill rubbed her hand on Trudy's arm.

"I'm sure Devin will call you as soon as it's over."

Jill laughed. "He better!"

Trudy sighed and looked over at her husband. "I suppose we better get this show on the road." She turned to Jill. "I am so not looking forward to the drive home, but we'll be back up for Thanksgiving, for sure. Maybe sooner if the baby cooperates."

Jill hugged her again, grateful they had worked past the jealousy that ate at Trudy until there was a confrontation. For months, Trudy believed Devin was in love with Jill, and it took that confrontation to show Trudy the error of her ways. Now, Jill felt she had a sister to go with her surrogate brother. She was content.

Devin helped Trudy into the car then stood with his hands on his hips. "You've got a good place here, Jill. I think you'll make a good life for you and the girls." He smiled at her, but worry rode in his eyes.

"Did you hear from Ben, yet?"

Jill shook her head. "Not yet. He'll contact me when he's ready. Until then, I have a lead on a couple of guys that could use the extra work. Zack and Jake both vouched for them, so if they're half-way as good as I'm told they are, they should work out okay."

"Maybe." Worry still creased Devin's handsome face.

"I'd feel better if Ben was here with you, but I get it. The guy always did march to his own beat." Jill laughed and turned to include Trudy in the conversation when she rolled down her window.

"Devin, you are such a worrier," Trudy said. "I'm sure Jill knows what she's doing." Trudy adjusted herself in the seat, trying to make herself comfortable.

"Devin, take this woman home. I'm sure she's anxious to be in her own house and sleep in her own bed."

Jill reached in and gently rubbed Trudy's arm. "If you find yourself up and about, call me. Sometimes, it helps to talk to someone who's been through it, including the late pregnancy insomnia."

Trudy laughed and squeezed Jill's hand. "I just might do that."

Marcus walked over and leaned in, kissing Trudy on the cheek. "You take care of yourself and my grand-baby. Make Devin cook tonight since he weaseled out of helping out around here, today."

Devin walked over and hugged his dad tight. The two men looked at each other, father to son. There was mutual pride mixed in with love in that look.

Marcus felt his heart swell. Hearing a sound, he turned to see Lavinia standing in the yard, watching. He held out his hand and pulled Lavinia into another hug.

Jill felt a twinge of envy. She would never have that with her own parents. Not ever again. She was grateful Devin shared his parents with her. It helped ease the grief that reached up at odd times to strangle her.

Marcus wrapped one long arm around her shoulders and squeezed.

"Let's go in and see what the ladies have whipped up for lunch. I'm starving."

Jillian grinned. "No surprise there, Uncle Marc. Seems like we didn't accomplish much. I feel like I'm spinning my wheels."

Marcus ruffled her short curls, a habit since Jill was a child.

"Well, maybe we'll be surprised and more got done than we think."

The two made their way into the kitchen and Jillian came to an abrupt halt. Helen Logan was busy setting the table. All the breakfast dishes had been washed and put away, and Lavinia was setting out bread, lunch-meats, and condiments.

"Where on earth is all this food coming from?" Jill wondered. Lavinia laughed.

"Thank Mary Lee. She keeps doing loaves and fishes miracles."

"Mrs. Logan, you didn't have to do that," Jill began, and Helen shushed her.

"I know I didn't. I also know you've bitten off quite a bit. This gave me something to do and gave me time to become acquainted with those two beautiful little girls. Now, we'll sit down, have some lunch and I'll get to know you as well. Everything happens for a reason, you know." Helen was a big fan of fate.

Helen called Zach, Jake and the boys in for lunch as Mary Lee came bopping down the stairs.

"You may want to see what I've done upstairs, Jill. I followed your diagrams and put the beds in the west wing together. Your towels and sheets are in the linen closets and the girls helped me unpack their toys and those are all safely on the shelves in their room."

Jill sat back and looked at the people sitting around her table. She knew there were people like this. She just didn't know any. Noah never allowed her to make friends. Now, she had Mary Lee and Zach. She supposed Helen could be considered a friend now, too. The jury was still out on Jake.

She thought he was overbearing and condescending. He considered himself a take-charge kind of guy. Helen thought he was a little of both.

Then there was Devin and Trudy.

Jill and Devin were as close as most siblings, joining and encouraging each other in their plot against parental units. If Jill didn't think of mischief to get into, Devin did. Jill guessed, between the two of them, they put more gray hairs on their parents' heads than anything life could have thrown at them.

Trudy completely misunderstood the relationship between Devin and Jillian until Jill spelled it out for her. The love she and Devin shared was the same as siblings. Anything else would have been incestuous. It took some doing, but Trudy finally understood and welcomed Jill into her life with open arms.

"Mom?" Megan tapped Jill's shoulder to get her mother's attention.

"What is it, sweetie?" Jill wrapped her arm around her.

"Can we take our plates outside and have a picnic? It's nice out."

Jill looked at her daughter, into eyes so like her own, and smiled.

"If you like. I hear you helped unpack some of your toys, so I think you guys deserve a little treat."

"Sweet!" Cody pumped a fist into the air.

Zack and Jake set up an impromptu picnic table for the kids, using some boards and a couple of sawhorses. The kids were in seventh Heaven.

The adults helped themselves to thick ham slices, rye bread, and condiments. Helen put together a fruit salad and Mary Lee brought out a large bowl of potato salad and a pot of baked beans.

A small mountain of miniature cream puffs sat on a counter. Jill knew she would be hitting those before going back to work.

Plans flew around the table. Suggestions and small talk added spice to the conversation. Jill couldn't recall the last time she laughed so much and so hard. Even Jake seemed to be getting into the swing of things.

"I see Steffi tracked you down," Helen said. It amazed Jill to see Jake shift uncomfortably. He frowned at his mother.

"Mom. Don't start. It's not like that."

"So, what's it like, then?" Zach asked, a wide smile on his face. "Enlighten us all."

Jake frowned at his friend.

"Steffi and I are friends." At that, Mary Lee gave a most unfeminine snort. Jake frowned at her, and she laughed in his face.

"Oh c'mon, Jake. It's *exactly* like that. Everyone sees it but you. I don't know if it's because you don't want to see what she's after or you really are that stupid. Since you're not a stupid man, it looks like door number one. You don't want to see. So, I guess that does make you stupid, after all!" Mary Lee said.

Jake scowled at her but, before he could comment, Jill dropped a little bombshell.

"I saw that man, again." The silence was deafening.

"What?" Marcus grabbed her hand. "When? Where?"

"He was standing at the edge of the lawn, watching Steffi when she drove away."

"Why didn't you say anything?" Jake wanted to know.

"Well, I turned to call to one of you but, when I turned back, he disappeared. Then. Devin and Trudy were leaving. Next thing I knew, it was lunch time… and, quite frankly, I didn't want the kids to overhear."

"Next time, you let me know. Don't wait. Don't hesitate."

"Right! I'll just cup my hands and scream at the top of my lungs, 'Oh, Sheriff, the peeping tom is back.'"

He struggled to keep his irritation under control.

"Did you get a decent look at him?"

"Short, slight build, sandy blonde hair. Since his back was to me, that's all I saw. Oh yeah, and he was really angry."

"If you didn't see his face, how could you tell he was angry?" Jake took a notebook from his pocket, made some notes, and fired questions at her. Jill thought he was probably very good at interrogations. She imagined criminals would quake in fear.

She was just irritated.

"Oh, I don't know. Maybe it's the fact his feet were planted wide apart and his hands were clenched in fists at his side. I would say those were pretty good indicators, wouldn't you?" Jill's voice was sickly sweet. Marcus and Lavinia exchanged looks and grinned. This was going to be fun to watch.

"Okay… next time you see him, call," Jake ordered and Jill rolled her eyes.

"Well, if everyone's finished eating, I'll get at these dishes and mosey on home," Helen announced.

"Oh gosh, Helen! You don't have to do that. I feel bad. You've been such a big help, and I've barely had a chance to sit down and talk with you. I feel terrible."

Helen reached over and patted Jill's hand.

"Don't you worry about that. We'll have plenty of time to get to know each other… and as to that, I'm available to watch those two beautiful girls any time you need me."

"Helen, why don't you come back for dinner?" Jill invited. "Then, we can sit and have a nice chat."

Helen's smile bloomed across her face. "I'd like that."

Mary Lee grinned as she ran a hand down Helen's arm. "We'll be eating at six. Just come back any time."

Helen left, and Jill headed for her study. Her computer sat ready and waiting for her. "I'm going to get my work place organized so I can get back to earning a living, and I thought after dinner, we could do a bonfire. We can get rid of all cardboard boxes and have fun doing it."

"Hey, now! That's a fabulous idea. I'll run into town and get supplies for S'mores," Mary Lee offered.

Jill went in search of her purse, pulled out some money, and handed it to her.

"This should take care of it." Jill handed several bills to Mary Lee. "In the meantime, I'm going to get organized, check my e-mail, and then head upstairs and finish putting my own stuff away and then get the girls' clothes hung up and organize their room a little more." Jill looked around. In spite of the busy morning, her house still wasn't home. Not yet. But it was getting there.

Jill stood in the middle of her study and looked around. Her computer was up and ready to go. That's a good thing, she thought.

She ripped open boxes and gathered the files nested in them, placing them on her desk before organizing them. She placed finished games on her upper shelves, leaving room for the games she intended to write.

It didn't take long before her study was put to rights. It was a workspace and one she only dreamed about. Now, it belonged to her.

Sitting behind her computer, she fired it up. There were two e-mails. One from her employers.

Congratulations girlfriend. Now, send us your address for our files.
Love Steven and Garrett.

The second e-mail came from Ben.

Hey little girl, happy to hear your news. Can't wait to hear your plans.
Send address and phone number. Talk soon.
Ben

Typical Ben, she thought. At least he finally got in touch. She couldn't ask for more than that.

She sent off replies to her bosses and Ben, and then got to her feet.

Jill paced from room to room. The good sounds of organization filled her home and she grinned. Without Mary Lee, Zach, Marcus, and Lavinia, the work wouldn't have been done so quickly. Because of them, she would be able to relax a little. Her house, almost completely organized, delighted her.

Jill decided this would be a good time to run into town and get her grocery shopping done.

"Aunt Vinia, I'm going to run into town. I'll take the girls with me."

Lavinia glanced up as she put the finishing touches in Jill's dining room.

"No need. They're up in their sitting room with the boys, video gaming their brains out. I'll keep an eye on them."

It began as a quick run to the store. It turned out to be a two-hour ordeal. People stopped her, asking questions and welcoming her to Molton. Their curiosity was gentle, but a little daunting.

Well, she told herself, you wanted small town living. This is it, so don't complain.

By the time she returned home, Zach and Jake were hauling the now-empty moving boxes out to the fire-pit. The fire would be a fine one, she decided, and just the beginning of new memories for the girls as well as herself.

"I found some old boards in the old barn out back," Jake told her. Once that cardboard gets rolling, we'll add it to the fire. Should be a good time."

Jill nodded as she opened the back of her truck. Jake took one look inside and shook his head.

"Good God, woman! Did you buy out the store? How much can one woman and two little girls eat?" He took in Jill's petite body and grinned. "You eat up all this food, you'll be as round as you are tall."

Jill's back stiffened. "I've about had it with men telling me what's wrong with my body. I plan on working hard on this place, and I'll need the carbs. My girls are growing and need the fuel. I buy healthy snacks and healthy food for them, not junk food, and what I've purchased is no one's business but my own!" She grabbed several bags and began hauling them into the house.

Jake grabbed a few more bags and followed her into the house. She turned on him like a small fury.

"I'm perfectly capable of carrying in my own groceries," she told him. "I don't need your help! I don't need anyone's help!" She knew she was being ungracious. She didn't care.

Jake came up behind her and put the bags on the floor. He grabbed her by her shoulders and spun her around.

He was at the end of his patience as well.

"Look. I'm being a friend. I figure after everything you've been through, you could use one. Doesn't mean I think you're incapable. Any woman who has been through the things you've been through is more than capable. I only want two things from you. Your friendship and the opportunity to rent out one of those stalls you have planned for a stallion. The one I have is okay, but my guy is a champion and deserves the best. You're building the best. So! What do you say? Do we have a deal?"

If Jake's intention had been to make her feel small and ungrateful, he succeeded.

"I'm sorry. I just haven't had much luck with men. If you know my history, you know that's true. I'll try very hard not to take exception, but you'll have to be patient with me. I've been taken for a very costly ride and, depending on certain circumstances, that ride could become even more costly. And, yes, you can rent out one of the stalls. We'll discuss price after they're built."

She gave him a rare smile. "What's your guy's name?"

Jake grinned. "Chief. He's a big beautiful bastard. Full Quarter horse with the classic look about him. Good-natured for the most part, too. The fact he's well-trained was a bonus."

Jake noticed Jill's face had gone bone white. "What's the matter?"

"Can I ask where you acquired him?"

"There was a sale. The owners died..." Jake stopped.

"What was the name of the agent?"

"Ben Lightfoot."

Jill closed her eyes as grief rose up and choked her. She felt Jake put an arm around her shoulders as he led her to a chair.

"Sit down here and catch your breath. I have more to tell you, but catch your breath, first."

"What? What else do you have to tell me?"

"I bought several of the mares, too. One had her foal this past spring."

A small sparkle lit Jill's eyes. "You have Gypsy?"

Jake nodded. "I never put it together. I have Jillian's Gypsy. We named her filly Jillian's Gypsy Rose. My mother is a big fan of the lady and the name sort of fits her. She's sleek and flirty."

Unable to sit still, Jill surged to her feet.

"Can I see them? Would it be okay if we came over after we're settled and see them?"

Jake reached up and played with her curls. "Sure you can. Anytime." He turned toward the door and then stopped. "Jill, I am a firm believer that everything happens for a reason. How about you?"

She occupied her hands, putting away groceries while her mind raced. She never heard Lavinia enter the kitchen.

"Jill? Are you okay?" Concern rode the older woman's lovely face. Jill smiled and nodded.

"Jake has Gypsy and Chief. He bought them at the sale after mom and dad..." she left the unspoken words hang in the air.

"It's something, isn't it?" Lavinia ran a soothing hand down Jill's arm. "You buying this place and then finding out who has your two favorite horses. It's something to think about, isn't it?"

"In what way?"

"In the way that you are meant to be here. In the way, that perhaps you and Jake should be friends. In the way that perhaps now you can see the rest of your life a little clearer."

Jill paused, her hand on her hip. "You're right, Aunt Vinia. You are absolutely right. It's interesting, too, that Jake said almost the same thing to me a few minutes ago.

Lavinia grinned. "Well, there ya go. Something else to think about."

Jill thought of little else while she worked to get her office together. She thanked all the fates for Lavinia and Mary Lee, who together organized the guest rooms according to her diagrams. She imagined she would go through the rooms later and fine-tune everything, but for the time being, her house was coming together and, most importantly, her workspace came together just as well.

It was, she thought, almost as if this place was meant for her and the life she was building for her daughters.

Her thoughts came around to Jake. What she took for arrogance was authority and responsibility. Both sat on those broad shoulders comfortably.

He made it clear. He wanted friendship, nothing more. She would be an ass to reject that friendship, especially since no strings seemed to be attached.

Her problem and she had to admit, it *is* her problem, was judging all men by the Noah standard. Not all men were like her ex-husband. She needed to remind herself of that from time to time.

By the time they all sat down to a dinner of roast turkey, baked ham, potato salad, a veggie tray and Helen's homemade apple pie, Jill thought she had a number of things sorted out.

"I know it'll be some time before you begin to build your herd," Jake said, passing a platter of turkey to Jill. "You'll need some help stringing fence. I can help with that."

"We all can help with that," Zach piped in.

Jill opened her mouth to object and then mentally slapped herself.

"I can get it started. You people all have other jobs to do, but I can at least get it started." Jill shifted just enough to face Jake full on and look into his eyes. "But, I'll accept any help you all can give me."

And that, Jake thought, was as close as it was going to get to her admitting she needed help. He could live with that.

Helen grinned. It was obvious that during her absence, her son and Jill made the first steps toward friendship. It was a start.

Eight

After dinner and after Jill's kitchen was put to rights, Mary Lee gathered her brood. The boys were tired and she noticed her oldest, Sam, was quiet. She didn't worry. She knew he would come to either Zach or herself and spill what was bothering him and, if he didn't, Cody would.

Mary Lee wrapped Jillian in a warm hug and squeezed tight. "You're just what this town needs," she said. "I'm so glad you're here!"

Those few words filled a spot in Jill's heart with warmth. Everyone she met in town let her know she was welcomed, and it made her battered heart sing.

"I'm glad to be here!" Jill said in a voice filled with emotion. "It's a good place. We'll heal here."

Mary Lee hugged her again before turning toward her crew and ordering her boys into the truck.

"I have several showings tomorrow but I'll give you a call later, you know, just to see how you're doing."

Jill laughed. "Thanks, mother hen, but Uncle Marc has to be in court first thing and then, after, he and Aunt Lavinia will be heading home. I'll give you a call early evening."

She walked over to the truck and gave Zach a hug.

"Thank you so much. We got a lot accomplished. It's a good day," Zach said as he wrapped her in a bear hug. "You need anything, just call. I'll be out tomorrow, first thing. We'll get those stalls framed in."

"All of them?" Jill asked, laughing.

Zach hugged her again. "I gotta tell you, girl. I appreciate the work. It's been pretty lean for my company these days."

Jill hugged him again. "I'm learning I can't do it all myself. That's what friends are for, right? Helping each other, right?"

Zach gave her a wide smile. "Yeah, but I'm not gonna bill ya for today." Laughing, he climbed into his truck. Mary Lee rolled her eyes and shook her head.

"Talk to you tomorrow," she called out as Zach carefully backed his truck down the sweeping driveway.

Arriving home, Mary Lee shooed her boys into the house while she and Zach unloaded the truck.

It didn't take long to get her own kitchen whipped back in order, but by the time she was done, Sam emerged from his room, smelling of soap, shampoo and toothpaste. He was dressed in striped pajamas, his grown-up pajamas he liked to call them.

"Well, Sam, my man. Something on your mind?" She draped an arm across his shoulders.

"I think I need to talk to dad. It's man stuff."

"Oh. Okay. I believe he's in the den, relaxing. Why don't you go in and talk to him. I'll keep Cody busy in here so you're not interrupted." As he turned to go, she called him back.

"Think you could use a snack after your man talk?"

Sam shook his head, surprising his mother. "I don't think so, Mom. Thanks."

She watched her oldest boy head for the den in search of his dad. Something mighty weighty was on her boy's mind, but she would wait and find out from Zach just what bothered their son so much.

Zach searched ESPN, looking for a game. His mood improved because of the work lined up. Pickings had been slim but, because of Jillian, it wouldn't be necessary to lay anyone off. Always a big plus, to his way of thinking.

Movement in the doorway had him turning his head. He watched Sam come into the room. His boy stood next to his recliner and studied him with very sober eyes.

"What's up, Champ?" Zach put an arm around Sam and drew him closer. Whatever the boy had on his mind had to be serious.

"Dad. You said we shouldn't ever hit girls. Does that go for ladies, too?"

"Yes, son. It does."

Sam nodded and studied his father's face. "Did you ever want to hit mom?"

Ordinarily, Zach would have given the kid a smart-ass answer, but obviously, this wasn't the time.

"No, Sam. I've never wanted to hit your mom. Want to tell me what brought all this on?"

"Bree said her dad hurt her mom real bad. She said Jill had to go to a hospital to get better. Why would he do that?"

Zach wondered how to explain something to Sam that he himself never understood.

"Sam, sometimes people just have a mean streak. You know what a bully is?"

Sam nodded. "Sure I do."

"Okay then. Men who hit women are bullies."

"Bree said she's afraid her dad will come and hurt their mom again. They're all alone out there."

And, there was the crux of the problem. Sam knew Jill and her girls were alone. His instinct would be to protect. Zach sighed.

His son was taking those first shaky steps toward manhood. His little boy was growing up.

Zach didn't know if he should be sad that his son was growing up or take pride in the man his son would become.

He decided to feel both.

"Okay, son, I can see you're pretty worried about this, so I'll fill you in on a couple of things. We're installing a security system. If Bree's dad tries to come in, the alarm will sound right down at the cop shop. Jake knows about everything that happened and he lives right up the road, so he would get there right away, and they have Jill's house on a regular patrol and, don't forget, Jill's pretty feisty. She's prepared and I have a feeling, between herself and her baseball bat, she could do some real damage."

Sam took a deep breath and nodded. He liked Bree and Megan, and he liked Jillian. His dad took a lot of worry off his shoulders, but he decided he would look out for Bree and her sister, Megan, at school. That would be his job, but he wouldn't let them know.

"I'll sorta, ya know, keep an eye on the girls at school. You know how some of the kids are," Sam said.

Zach ran his hand over the boy's head, then ruffled his hair.

"You do that, Sam." Zach slid a glance in his son's direction.

"Want to watch some of the game with me?" he asked. Sam's face flushed with pleasure. "Thanks, dad, but I'm kind of tired. I think I'll go to bed."

Zach hugged his oldest and wondered how long it would be before Sam would insist on manly handshakes instead of hugs.

Zach thought it wouldn't be long.

"Night, son," he called as Sam made his way out of the den. Something tightened in his heart and then released when Sam turned and waved.

Yep, Zach thought, his boy was growing up.

"I'm heading on home," Helen announced. "I need to feed the horses and then I think I'm going to make it an early night." She walked over and gave Jill a hard one-arm hug.

"You need something, you call. I'm almost always home."

"Thank you and I will," Jill promised.

"I'm going up and grab a fast shower before Marcus comes in and hogs the bathroom," Lavinia announced. She held out a hand to Helen.

"I have so enjoyed meeting you. I hope to see you again, often."

Helen laughed. "Oh, you will, Lavinia. That's a promise."

Helen walked to her car, flashing a jaunty wave to her son and Marcus.

The two men returned her wave and resumed their conversation.

"I need to be in court first thing and, after that, Vinia and I will be heading home. I'm going to leave Jill in your capable hands, but I want you to call me if anything develops."

"Not a problem, Judge. I have her on our route, so we'll be keeping a close eye on things around here." Jake sighed. "I'd tell you not to worry, but you and I know that no matter what I promise, if the ex has it in his mind to get to her, he'll do it."

"You're not reassuring me."

"I don't mean to. We need to be realistic. I'll have my mom keep a close watch on things here as well. She's sharp. She'll let me know if there's anything off around here. But, as we know… a restraining order is just a piece of paper. If he wants to risk jail time for breaking it, he will."

Marcus sighed. "It just never ends for her, does it?" He shook his head. "To lose her folks in that way, and then finding out her husband is the prime suspect… it just never ends."

"Any progress on the investigation?"

Marcus shrugged. "Not really. He's got an alibi, and they can't seem to break it. He's still their number one, but they are still looking into other avenues as well. Maybe a serial arsonist who wanted to add to his kicks. Who the hell knows?"

"Just how bad was it?" Jake asked.

"You saw the pictures, didn't you? I know I faxed them to you."

Jake nodded. "Yeah, I got 'em. Was it as bad as it looked?

Marcus sighed. "Worse. Much worse."

"Why don't you fill me in?"

"Yes, okay. It all began after the double funeral for Jill's parents. They were killed on Thanksgiving night, and Jill was notified the next morning. She was devastated." Marcus's eyes reddened as he remembered. "Before that, the week before the killings, her parents sat her down and explained about changes in their will. God! They hated Noah, but I am confident that if they had known what he would do to her, they would have given him everything."

Marcus ran a hand through his thick white hair and gave a deep sigh. "Anyway, Noah gave Jill all of his attention at the funeral. We knew he did it for show and he put on a good one. He was oh so attentive at the funerals. It was sickening, really."

Marcus slid a glance toward Jake, and his estimation of the man rose considerably. Jake gave Marcus his full attention, his craggy face tense. Marcus could only wonder what was going through the man's mind.

"So, we knew Jillian would be receiving a hefty royalty check. Her employers notified her and she told me. I called them and asked them to hold off on that for the time being. They were apprised of the situation and agreed."

Marcus kicked a small stone and turned to Jake. "You see, Jillian had decided Noah would never change. She intended to file for divorce right after the holidays." Marcus shook his head. "She didn't get the chance. Not then, anyway."

Marcus faced Jake straight on and gave him the rest of the story.

"After the funerals, we waited a few days until I read the will. Noah began drinking heavily. Lavinia, Devin, and I begged her to stay with us, but Jill does have a mind of her own."

Jake still said nothing, listening and wondering what kind of man would raise his hand to a woman. Oh, he knew. He just wondered what it took for a man to beat on a woman and apparently in front of their children.

He would never understand it.

"Where were the girls?" Jake asked and Marcus sighed again.

"That's the hell of it. They were there when Noah tore into Jill. I have often wondered where Jillian got the strength to get those girls out of that hell, but she did."

Marcus shook his head, his eyes hazy as he remembered.

"The girls ran to a neighbor they trusted, and the neighbor called nine-one-one and then called us. We got there shortly after the uniforms did. One of them told me it took three of them to get Noah away from Jillian."

"How bad was she?" Jake asked and Marcus's eyes filled with tears.

"Broken left leg, dislocated left knee, three broken ribs, dislocated right hip, and a concussion."

Jake whistled. "How the hell did she survive something like that and come out whole?"

Marcus shrugged. "That girl has more heart than anyone I've ever met and maybe now you understand her mistrust. She's never going to let anyone be in charge of her again. You can count on that."

"What about after she was released?"

"Oh well, of course she and the girls stayed with us. After she woke up, she signed papers giving Lavinia and I temporary custody so it followed that on her release she stayed with us until she was stronger. Then, we moved her into an apartment we own." Marcus gave a half laugh. "Between Lavinia and Devin, they deviled her, forcing her to make decisions, take an active part in her rehab, that sort of thing."

"So, she didn't wallow."

"No, she didn't wallow. You need to understand. Jillian was an only child. Her parents were like brother and sister to me, and Jillian was like another child to us. Her parents felt the same about Devin."

Marcus gave a full laugh, remembering. "Once, we hoped they'd get together but when it was suggested to them, they were both horrified. In their minds, they were brother and sister." Marcus ran his hand through that shock of white hair.

"Once we understood, we left it alone. Trudy had some bad moments in the beginning, but Jill sat her down and explained it all to her. That's just how Jill is."

"Straight shooter," Jake said and Marcus nodded.

"Anyway, somehow, Noah always manages to know just what Jillian is doing and manages to keep in contact with her."

"Yeah, doesn't want to lose his meal ticket," Jake said in a voice filled with disgust.

"Got that in one. He called her last night, demanding money. Somehow, he found out about her big fat royalty check. He wants it for himself. Knowing Noah, he wants to buy some flashy place where it's warm or some damn thing."

"What did Jill do?"

"She politely told him to go to hell." Marcus looked off across Jill's fields.

"She has strong plans for this place. I have every faith she'll make a go of it, but only if Noah leaves her in peace."

"You said he is the cops' number one. Any progress on that?"

Marcus shook his head. "Not yet. They won't go after him until they have a rock solid case."

Jake nodded. If he was sure of anything, he was sure the Milwaukee cops would be thorough.

"Well, son, this old man is tired. I'm heading inside, taking a shower before Lavinia uses up all the hot water and relax. Will we see you tomorrow?"

Jake nodded. "I'll be in court. I want that order in my hand as soon as possible. See you there."

Marcus strolled to the house while Jake made his way to his truck. Jill's voice stopped him.

"Look. I just want to say I was out of line earlier and I'm sorry."

Jake shook his head. "No you weren't. You are cautious. That can be a good thing. Let's get one thing straight, though. You receive any weird calls or see anyone here that shouldn't be here, you call. Dial nine-one-one and then call me. Okay?"

Jill peered up at him and realized her mistake.

His attitude was not chauvinistic; it was the wanting to help. He trusted that she knew what she was about, and only wanted to help her.

She would have to work on not making snap judgments.

Jake could almost see the wheels turning in her head and smiled. He held out a hand to her. "Friends?" She took his hand and smiled up at him. "Friends and neighbors."

"It's a start, Jill. A lot of us are here for you. Don't forget that."

"I won't forget."

Jake climbed into his vehicle, gunned the engine, drove down the drive, and headed home. He hoped like hell she'd follow through.

Jillian hurried up the stairs and found Bree in the shower. Megan sat on her bed, playing with Charlie.

"C'mon, honey. Bath time," Jill sang out, making Megan giggle.

Jill added some bubbles and helped Megan into the tub while Bree emerged from the shower.

"Mom?" Megan pulled on one of Jill's curls to get her attention.

"Yeah?" Jill began shampooing Megan's hair.

"I like it here. Sam and Cody are nice and we all had fun, today."

"Well, that's good, honey. I'm glad you like it here. Once we get everything situated and we start getting horses, I hope you'll like it even better."

Megan nodded. "Can I get a pony for my own?" She wanted to know.

"I think that can be arranged, but you'll have to learn to take care of it. It's a big responsibility. You will have to feed it and exercise it and groom it."

"I know that, mom. I think that would be good for me, don't you?"

Jillian grinned at her daughter and wrapped her in a big hug, not caring that now her own clothes were soaked.

"I think it would be very good for you."

Jill noticed Bree standing in the doorway in a fresh nightie and smelling of toothpaste, looking all pink and fresh.

"I think I'm too big for a pony, mom. I think I'd like to have a regular horse," Bree announced.

Jill held out an arm and Bree came into the hug she knew her mom had waiting.

"I think you could be right. Would you like a horse, Bree? I wasn't sure. You never said anything before."

Bree nodded. "I know I have to learn to take care of it, too. It would be awesome to have a horse of my own."

"Okay then. As soon as I get the land fenced off, we'll start looking. All right?"

Both girls nodded so vigorously, Jill thought their little heads would pop off their shoulders.

"Okay, Megan. Get into your night shirt and we'll read for a little bit before bed."

Reading before bed became routine only after leaving Noah. He never allowed it. Every time Jill bought books for the girls, he managed to destroy them.

Time to put that behind them, Jill reminded herself. That part of our life is over. New days, new ways.

After reading a little Harry Potter for an hour, Jill kissed the girls, knowing they'd be asleep before long.

She headed into her own rooms, gathered her things, treated herself to a long hot shower, and then snuggled into her bed. Tomorrow, she and the girls would be on their own for the first time since November.

Excitement and determination coursed through her body, and she hugged herself. She would succeed on every level.

Jill fell asleep, content in the knowing she would make a go of things, for herself and her daughters.

She slept peacefully until three in the morning. Her phone's incessant buzzing woke her, but it went to voice mail before she answered.

She listened to the message with growing horror. A voice, a child's voice screamed, begging for help.

"Help me mom! Please, please help me!"

Bree, she thought, Megan!

Jill bolted from her room and ran into her daughters' room. Her breath shuddered out seeing the girls in deep sleep.

Charlie, curled at the foot end of Megan's bed raised his head and gave a half-hearted thump with his tail before going back to sleep.

She made her way back to her own room on jelly-filled legs, her body shuddering uncontrollably.

Jill almost had herself under control when the phone buzzed again. She looked at the display but couldn't place the number.

"Hello?" She hated that her voice quavered.

"Hello, Jillian. Did you like my little message?" The electronically altered voice taunted.

"I'm close, Jillian. Very close. One day soon, I'll be coming for you and those two little bitches. Your little dog, too." The laugh was filled with pure malice as the caller ended the call.

Jill tasted copper. She was terrified as she dialed Jake's number with shaking hands. He picked up on the second ring.

"Can you come? I've had two calls tonight. One I have on voice mail. Please. Can you come?"

"I'll be right there. Stay in the house. I'm on my way, Jill. Just sit tight."

"Yes, all right. I'll be up in the girls' sitting room. I'll come down when I see your lights."

"That's fine. I'm leaving my house now. You should see my lights. Stay on the line with me, Jill."

"Yes. Yes, I'll stay on the line with you. I see your headlights now. I'll come down to let you in. Should I wake up Uncle Marc?"

"No. Just come on down and let me in. I'm pulling into your driveway now."

Jill could see his lights sweep the front of her house as she dashed down the wide staircase. She hit the foyer at a dead run, raced through the kitchen and did not slow down until she reached the back door.

Her trembling fingers fumbled with the locks and it took some time to get them open. She was about to throw open the door as Jake walked up the porch when a hand on her shoulder caused her to spin around, a small scream escaping.

"Easy, Jill! What the hell is going on around here?"

Marcus stood in his robe, his hair sticking out at odd angles, looking like a perturbed scholar.

Lavinia, blinking like an owl, stood just behind him.

"I'll tell you. I'll tell all of you at once, but just let me let Jake in."

He came through the door and she grasped his powerful arm with shaky hands.

Jake took one of them in his large hand and patted it. It struck him how small she was and how vulnerable.

"Okay. Take it easy. Let's sit down at the kitchen table and talk about this."

"Yes. We'll talk about it. I want you to hear it. It was brutal."

"What the hell are you people talking about?" Marcus wanted to know.

"Jill got a couple of phone calls a little while ago," Jake explained. He kept her small cold hand in his large warm one. "We're going to listen to the one on her voice mail and then we're going to figure out what to do."

"I'll make coffee," Lavinia offered, and Jake gave her a grateful smile.

"I'd appreciate that."

Jill sat at the table, placed her phone in the middle, and then clasped her hands together between her knees. This way, she hoped no one would see them shaking.

They gathered around and listened to the voice mail. No one said a word until it was over.

"Anyone care to bet that was an altered voice?" Jake said. "Does that sound like something a kid would say if he or she happened to be in danger?"

Jill sat quietly and then shook her head. "No, not really. I guess I just panicked. It fits with the follow-up call, too."

Lavinia sat stone faced, her dark eyes snapping with anger.

"That was monstrous. Just plain evil, not to mention sick!" Lavinia said before reaching over and patting Jill's shoulder. "I can see, though, how that would upset you."

Those glittering eyes settled on Jake. "What do you propose to do?" Lavinia asked.

"I'm going to write down Jill's number and see if we can trace it. Not too much hope there. Whoever did this would be smart enough not to use their own personal phone, but we'll find out which towers it bounced off. It's a start."

He looked over at Jill. She looked so young and scared.

"You said there was another call," he prompted, and Jill nodded.

"Care to fill us in on that one?"

She carefully relayed the second call. Calmer now, she wanted to make sure she got it just right.

"So, he's letting you know he's coming for you. Interesting. Why would he warn you?"

Jill shrugged. "I don't know. It doesn't make much sense, does it?"

"Sure it does. It's done to provoke. He wants you good and scared, thinking you'll panic and do something stupid. Care to make a guess who's behind this?"

"Noah!" Jill clenched her fist and brought it down on the table. "Noah would do something like this!"

Jake looked across the table and met Marcus's eyes. "Mind telling me what you're doing up, Judge?"

Marcus glanced at Jill before answering.

"I wasn't going to bring this up right now, but I was about to call you as well."

Jake sat back and waited.

"Someone was shaking the hell out of our balcony door. I thought it was going to fly right open. When I got out of bed and looked, there wasn't anyone there, but the shaking woke both of us out of a deep sleep."

Jill's face turned bone white. "Oh my God!" Her voice was low and tense.

"Take a minute, Jill. Let's hear the rest."

"There isn't any more. Just that someone shook our door hard enough to wake us up. I was about to call you when I heard Jill run past the hallway door. I thought I'd better check on her, first. Seems like it's been a night for weird goings on."

"Damn it, Judge! You should have told me right off!" Jake reached for his own cell phone and punched in a number.

"Hey, Del. I need you to come out Ms. Tolivar's house and do a walk around." Jake paused. "Yeah, that's the one, and I need you to do it now." He clicked off. "Whoever it was is probably long gone, but it won't hurt to make sure."

Jill rubbed her hands up and down her arms as she got to her feet. She paced around the kitchen, trying to calm down.

So many doubts surged through her. Had this been a bad decision? She just didn't know.

Lavinia stood and reached out, pulling Jill close. "Don't even go where I can see you're going. This is a good place. Let Jake do his job and we'll get to the bottom of it all." She gave the younger woman a hard squeeze before letting her go.

Headlights broke the darkness and Jill turned as Jake surged to his feet. "That'll be Del. You all stay inside. We'll do a sweep. I'll be back soon."

He went out and met his deputy. Together, they walked around the house as well as the outbuildings.

To Jill, it seemed he had been out there forever, but only a few minutes passed before Jake made his way back to the house.

"If someone was here, he's gone."

Jill sank to her chair and he put a gentle hand on her shoulder.

"Jill. You have some of the best security I've ever seen. Zach will get it installed tomorrow, so don't worry. Try to get some sleep. You're going to have a trying day tomorrow. You don't want to come into court looking like something the cat dragged in."

Jill nodded, too tired to argue. "Will you just come up and double check all the doors up there? I'll sleep better."

"Sure. C'mon. Let's get it done and then you get some sleep."

They started at the vacant wing and double-checked. All doors were secured.

They made their way down the long corridor to the wing Jill occupied and she came to a dead stop, grasping Jake's arm.

"Do you smell that?"

Jake pushed her against the wall and drew his weapon.

Marcus joined them and his head came up. "Is that cigarette smoke?" He kept his voice low.

Jill nodded. "Yes," she whispered, "and it's coming from the girls' room".

Nine

Jake sent a text to Del, telling him to come back. He told him which wing to come to and which doors to wait at, directing him to the French doors leading into the girls' sitting room.

Jake waited until Del signaled him that he was ready, and then he eased into the sitting room, waving for the small group to stay where they were.

Using the glow of the small night light Jill provided for the girls, he walked over to the French doors and unlocked them, waving Del in and putting his fingers to his lips, signaling for absolute quiet. Del nodded.

Del is young, Jake thought, but damn, he's quick. I could use a few more like him.

Jake motioned toward Del's weapon and the young deputy nodded.

Del eased his weapon from its holster and nodded again. He was ready.

If Del was afraid, he didn't show it, keeping his cool as he followed his boss toward the bedroom.

"Boss! You smell that?" Del whispered.

Mingled with the cigarette smoke, the men picked up the scent of a man's cologne. One that hadn't been produced in years.

The cold in the room hit them like an icy wall. It was so goddamned cold. The air was *freezing*. Their breaths huffed out in little balls of vapor.

Jake fought shivers racing up his spine and glanced over to where Del stood. He looks spooked, Jake thought. He didn't want to think what it took to spook an infantryman with a couple of deployments under his belt. Jake couldn't believe how damn cold the room became.

"What the hell, Boss?" Del whispered. Jake signaled again for quiet as he eased the bedroom door open.

Another night light gleamed in the dark and the men could see the two girls, sleeping peacefully.

It was warmer in the bedroom, but Jake felt the cold hovering at his back.

Charlie raised his head and let out a low growl. Jake hurried over to the bed and patted the little dog's head.

Jake's scent was familiar to the little dog and he laid his head back down, but kept his eyes on Del. He growled again, softly, and Jake, not wanting to wake the girls, waved Del out of the room.

Before exiting, Jake checked under beds, in the closets and every little cubby someone could be hiding. He found no one.

He joined Del in the sitting room and, together, they moved about the room.

"Can you feel that, Boss?" Del whispered. Jake nodded.

"Yeah, feels like someone's watching us."

Jake stood in the middle of the sitting room and let his senses take over. Those senses were honed and, over time, he learned to trust them.

"Let's do another go-over in these rooms. Concentrate on the bathroom and the bedroom. If someone's in here, we'll find him."

Jake moved on silent feet and eased into the bedroom again. Charlie let out a soft woof before returning to sleep.

Again, the two men found no one lurking about in the house, but neither Jake nor Del could shake that uneasy feeling of being watched.

Del, the survivor of two deployments into hell, knew that feeling. He stood still as a statue and Jake followed Del's lead.

Del turned, facing the French doors, but still did not move.

The feeling of someone watching was overwhelming, now and with it came a feeling of danger.

Del stared out the doors and into the overgrown garden, his golden eyes wide.

He kept his breathing soft and just stared into the blackness beyond those French doors. He motioned to Jake to wait, and then was out the doors like a shot.

A form seemed to meld into the shadows as Del raced down the outside stairway and into the garden.

Jake considered following him, but decided to wait. His confidence in Del was unlimited. Del motioned for him to stay, so stay he would.

After what seemed to be an eon, Del rejoined him in the girls' sitting room.

"I could have sworn I saw someone standing out there, Boss. If there was, by the time I hit the ground at a dead run, he was gone."

Jake nodded.

"That feeling is gone, now. Do you feel it?" Jake whispered. Del grunted in agreement. "Room is warmer now, too."

"Let's not mention this to the lady of the house, but I want an extra patrol on this house, Del. I want you to take care of it and on your off days, I'll handle it. There's no need to alert the whole damn department. Word gets around, so we'll try to keep this between you and me."

Del grunted again. "Sounds like a plan, Sheriff. Tell you what, though. I got nothing going on, so I'll take a spin out here on my off days, too."

Jake shrugged. "Sounds good, but I don't think it'll be necessary. You're one of the best I have, Del. Let's not burn you out."

Del grinned. "You *are* the boss, Boss."

Emerging from the sitting room, Jake and Del joined the others in the hall.

"Except for the girls and Charlie, the room is empty."

"Oh, but..." Jill began and Jake raised a hand.

"I know. I smelled it too. I'm going to call Zach in the morning and have him check the wiring and such. It could be something as simple as chafed wiring." It sounded good, but Jake didn't believe his own words for a minute.

Del stood next to his boss and slid a glance toward him. If his boss didn't want to mention the scent of a man's cologne *and* the mind-numbing coldness, that was fine with him.

The little group headed down the main staircase and into the kitchen.

Jill offered to make coffee for them, but they politely refused.

"You need to get some rest. Big day coming up tomorrow," Jake said.

"I, for one, plan on getting a little more sleep," Marcus announced to the room in general. "I'm getting too old for all this excitement."

Lavinia was uncharacteristically quiet, and Jill sent her a speculative glance. Something's up, Jill decided, but until Lavinia chose to tell them, waiting would be the name of the game.

Still, Jill wished she knew just what traveled around in Lavinia's large brain.

"I don't think I'll be sleeping much, tonight," Jill said and proceeded to make the coffee.

"I could go for a cup of that," Jake said as he delved into her cabinets and retrieved two mugs.

"Boss!" Del caught Jake's attention, "I'm heading on out. I'll take one more walk around the area and then go back on patrol if you don't need me here."

"Yeah, go ahead." Jake wanted a private word with his deputy, "I'll walk out with you."

Del raised an eyebrow, but said nothing.

Jake waited until they stood next to Del's cruiser.

"Something really weird is going on out here, and I don't think it's her ex-husband. I could be wrong, been wrong before, but until we figure this mess out, let's keep it under wraps for the time being."

"No problem, Boss. It won't come from me but, sooner or later, the others are going to want to know what the hell is going on out here."

"Yeah, and when that time comes, we'll just say it's the ex-husband playing tricks on her. We don't want word of the weird shit getting back to Ms. Tolivar until we have a handle on just what that weird shit is."

"How do you want me to write this up?"

Jake thought for a minute, then shrugged one muscular shoulder.

"Just write it up as a possible intruder and threatening phone call. That'll look good in court tomorrow."

"Court tomorrow?"

"Yeah, she has an order in Milwaukee County, but needs one here. Judge Brentwood is representing her in court. He has a lot of documentation and our own Judge Maddox is a friend, so it's pretty much a done deal. Extra documentation won't hurt."

"Okay, Boss. I'm outta here." Del opened the cruiser's door, and then paused. "You be careful out here, Jake. If the ex-husband is behind this, he could be dangerous."

Jake's grin was wintery. "I'll be careful, Del. I have to admit, though. I wouldn't mind getting my hands on whoever is responsible. My money's gonna ride on the ex, though."

Jake watched as Del backed down the drive. His crew was excellent. He couldn't ask for a better bunch of deputies, but out of the dozen men and women working for him, Del was his most trusted.

Del's boyish face hid a razor sharp mind along with some impressive guts. Not much phased the younger man, and panic didn't seem to be in the guy's vocabulary.

Jake wondered how long Del would be satisfied working for a Sheriff's Department in a small county. The way Jake figured it, he would be losing Del in a year, two at the most.

Sighing, he made his way back to the house. He supposed he couldn't blame Del. After all, he thought, he had put his time in Milwaukee working homicide/robbery. He would probably still be there if his dad had lived through that heart attack.

His dad didn't survive, though, and his life changed. His mother needed him, so he brought her home.

Now, he was home and all in all, satisfied. Every once in a while, something came along to keep him on his toes. Just like now but, for the most part, he liked the quiet.

Lavinia, Marcus and Jill sat at the kitchen table. Marcus broke down and grabbed a cup of the hot brew for himself. All three of their faces reflected the tension hovering around the room.

"You three look terrible. I'd ask what the problem is, but it's pretty obvious." Jake kicked back into his chair and let his eyes roam around the three of them. "I could tell you not to worry. That won't do any good, either."

"Did Jill make a mistake?" Lavinia wanted to know, and Jake shook his head.

"No. I don't think she did. We may be a small department compared to the big city, but our response time is faster than it would be in Milwaukee. If she calls or if her alarm goes off, we're going to be here faster than they can respond in the city."

Lavinia nodded but looked far from reassured.

"I could smell the smoke in the hall. I also smelled a man's cologne." She shot a sharp look at Jake. "That's something you weren't going to mention."

"No, ma'am. I didn't plan on bringing it up. Now that you have, we'll deal with it. We went over every inch of the sitting room, the sleeping room and the bathroom. We looked under beds, in closets and behind drapes. Nothing."

Lavinia opened her mouth and Jake held up a hand.

"Let me finish." Lavinia's mouth snapped shut. She didn't know if she should be amused or angry.

"I'm not saying you shouldn't be concerned," Jake went on. "What I'm saying is we're very competent. We know the score with the ex-husband and we're going to be very vigilant."

"I love the way you all are talking about this as if I'm not here," Jill snapped. "The decision is mine! I'm staying! If Noah is behind these things, I won't give him the satisfaction of cutting and running!"

"Okay then," Lavinia said. Her eyes sparkled, and Jill worried her surrogate mother may be angry. Then, Lavinia cracked a smile and began to laugh.

"Sometimes, I forget you inherited your dad's temper." She leaned forward and stared hard into Jill's eyes. "Promise me you'll be careful. You know better than anyone just how wily Noah can be."

"Yes, I know and I will be careful. He won't make me run, but I won't do anything to put the girls and myself in danger."

"Now that we've established that Jill is not an idiot, I think I'm going up and get some sleep before court." Marcus got to his feet, walked to the sink and rinsed out his cup.

He leaned down and kissed his wife, patted Jill's head and gave Jake's shoulder a friendly squeeze before heading up the stairs.

Lavinia let loose with a large yawn, patted Jill's cheek and placed her cup in the sink. "I'm following Marc's example. See you in the morning."

Jake drank the rest of his coffee, and then got to his feet.

"I should let you get some rest. Don't worry about tomorrow. It should be pretty cut and dried."

"What happens after I get the restraining order?" Jill folded her hands in her lap and waited.

"We'll fax a copy of the order down to the Milwaukee County Sheriff's Office. One of their people will serve it. Like I said, simple. No reason to worry."

Jill sighed. "I can't help but wonder if I'll ever be free of him."

"Sure you will. Eventually, he'll find another paycheck. Guys like that only know how to do things one way. He won't change, but the times will. Keep that in mind."

Jill walked him to the back door.

"Anything happens," he told her, "you call me".

Jill nodded. "I will. I promise."

Jake grinned. "Good enough!"

She made sure to lock the back door and moved to turn out the kitchen lights and then, her phone rang.

Ten

"You having a party and not inviting me?" A familiar voice boomed out, and Jill's heart sang.

"Ben! Oh Ben! Where are you?"

"I think I'm outside your house, or I've found myself one hell of a fancy bordello."

Jill raced to the door and threw it open. Ben stood on the other side and she launched herself into his arms.

Jill took in the beloved figure of a man she loved with all heart. Here was one of the last reminders of home.

Tall and lanky, his hair as black as midnight and pulled back into the usual ponytail that traveled halfway down his back. Sharp black eyes took in everything and everybody with one sweep. His craggy face held a hint of cynicism mixed with a touch of toughness to his slightly irregular features.

Dressed in well-worn jeans and a black t-shirt, he looked every inch the wrangler.

"Ben! I can't believe you're here!" Jill's voice sang with happiness.

"Well, little girl," he said, using his pet name for her, "Here I am. What the hell's going on? It's after four in the morning, and it looks like you've got yourself one hell of a party happening." He gestured toward Marcus and Lavinia's Escalade, the moving truck and her own SUV parked in the drive. "And look, here comes another guest."

Jill saw Jake's cruiser pull in directly behind Ben's truck. She watched as he launched himself from his vehicle. His long legs quickly ate up the distance between Jill and himself.

Jake saw the headlights from the huge diesel driven truck in his rear view mirror. He spun his car around on a dime and headed straight back to Jill's house, unsure of what he would find.

Jake found himself under scrutiny from those unreadable black eyes and stepped forward. Before he could say anything, Jill, blushing with happiness turned and introduced the men. Ben's sharp eyes searched her face. "You got trouble, little girl?"

"I don't know. I think so, but let's not think about that right now. You're here! I'm so happy to see you!" She squeezed him, hard.

"I think I'm glad I'm here, too. Give me coffee and I'll know for sure."

Jake watched the older man, closely. He noticed a brief glimpse of worry mingled with confusion flash from the deep dark depths of Ben's eyes and positioned himself so they could speak without Jill over-hearing as she dashed off to make the required beverage.

Jake quickly briefed Ben, and Ben spat out a pithy remark, suggesting that perhaps Noah had intimate knowledge of his own mother.

"Yeah, I got that he's a real piece of work. I'm glad you're here, Mr. Lightfoot. She'll sleep easier with you around."

Ben studied the sheriff a little harder.

"Don't I know you?"

Jake nodded. "I bought some horses from you last winter. The mare foaled late this spring. She's a pretty little filly. My place is just up the road. Feel free to come on over and take a look."

"Yeah, I remember now. So Gypsy had a filly. Mom and daughter doing well?"

Jake nodded again and then gestured toward the outbuildings.

"After Jill gets her stalls up, I'll be bringing Chief over to board. I figure Jill could use a hand up on her new venture, and it's going to save me tons of work repairing stalls every time one of those mares comes in season."

Ben grinned. "He does have a mind of his own."

"Come on! I have fresh coffee brewing!" Jill called from the back door and Ben's grin blossomed into a smile.

"She always was a bossy little thing," he said.

Jake's lips twitched. "Yeah, well... obviously, she hasn't changed much," Jake quipped.

Ben flashed a white smile and shook his head.

"If you knew her momma, it wouldn't surprise you." He looked to where Jill stood, all but tapping her foot with impatience.

"It's best if we get on in there before she throws a fit."

"You go on ahead. I'm going to get myself home and hopefully catch a couple more hours of sleep." He glanced toward Jill again and shook his head. "I'm pretty sure we'll be running into each other now and then." Jake turned to leave and then turned back again. "If something happens, I want to know about it. Phone calls, possible intruders, anything."

Ben nodded, but he looked puzzled. "Count on it."

Jill waited in the doorway until Ben finally joined her.

"Jake isn't coming in?" she asked.

Ben shook his head. "Nope. Said something about wanting to get a power nap in before work."

"Oh well, come on in! I'll give you coffee and some food. We'll bring in your stuff after you've relaxed a little.

Ben shrugged. "Not much to bring in. I still travel light." He took his first sip from his mug. He sat back and stretched out his long legs. "Care to tell me what the hell is going on around here?"

Jill grinned. Ben never did mince words, preferring to get to the heart of the matter, so she filled him in. She told him of the phone calls. She even told him about the smell of cigarette smoke.

"I don't know, little girl," Ben said after she related everything to him. She held back and was aware of those shrewd black eyes, watching her so closely.

"Maybe, this place isn't such a good idea," Ben said, shaking his head.

"I'm not leaving here, Ben. This is our place. I like most of the people here and I love this house. I can do everything I want to do here."

Jill frowned, and Ben had to suppress a smile.

Ben gave a mock sigh and shook his head. "You always were a stubborn one. So, fill me in on what you have planned."

She told him about therapy horses and renting stable space. "Eventually, I'll get into breeding. That's down the road, but maybe not too far."

"That road is a rough one. You know that."

"Yes I do." She gave him a bright smile. "But now I have you here! It'll be a piece of cake."

"How do you know I plan on staying?" he asked and Jill laughed.

"If you had not been interested, you wouldn't be here."

Ben grinned. "Caught me. Okay, how about you show me where I can bunk, and I'll get my stuff out of the truck."

Jill started to lead him to the main staircase, and he stopped her.

"Listen. I'm going to be wrapped up in those horses you are planning on getting. I don't want to be doing stairs in the middle of the night if one of them decides to throw a foal. Got something down here?"

Jill led him to the bedroom off the kitchen and Ben nodded in approval.

"This'll do just fine." He walked out to retrieve his things from his truck and Jill quickly found sheets, blankets, and pillows.

Together, they made up his bed.

"That should do it," he said as he hefted a large and very heavy duffel bag onto the bed.

"I'm just gonna put my stuff up and get some sleep. You should do the same. You've got at least three hours of sleep coming to you before court. You want to be on your game, just in case." Ben left the rest unsaid. Noah could be unpredictable. God only knew if he had something planned, some way to fight her.

Jill nodded and gave Ben another hard hug.

"I'm so glad you're here!" she told him in a watery voice.

Ben hugged her back, lifting her off her feet. "Me too, little girl. Me too!"

Jill woke, took a fast shower, and dressed for her court date.

She knew she looked smart dressed in crisp white pants, a red camisole and matching lightweight blazer. A pin that once belonged to her mother in the shape of a leaf and studded with diamonds rested on her lapel.

Small diamond studs sparkled in her ears, a gift from Ben when she turned twenty-one.

As she came down the stairs, she could hear happy and excited voices coming from the kitchen.

Her girls were giggling, and Ben's deep laugh mingled with their squeals.

"Well, good morning!" Jill sang out. Bree and Megan rushed to her, wrapping their little arms around her slight frame.

"Look who's here, Mom!" Megan jumped up and down on her toes.

"Yes, I know." She hugged her daughters tightly.

"Ben said after the stalls and stuff are done, we can go find me a horse and a pony for Megan 'cause she's still little."

"Nuh-uh! I'm big! Right, Ben?"

"Well, Squirt. You're bigger than the last time I saw you, but I'd guess you still got some growing to do."

"But I can get a full-size horse, right Ben?" Bree chimed in, and he shook his head.

"That's all gonna be up to your momma. Now, sit down here and eat your breakfast before it gets cold."

Jill looked at the table and the food piled on it with wide eyes.

"Good Lord, Ben! You made enough for an army!"

He cooked scrambled eggs, bacon, french toast and pancakes, along with orange juice and coffee for the adults.

"Girls need a hearty breakfast, don't they? They're growing. You need to eat more than toast! I know you, little girl! You get upset, you won't eat. Now sit down before this gets cold."

Lavinia came through the door, followed by Marcus. She ran a hand through her hair as she looked at the immense breakfast Ben provided.

"Good thing we're going home today. With Ben cooking, they'd have to roll me out of here and none of my clothes would fit," Lavinia said.

"Looks and smells terrific to me," Marcus said as he took a seat at the table. "And I'm not waiting for any of you. I'm starving!"

"Yeah? What else is new?" Lavinia asked her husband before walking around the table and hugging Ben. "I'm so happy you're here," She told him.

"I've been getting a lot of that lately," Ben told her. "Nice to know I've been missed."

He poured out two mugs of coffee and handed one to Jill and the other to Lavinia.

"Hey! Where's mine?" Marcus wanted to know.

"I serve beautiful women. Men are on their own," Ben quipped.

During breakfast, they kept the conversation light and let the girls lead the breakfast talk. There was no point in upsetting them now that they were beginning to relax in their new home.

"Are Sam and Cody coming today?" Bree asked.

"I don't think so, sweetie. Zach's coming to work and he'll have his crew with him. I imagine the boys will stay at home," Jill told her. Megan pouted.

"It's fun when they come." She felt the need to point that out to her mother.

"I know, honey, but today's a work day for Zach. But, I'll tell you what. When I get back, I'll call their mom and see what they have planned for the day. Maybe we can have them come over for a picnic or something later in the afternoon. How does that sound?"

"I think I'll take the girls shopping while you're busy at the courthouse," Lavinia said. She turned to the girls. "What do you think? Think that will be fun?"

Bree nodded, but Megan wasn't too sure. Shopping for clothes and junk didn't sound like a lot of fun to her.

"How about you, Ben? What are you going to do?" Jill asked.

Ben shrugged. "Me? I'm gonna supervise this crew you hired and make sure their work is up to snuff. After that, I'm going into town and have a look-see around town and see what's what."

"We shouldn't be that long," Marcus chimed in. "This is actually pretty cut and dried... or it should be."

Yeah, Ben thought, unless Noah threw a monkey-wrench into the works. Then, this could take all day.

Jill managed to swallow a few forkfuls of scrambled eggs before her stomach began to churn. Nerves were trying to take over.

She sipped her coffee, hoping everything would stay down.

Jake popped in on his way to work. He gave Jill a quick glance and felt a wide and foolish grin split his craggy face. She sure does clean up well, he thought.

"Are you coming to court with us?" Jill asked. She felt a pang of disappointment when he shook his head, and that annoyed her.

"You won't need me there. Judge Brentwood here has everything covered. You'll do fine."

"At least have some coffee before you go," she advised. "After all, it's my fault you lost a night's sleep."

"No one's fault. Part of the job," he told her and, seeing her face fall, grinned. "But I could use a cup before I head off to work."

Jill got to her feet and poured him a mug, handing it to him, all the while wondering what had gotten into her.

She had two girls to raise, for God's sake! She had her horse business to get off the ground and work on her expansion of her game to complete. Add in she had just shed herself of an abusive husband, a man should be the last thing on her mind, but there he was, popping into her thoughts at odd times.

Get a grip, she told herself, and get back to business.

Court went pretty much as they expected. Noah hadn't bothered to show up and Judge Maddox, after seeing the police reports and the pictures of her injuries at the hand of her ex-husband, promptly issues the No Contact Order.

"If he attempts to break this order, young lady, you are to notify the Sheriff's Department of this county, immediately," he told her.

"Yes, sir," Jill said in a soft voice. She wondered, though, just how much this order would be worth if Noah went on a tear and decided to come after her.

No point in worrying about that now, she told herself. Jake lived close enough, should Noah show up.

For now, she and the girls were safe. That's all that mattered. Her girls were safe.

Mary Lee Connor emerged from an early morning meeting with her staff. A small headache nagged at her, so she wasn't pleased when she spied Steffi Brandt sitting in her waiting area.

"I need to talk to you," Steffi announced. Mary Lee silently groaned.

"Fine. I don't have a lot of time, Steffi. Make it quick."

"I think you cheated me. You listed my aunt's house for less than it was worth."

"Yes, I did. At your insistence." Mary Lee walked to her file cabinet and took out a file. She paged through the contract until she found what she was looking for.

"This is the original listing agreement. One you signed, Steffi." She pulled another page from the file and held it in front of the other woman. "This is the amendment to that listing agreement, stating the house was listed, at *your* insistence, under market value."

Mary Lee pulled one more page from the file and held it in front of Steffi, as well. "This is the final offer from Ms. Tolivar with another amendment stating you knew and agreed to sell her the house for the agreed-upon amount."

Mary Lee dug out a couple of Motrin and dry-swallowed them. "I didn't trust you, Steffi. I made damn sure I covered my ass."

Steffi's face burned and fire shot out of cold blue eyes.

"I need more, Mary Lee. That nursing home I have her in is costing a bundle to keep her there. I have to have more."

Mary Lee gave Steffi a stony stare. "Not my problem. Maybe, you should get a job to fill in the gap," she suggested and watched Steffi stiffen.

"Maybe, you should follow your own advice. When I'm finished with you, you'll be lucky to sell an outhouse to out-of-towners."

"Yeah, Steffi. Whatever. Now, if you'll excuse me, I have things to do."

Steffi planted her feet, drawing a long drawn out sigh.

"Something else on your mind?"

"Where's Jake been spending his time these days?" Steffi's tone was so snide, Mary Lee wanted to smack her.

"If you want to know where he's been, then ask him. I'm not his keeper."

Steffi tossed back her hair and picked up her red leather hobo bag. She looked Mary Lee square in the eye as she draped the strap over her shoulder.

"We're not finished, Mary Lee. Not by a long shot."

Steffi sashayed out the door, leaving Mary Lee fuming.

"Jan. Get Mr. Lawrence on the phone for me," Mary Lee told her office manager.

"You think you're going to need a lawyer, Mary Lee?" Jan said.

"I think she's going to try to make trouble. It's what she lives for. I want to make sure all my bases are covered."

After her long and reassuring conversation with her attorney, Mary Lee felt relief, if not for the headache still plaguing her.

"If I have nothing on the books for today, I'm going back into the house and see if I can shake this headache."

"You're free as a bird for today. Tomorrow is another story."

"Yeah, thanks. If I remember, I have two listings and four showings. Let's hope this damn headache is gone by then."

"It will be. You won't have to put up with Steffi Brandt tomorrow," Jan said, a small smile playing around her lips.

Mary Lee walked down a short hallway and into her home. Closing the door, she headed for her bedroom.

The boys were with her mother-in-law for the day, and her bed seemed to be calling to her. She turned off her phone, pulled the duvet from the bed, and made herself comfortable.

She was asleep before she knew it.

Some days, Jake Logan thought, his job just sucked out loud. Today was one of those days.

With his face grim, he headed to his cruiser and drove out of town.

He pulled into Jill's drive and saw the judge's Escalade parked close to the house.

He noted the doors were open and watched as Lavinia came out with a couple of small bags. She gave him a friendly wave before returning to the house.

He waited for a moment, getting his thoughts together before opening his door and following her into Jill's house.

This was not a social call.

Jake Logan was there to tell the judge and his wife that their son, Devin, had been killed in an accident last night and although Trudy survived, she lost the baby.

He would wait to tell them about the witnesses who saw a large SUV push them off the road, over a bridge and into the train yards down below.

That news could wait.

Eleven

Devin and his unborn child, dead! It couldn't be possible. By some miracle, Trudy survived, Jake told Jill and the Brentwoods. Devin died on impact. Trudy was in ICU, and they were treating her for internal bleeding. The baby didn't make it.

Jake wished he could have been anywhere but standing in this kitchen, telling these people the awful news.

"How?" Jill asked. He didn't want to tell her. He didn't want to tell any of them, but he didn't have much choice.

A small groan escaped Lavinia's lips, and she clasped Marcus's hand in a hard grip.

Marcus could only stand and stare at Jake while his mind tried to process the information. He failed. He couldn't grasp the things Jake was telling them.

Jill's body trembled and he eased her into a chair.

"Where are the girls?" he asked quietly.

"They're with your mom, actually. They went shopping with Aunt

Vinia and then your mom swiped them. They're going to learn how to make pies and visit the horses."

"Okay. Good." Jake looked around the room while his brain searched for the proper words. Please God, he thought, help me out here.

Lavinia cleared her throat and pinned Jake with her dark, expressive eyes.

"I believe Jillian asked you a question," she said, and Jake nodded. Okay. Fair enough. They were entitled to know what he knew.

Jake believed bad news should be delivered the same way one would rip off a bandage. Quickly and decisively.

"According to witnesses, Devin's SUV was forced off the road, over the guardrail and into the old abandoned rail station below the expressway." Jake flipped open his notebook. "According to witnesses, it was deliberate. The Milwaukee cops were able to track down the owner of the truck. He had reported it missing two days ago. They haven't found it yet."

Deliberate! The word raced through Jill's mind on spiked hooves. Deliberate, she thought. As the word penetrated the fog of misery in her mind, the next word followed; murder.

Lavinia sank to her knees, sobbing. Marcus reached for her, wanting to give her comfort.

"I'm going to make arrangements to have you driven back home," Jake told them. "Neither of you is in any shape to drive."

Marcus, kneeling next to his wife, his arms wrapped around her could only nod.

Jake stepped outside and flipped open his phone. The first call he made was to his mother and explained the situation to her.

"Can you keep the girls for a little while? Jill's pretty rocky, and I need to make arrangements for Del and another deputy to drive the Brentwoods home," he asked.

"Yes, of course," Helen agreed. "I'll keep them here and busy until you or Jillian tell me different." She sighed. "This is terrible news. I liked them, and that poor woman, losing her husband and her baby. That's beyond terrible, Jake."

The next call was to Del. The weight in his deputy's voice told him he had awakened the young man.

"I'm going to ask you to drive the Brentwoods vehicle back to Milwaukee, Del. Call one of the deputies, and he can follow behind to bring you back."

"No, Boss. We don't have to pull anyone off duty for this. My brother's visiting. He can drive my truck and bring me back."

Jake didn't even know Del *had* a brother. "Okay, that's fine. I'll meet you at Jillian's house; give you the credit card. You put your gas on the county. I'll square it with the powers that be."

"Okay. I'll be there in twenty."

He tucked his phone in his pocket and went in to find Jill. He managed to do all he could for the Brentwoods, but Jill's devastated face stayed in his mind. She needed tending.

She sat at her kitchen table, afraid to move.

The insane thought that if she moved, she would splinter into a million pieces ran through Jill's mind.

Jake found her sitting, crying and rocking and put an arm around her shoulder.

"Do you want me to call someone?" he asked. Jill shook her head.

"There isn't anyone to call," she told him.

He watched her get herself under control. It took a tremendous effort and showed the depth of her character.

"Uncle Marc and Aunt Lavinia need me. They can't make that drive home, so I'll do it. Could you call your mother and ask her to send the girls home? They need to be told, too."

"Jill. Arrangements are in the works. Del will drive them home, his brother will follow to bring him back." He ran a hand through his hair. "But, you're right about the girls. I can run up the road and get them, bring them home."

"That's really nice of you, Jake. I'd appreciate it. Thank you, but wait until… well, until things settle down a little."

"Okay. That's not a problem."

Jake patted her shoulder on his way out the door.

Yeah, he thought, sometimes his job just sucked.

In the week following Devin's death, Jill was in constant contact with either Lavinia or Marcus.

"I thought I'd drive down and see Trudy." Jill mentioned the idea to Marcus and he immediately nixed it.

"She doesn't want to see anyone, honey. She doesn't even want to see us. Give her some time. She's grieving so hard."

So, Jill threw herself into her work. The stables were coming along quickly. She would be able to rent a stall before too long.

Her days took on a routine that was a killer.

She woke early, worked on her game's expansion program until the girls woke up. After breakfast, she could be found in the field, roping off twenty-two acres and marking where the fencing would go. At night, she bathed her girls, read to them and then retired to her room to try to sleep.

The pace was grueling and she caught Ben watching her, worry all over his face.

"Little girl, you need to slow down. We'll get it all done, but killing yourself won't help."

"Ben, it's like November all over again." She referred to that terrible Thanksgiving night when her parents died.

"I so want to see Trudy, but she doesn't want visitors."

Ben shrugged as he hammered in a post for the fencing. He had his own thoughts about Trudy Brentwood. He kept them to himself.

"That's to be expected." He stopped to wipe his face with a bright red bandana. "Any new leads on what the hell happened?"

Jill shook her head. "Not that I know of. Uncle Marc said they found the truck, but all the prints were wiped clean."

She pulled a bottle of water out of the cooler they hauled out to the field and drank deeply.

"Why Devin?" she asked. "I keep asking myself that question. Why Devin? Why would someone want to kill him and Trudy?"

"Lots of sickos out there, little girl. Who the fuck knows."

They worked in silence for a while getting many of the posts up, waiting for the white tape that would serve as fencing.

"I'm just going to go ahead and put the mountings up for the electric stuff. Why don't you go on ahead and get dinner ready," Ben suggested.

"Are you sure? We could do a few more posts before calling it a day." Jill stood with her hands on her hips and took stock.

"It's hot and muggy as hell, little girl. You go on and do what I said. It's enough for today." Ben gave her a stern look as he took her tools from her hands.

"Go on. Get inside. Take a shower and we'll eat. Good thing we decided on a tuna salad. Too hot to eat a heavy meal."

Jill didn't have much of an appetite, but did as Ben told her to.

After her shower, they sat down in the kitchen and feasted on Jill's tuna salad and fresh fruit. Strawberries and ice cream worked well for desert.

"I'll take care of the dishes. Those girls need a little mom and me time," Ben told her.

"They're so upset," Jill said. "They loved Devin so much. Now another constant in their lives is gone."

"Those girls will be fine, Jill, as long as you are," Ben said.

"I'll be fine. What choice do I have?"

"None." And there was the crux of the problem.

With the exception of Ben, Jillian didn't have anyone to take some of the burden from her slight shoulders.

That was okay, she decided. Her parents raised her tough. She had herself and her daughters and now Ben.

Mary Lee and Zach were becoming good friends. So it seemed was Jake and his mother. Maybe, she wasn't quite so alone after all.

She sat between the beds and read *Black Beauty*. Bree's pick. The girls became sleepy and Jillian quietly closed the book and placed it on the little table, which held so many of their favorites.

Bree dreamed of flying over fences and Megan dreamed of riding with the wind. Charlie dreamed of running through meadows, chasing bunnies.

Jill fell into bed and was asleep until three in the morning.

The buzzing of her phone woke her, and she felt a spike of fear, but mixed in with the fear was annoyance.

She didn't recognize the number on her display. She clicked the on button and promptly shut it off, hoping that would take care of it. It didn't.

"What?" she barked into the phone.

The electronically altered voice came over the phone.

"One down and three more to go. Don't think the old man's gonna save you, bitch. He won't." The caller clicked off.

She thought about not calling Jake. On second thought, she decided that would be a bad idea.

He answered on the second ring.

"I had another one of those calls," she told him, and then proceeded to tell him what the caller said.

It's interesting, he thought. Most of the fear was gone, but she sure sounded pissed off. He grinned. It was good to hear.

"Okay. I'll take a run up the road just to make sure everything's as it should be. Stay in your room. I won't come in unless I have to."

From her verandah, she watched as his lights came up the road and turned into her drive. She watched as he made the rounds of her property.

With relief, she realized he was coming up the outside stairs.

"Everything is okay here, Jill," Jake said as he joined her.

"Thank you for coming. I didn't want to disturb you, but thought better of it." Jill sighed heavily. She turned to him and placed her hand on his arm.

"It's never going to stop, is it?"

Jake patted her hand. "Sure it is. We'll find out who's behind this, Jill. I promise you. We will get to the bottom of this."

She nodded but didn't feel too reassured.

"If I ever get my hands on him, I'm going to strangle him, Jake."

His grin flashed in the moonlight. "Can't say as I blame you."

He became aware at the same time Jill did that she was standing outside in her nightshirt. She took a step back.

"You go on in and get settled. Get some sleep."

She turned to go in and then stopped.

"Thanks, Jake."

He smiled. "You're welcome."

Jill decided to check on her girls before returning to bed. As she entered their sitting room, she could hear Megan having a conversation. She also smelled cigarette smoke.

"No, we don't have a birdie," Megan said, "but we have a Charlie and you shouldn't smoke. It's bad for you."

Frightened beyond belief, Jill bolted into the room and looked around.

It was empty, but the smell of cigarette smoke mixed with a man's cologne still lingered.

Jill checked all the doors and found them still locked.

She returned to the bedroom and found Megan sitting up in her bed.

"Megan, who were you talking to?"

"The man that was here. He keeps asking for his birdie. I told him we don't have a birdie and he got mad."

"What did this man look like?" Stay calm, she told herself. Don't freak out the kid. That was not an easy thing to do since she herself was freaking out.

"He dresses funny and he smokes."

"How does he dress funny?"

"He has this funny green suit on with shiny things on his shoulders and here." Megan pointed to where lapels would be.

"How is he getting in, Megan? Are you letting him in?"

"No! I don't let him in. He just comes in through the door." Megan pointed to the verandah doors.

How can that be, Jill thought. Those doors are locked.

"Okay, sweetie. Go back to sleep."

Jill sat with her daughter until Megan drifted off again.

Should she call Jake? No, she decided. She would tell him about their late night visitor in the morning.

Now she had another mystery. Who was entering her house at will? What did he want? What the hell is going on in her house, she wondered.

If it took the rest of her life, she would get to the bottom of this mystery, too.

Twelve

The day of Devin's funeral dawned cloudy, humid, and hot. She dressed in a cool blue dress, the color of lightening, and black pumps with a small bag to match. Jill didn't bother with make-up. It would just wash away, anyway.

She gathered her girls and the three walked down the main staircase. Ben, watching them walk toward them, thought they sure did make a picture.

"Are you going with us, Ben?" Bree asked, taking in his black suit and tie. Ben nodded.

"We can take my truck. More than enough room," he said.

Thankful, she wouldn't have to drive. Jill nodded.

She felt ill and a wreck, emotionally. They would bury the surrogate brother she loved and, as much pain as she was in, she wondered how Lavinia and Marcus would hold up.

She also wondered if Trudy would be there. The last she heard, Devin's wife was still in the hospital.

"Eat something, Jill," Ben ordered, and she managed to choke down a piece of toast. She washed that down with coffee.

The girls ate their breakfast in silence. To all three of them, it seemed black tinged their whole world.

They made the two hour drive to the city in silence. What was there to say, after all?

"Want me to drop you off at the door?" Ben asked as they pulled into the funeral home's driveway. Jill shook her head.

"No. We'll go in together."

Ben parked and turned as he left his vehicle, lifting Megan and placing her gently on the ground. Bree hopped down on her own.

Walking into the foyer, Jill saw Lavinia and Marcus waiting for her.

"Jill. You can't come in here," Marcus told her, gently taking her hand.

"What? Why not?"

"We tried to call you before you left the house." Lavinia ran a hand down Jill's arm, offering comfort where there was none.

"My battery went dead. It's on the charger. What's going on?" Jill wanted to know.

"Noah's here. He's been with Trudy ever since the accident."

The news hit Jill in the pit of her stomach.

"Why is he here? He never liked Devin." Jill wished she could take the words back, seeing the pain on Marcus's face.

"The better question is why that son-of-a-bitch still isn't in jail," Ben barked.

Lavinia sighed. "He was at the hospital when we got back into town. He hasn't left her alone for a moment."

"Jillian," Marcus began, running a shaky hand through his white mane. "If you stay, you're breaking the No Contact Order. It will be null and void."

And there was the crux. This was Noah's way of trying to control her actions.

"It's okay. We'll go home. I don't have to be here to mourn Devin. I can do that anywhere. Noah doesn't get to score points off of me. Not today. Not any day."

She turned to go and caught a movement out of the corner of her eye. Noah was striding toward her, a satisfied smirk on his face.

Ben took a step toward Jill's ex-husband, but a hand on his arm stopped him.

"It's all right, Ben. Let's go home. Suddenly something stinks here."

Ben smirked. "Yeah," he said. "Smells like loser."

Noah heard the remarks and his face turned purple with rage. He lengthened his stride, intent on confronting his ex-wife, but Marcus thwarted him by stepping into his path.

"Don't be stupid, Noah. This isn't the time nor the place for a scene. She's leaving. You won this round. Be satisfied with that."

"I'm no loser!" Noah stormed, and Lavinia gave him a cool smile.

"That's a matter of opinion," she told him. "We know why you are hovering around Trudy. You may have won this round. You won't win the war." Lavinia turned on her heel and entered the chapel where her only son lay.

Having Noah there galled, but Trudy seemed to take comfort from him. For now, she and Marcus would let it go. Eventually, though, they would find the underlying cause of this unholy alliance.

Jill and Ben walked back to his truck, the girls walking between them. Glancing down, she noticed Bree's pale face and the fear lurking in her eyes.

She put a comforting arm around her oldest daughter and held on tight. Megan clung to Ben's hand. Both girls were in a panic brought on by the mere sight of their father.

"Ben, why was dad here?" Bree wanted to know. Ben shrugged.

"Just to cause grief for your mother, little one. Nothing more and nothing less."

"Will he come after us, now?" Megan asked in a thin, wavering voice.

"No, darlin'. He won't come after you. Don't you worry about that."

Noah stood on the portico, watching Ben and Jill shepherd the girls into Ben's truck. A wide smile split his handsome, cold face.

Driving past, Jill make eye contact and with her next action, Ben roared with laughter.

Jill raised her middle finger and mouthed "fuck you" directly into Noah's face, wiping the smile from his face.

Noah's anger choked him. The day of reckoning would come, eventually. Then she would see just who won the war.

Steffi Brandt watched as Jill, Ben and the girls drove back into town. The whole town knew they had left to attend Devin Brentwood's funeral.

Back so soon, Steffi thought. Must have been a real short funeral.

Steffi didn't like Jillian Tolivar. She didn't like the amount of time Jake spent with her.

It became Steffi's mission to get rid of the divorcee and her two brats, one way or another.

She decided to begin her campaign, immediately. Luckily, she was sitting at the counter of Mike's Diner, and her lunch companion just happened to be one of the town gossips.

"I wonder just where Jillian Tolivar got the kind of money to do all the things she's doing," Steffi mentioned. "And, she had the nerve to offer me below market price for my aunt's house."

Steffi tossed back the spill of hair currently an interesting shade of auburn and looked the old woman in the eye. "She cheated my aunt." Steffi managed to work a tear into her eye.

The elderly woman almost laughed in her face. "You've got to be kidding. Everyone in town knows you listed that house for a quick sale. As for where Jillian got her money, she worked for it. Perhaps you should try that." The old woman got to her feet, laid a couple of bills on the counter and left.

Well, hell. That didn't go as planned. Perhaps, misinformation wouldn't be wise. Jillian seemed to have the town on her side, but there was still Jake.

She decided she needed to work on him a little harder. Once she got him in her bed, he'd be putty in her hands.

Feeling better with a half-assed plan in place, Steffi finished her iced coffee and sailed out the door, forgetting as usual, to pay her bill.

Moving on impulse, Steffi climbed into her car and pointed it in the direction of the sheriff's office. There was the odd chance he would be out on patrol, but she'd take a shot.

Pulling into the parking area, Jake's car was nowhere in sight. She gave her steering wheel a bad-tempered slap.

"Damn!" she muttered as she headed back out again. Playing a hunch, she headed for Jillian's house.

Not wanting to waste the day, Jillian decided to run into town. School would be starting soon, she needed to register her girls and, after that, she swung over to the grocery store and picked up a few things.

She was loading her groceries into Ben's truck when Jake pulled up behind them.

"Heard what happened today." He watched her closely, looking for some kind of reaction. Surprise flitted across her gamin features.

"How did you hear about that so soon?"

"Marcus called. He was worried about you."

"I'm fine. Noah scored some points off of me, but he's still the loser." She ran her hand through her short curls. "I just hope Trudy doesn't get sucked in. He can be very charming until he gets what he wants."

"Yeah, I figured that out for myself."

He walked over to Ben's window to include him in the conversation.

"I also heard you gave him the one finger salute." Jake's lips twitched, and he fought hard to keep a sober face.

"Yeah, I did. It felt good. I know I shouldn't have done that, but I did it anyway. I'm not sorry, either."

"Marcus saw it. Almost made him laugh which, let's face it, he needed. He said Noah stormed back into the funeral, absolutely fuming."

"Is there a purpose to rehashing this?" Jill wanted to know.

"Yes, there is. You don't want to antagonize him at this point. You're still in the driver's seat. That's gonna bug him. He may do something stupid."

Bree leaned forward, and Jake wished he could bite his tongue in two.

"Dad might hurt mom?" The fear in Bree's voice arrowed straight into Jake's gut.

"No, honey. He won't hurt mom again." Jake hoped he sounded reassuring.

Bree's eyes searched his face, looking for the truth. Whatever she saw there did a lot to reassure her.

"If dad tries to hurt mom again, I'm gonna punch him!" Megan announced. Jill grinned.

"Dad won't hurt me again. I promise you."

"Look. I've got to get back on the road. Why don't I pick up some pizzas and we can all chow down," Jake suggested.

"Sounds good," Ben piped in. "We can have an outdoor pizza party, after which we'll fire up the burn-pit again and get rid of the rest of those boxes. Where do you think you're going?" Jill was heading back into the store.

"If we're going to do a bonfire, we need stuff for S'mores. I'm going to get some."

Jill turned to Jake. "I'll call your mom and have her come over, too."

"Might as well call Mary Lee and have her bring the boys. Tell Zach, too. He's working today, isn't he?"

Jill nodded. "We'll make a party out of it. A party is exactly what we need right now."

Jake shook his head. What began as a little get-together turned into a full-fledged party. He had better order plenty of pizzas. Those boys of Mary Lee's eat like stevedores.

Ben and Jill pulled in behind Mary Lee's SUV. It didn't surprise either of them to see her there. It's just something Mary Lee does. Mary Lee's a good friend, Jill thought.

"Mary Lee! I'm so happy you're here." Jill jumped from Ben's truck and embraced the tiny blonde.

"I wanted to make sure you're okay. Today had to be rough."

"You have no idea," Ben quipped. He turned to the two girls exiting his club cab. "Why don't you two go change clothes and meet me down here in ten minutes." He turned to Jill. "I'm gonna get outta these duds and get into some comfortable clothes; check and see the progress on those stalls."

"Let's walk on back to the stables. Jake's bringing pizza, I picked up stuff to make S'mores, and it looks like we're going to have a bon fire tonight."

"Are you up for that? Today had to be devastating." Mary Lee searched Jill's face, looking for signs of fatigue and grief.

She found the grief in Jill's expressive eyes, but that was all.

"I'll tell you about it as we're walking back."

Mary Lee exploded on hearing that Noah had been at the funeral, effectively banning Jill from saying her final good-bye.

"Mary Lee, he's up to something. I just know it."

"I agree but, until he makes the next move, you won't know what."

Mary Lee played with the fine gold chain she wore around her neck.

"What's up, girl friend?" Jill asked, and Mary Lee gave her a wry smile.

"It appears we have a female version of Noah in our midst." Mary Lee cleared her throat. "Steffi Brandt is making noises about the sale of this house. She's hell-bent to cause you trouble."

Jill sighed. "Good luck with that. I'm not stupid, Mary Lee. The sale went through, and she signed everything without complaint. What's her deal?"

"I suspect it's a two-fold deal. She's probably gone through the money from the sale of the house, and she sees you as competition."

"Competition for what?"

"Jake Stone."

Jill let that stew for a moment before making a pithy remark. It seemed to be her day for cussing.

"Oh for God's sake! He's the county sheriff. He's a neighbor, and we're working our way up to being friends! What the hell is there to be jealous about?"

"Sweetie. You're young, you have goals, you are cuter than a bug's ear. Those are just three of the reasons she is jealous. Mostly, she's jealous of your money and the time Jake is spending with you."

Jill dug her fingers into her forehead. "For the love of God! I just got out of a bad marriage. I'm certainly not looking to jump into another."

"See? There's the difference. She thinks money is the answer to everything, and Jake's got plenty in his own right." Mary Lee gave Jill a hard one-armed hug. "Let's not let her spoil tonight. I just wanted to make sure you are okay. Since you are, I'm going home and changing into something more casual." She looked down at the white skirt, blue tank top, and white blazer she was wearing. "I suggest you do the same." Mary Lee gestured to Jill's blue linen dress.

"Good thinking. The weather is humid, today. I'm going up and getting into something cooler before I melt."

"Tell that husband of mine I'll see him in a few."

She waved as she walked back to her vehicle. Jill walked into the stable, deciding to deliver the message before going up to change.

She took one look, and her jaw dropped. Zach and his crew had a great start. Two stalls were almost finished, just needing the steel-reinforced gates.

"We'll be starting on the birthing stall tomorrow after installing the gates on these two. Soon as you get some of this land fenced in, you can begin to take boarders," Zach told her.

"I can't believe how fast this is going." She stood in the middle of the stall and turned in circles.

"You have a good design. It's easy to follow and easy to build."

"I used the same plan my dad used. It worked well for him."

"I can believe it." Zach grinned down at her. "Didn't I hear the love of my life outside?"

"Yes, yes you did. She's going home to change. It appears we're going to have a pizza party here, tonight, followed by S'mores and a fire. You up to it?"

"Pizza and S'mores? Hell yeah!"

Jill laughed and headed into the house. She took the back stairs up and, as she turned toward her room, she smelled cigarette smoke and old-fashioned cologne. She could hear Megan and Bree talking, but not to each other.

"I told you! We don't have a birdie! We have a Charlie!" Megan sounded out of patience.

Jillian dashed into the room and looked around. Both of her daughters were facing the doors leading out to the verandah.

"Who was here? Who are you talking to?" Jill demanded.

Bree pointed toward the doors. "That man in the funny green suit was here again. He went out the doors. How can he go out the doors without opening them?

Jill opened her mouth, and then closed it again. How could you answer the unanswerable?

Thirteen

Jill's knees turned to jelly as she sank down to Bree's bed.

"What do you mean he goes through the doors without opening them?"

"You know, he just kinda melts through the door." Megan gestured with her little hands.

Dear God, she thought. What in the hell is she telling me? How can someone 'melt' through the door?

"Bree, are you saying he's been here before?"

"Yeah, mom. He comes in and talks to me and Megan a lot."

Don't look scared, Jill told herself. Don't freak the girls. Keep it sane. Stick to facts, girl.

"He usually comes at night," Megan said, wanting to be helpful.

"And he's looking for a bird?" Jill asked. Both girls nodded enthusiastically.

"We keep telling him we don't have a birdie, like he calls it. We told him we only have a Charlie. That makes him mad," Bree said.

"Okay. Tell you what." Jill's mind raced. "Get changed into play clothes. We're going to have a party and bon-fire, tonight, and then we're going to camp out in my room. Won't that be fun?"

Her girls would be staying close until Jill figured out just what the hell's going on in her house.

Jill headed into her room, changed her clothes, and then ran down the stairs, Charlie hot on her heels. She opened the back door and the little dog bombed out into the back yard, almost desperate to run and jump and get rid of some of his excess energy.

Jill made a detour into her office and checked her e-mail before heading outside.

She stopped in the kitchen before heading outside and into her stable. She watched with pleasure as Zach and his crew completed the birthing stall.

"Wow! This is really coming along." She touched one of the gates and beamed at Zach.

"Yeah. Few more days and we can rough in the tack room and mount the feed boxes."

She gave him a quick one-armed hug. "I'm so pleased."

He looked into her eyes, saw the pain there, and flinched a little.

"Rough day, huh," he said. Jill nodded.

"My ex-husband was there. I couldn't go in. The louse did it on purpose." She shook her head, a wry grin on her face. "I saluted him and mouthed 'fuck you', so that was something. Petty, but I felt better."

Yeah, he thought, but it hurt you. Zach thought he'd like to give the ex-husband a nice pat on the head… with a hammer.

"Looks like we're going to have a get-together," Jill said, changing the subject. "Jake's picking up pizza and Mary Lee is going to pick up the boys. Helen's mother is bringing something for desert." She peered up at him. "It feels like a party. Is that so wrong?"

"No!" Zach said, shaking his head. "Look, I didn't know your friend, but you did. From what Mary Lee's told me, you two grew up together. What would he want you to do?"

"That's a good question. The answer is he would want us to celebrate his life, not grieve. Oh, don't get me wrong. I'm going to grieve for him the rest of my life, but he wouldn't want us to be all morose and stuff. Devin wasn't like that."

"Looks like you've answered your own question, then." Zach reached out and patted her shoulder.

Jill took a deep breath and plunged ahead. "Invite your crew and their families. We have enough room, and we can fill in the pizzas with other stuff. I don't know." She gave him a wry grin. "We'll figure it out as we go."

It's a last minute thing, Jill thought, but sometimes those are best.

She set aside any guilt she felt over a party on the very day of Devin's funeral knowing he'd appreciate it. That had been Devin's way. Face it, analyze it, and get on with it. That had always been Devin's motto.

She turned as Jake pulled into her drive. Walking over, she reached in to help with the pizza boxes. Not surprising, he had brought beer with him.

"I think we're going to need more beer," she told him.

"Why is that?"

"It appears we are going to have a full-fledged get-together. I can't call it a party, I'm not sure it is a party, but it's something."

Jake grinned. "Good thing I told Del and his brother to join us." Jake reached into his pocket and pulled out his phone.

He punched in a number. "Del. Grab a case of Bud and a case of Coke." He paused, listening, then laughed. "You're not working tonight, are you?" Jake asked and laughed again. "Good. I'd hate to nail my deputy for drunk driving. See you in ten."

Even as he spoke, other cars turned onto Jill's property. Word had spread like wildfire.

For a moment, Jill's mouth felt like cotton. She took a deep breath and went to greet her impromptu guests.

"Hello! I'm Jill Tolivar! Welcome!"

The women and children of her work crew hurried towards her, anxious to get a good look at the woman who is providing their husbands and boyfriends with work.

"We're so happy to meet you!" The women gushed while their children hung back, a little shy.

Ben strolled over and the women flushed, getting a good look at the newest newcomer. His craggy good looks and the air of mystery that surrounded Ben had more than one woman sighing.

"I'll get things set up, little girl. We better get this show on the road and get those kids fed before they start gnawing on us."

Ben strolled away, and Mary Lee fanned her face with her hands. "Not exactly handsome, but ho boy! He sort of smacks ya right in the hormones." The women laughed and agreed.

"Who is he?" Sara, the wife of Zach's foreman, asked as she herded her kids away from the pizza boxes.

"He was my dad's best friend as well as his right-hand man. There isn't anyone alive who knows more about horses and teaching than Ben."

"Speaking of horses," Jake began as he walked over to the little group. "Chief wants to know when you're gonna come visit."

"Soon. Maybe in a day or two," Jill told him.

He nodded. "Sounds like a plan."

As they spoke, more pizza boxes added to the mountain already waiting told Jill she needed to get things organized.

Helen arrived with four huge apple pies, and a few of the women added their supplies for S'mores to Jill's.

"Looks like we've bought out every pizza in fifty miles," Helen quipped as she added her desserts to the feast.

Jill grinned. "This is going to be fun. And, this is exactly what the girls and I need."

Moving quickly, she brought out paper plates, napkins, and forks for those who chose to eat pizza with utensils rather than their fingers.

Del drove up and quickly unloaded cases of beer, Coke and Sprite.

"Thought some may not want the caffeine."

"Good thinking!" Jake smiled his approval.

Before long, the children were settled with food and drink, and the adults began to fill their own plates.

"This is a great idea!" Mary Lee gushed. "We should have done this before."

Jill nodded. "I like that idea. Let's make this a Friday night deal."

Everyone agreed.

"Of course, it won't always be pizza, will it?" Ben asked.

Jill shook her head. "No, of course not. We can do barbecue and whatever."

As they ate, talk centered on school. "These kids will be back in school in a couple more weeks. I'm always sad to see them go back, because I know winter is coming. I dislike winter," Sara announced. She slid a glance toward Jill. "I imagine you have your girls all registered."

Jill nodded. "Took care of that today," she said around a mouth full of pizza. Jill quickly swallowed and washed it down with Coke.

"Good! I was a little hesitant to bring this up, but I'm gonna do it anyway," Sara said with a wide grin. "If you don't want to do it, just say so."

Jill looked at her with big question marks in her eyes.

Mary Lee grinned. She knew what was coming.

"I was wondering, since you have all this room and all, if you would consider hosting the school's Halloween party. We usually have it at school, but the kids aren't real happy about that. They'd like it somewhere else."

Jill sat quietly for a moment. She looked over to her old barn.

The building was huge and she thought it could work for a haunted house type thing.

"We could do that. We could fix up that old barn for the older kids and the second pole building for the younger kids," Jill said.

"You'll do it?" Sara asked, her excitement pouring out of her. She had hoped but didn't dare believe this new citizen would want to take something this big on.

"What do you think, Ben," Jill asked when he sauntered over to join them.

"I think it's a fine idea. It's going to take time to get it all set up but, yeah, we can do this." He glanced toward the road. "We got more company coming," Ben announced, gesturing toward the end of the driveway.

"You have got to be kidding me," Mary Lee said. She rolled her eyes in absolute disgust.

"Who is that?" Ben asked.

Mary Lee gave an irritated shoulder jerk.

"Steffi Brandt!" The name evoked groans, and even more groans erupted as the woman in question parked behind Jake's vehicle and slithered out.

"You're having a party and didn't invite me?" she called out, a pretty pout on her lips. Her remark was met with stony silence and dirty looks from all the women present. Wisely, the men kept to themselves.

Steffi pinned Jillian with her cold eyes and smirked. "Don't you think it's a little tacky? I mean, throwing a party on the very day your best friend is buried?"

Jillian felt the blood rush to her face. "It's not a party," she murmured. "It's a get-together."

"Hmmm. Beer, soda, and pizza. Looks like a party to me," Steffi said, enjoying herself, enjoying the discomfort of the other women.

Her smirk in place, she glided over to where Jake sat. His face resembled something carved out of stone.

Jake stood before she could perch herself on his lap. A frown flitted across Steffi's cold face.

"If you're finished with children's hour," she began, "why not come over for a little adult time?"

Jake shook his head. "I'm happy where I am, Steffi." He took her arm and led her, not too gently, toward her car.

Steffi tried to wiggle loose, but his grip was firm.

"I don't know what you're trying to do, Steffi, but that was completely uncalled for."

"What? What was uncalled for?" She slid a glance and noticed the anger simmering behind his eyes. "Does the divorcee have her hooks in you? You no longer have time for me?"

Jake watched her petulant face closely. Now, he could see the greed lurking just underneath. As much as he hated to admit it, his mother was right. Obviously, Steffi was looking to sink her hooks into him.

Jake shook his head, wondering how in the hell he missed the cues everyone else noticed.

"No one has their hooks in me, Steffi. I suggest you go home and re-think your life. You're making a mess of it."

Steffi's face resembled a thundercloud, all dark and stormy.

"My life is just fine. If you care to spend your time with those beneath you, that's your problem. I'm leaving, so you can let go of me. When you come to your senses, you know where to find me."

She turned on her heel and yanked open her car door. She shot one last disgusted look before placing herself behind the wheel. She didn't bother looking behind her but, rather, gunned the engine, threw the vehicle in reverse and tore down the driveway.

Jake shook his head as he walked back to join the group.

"I'm sorry about that, Jill," he said, and she shook her head.

"You don't have anything to apologize for, but now I think we should gather up the cardboard and find some wood. Let's get this bonfire going."

Jill wanted to shake off Steffi's words, determined not to ruin the evening for her girls as well as her guests. It was difficult. She turned toward the road as Steffi's car spat gravel as she burned away from the house.

Jill grabbed Jake's arm and pointed. Standing just outside of a stand of trees was the man, staring after Steffi, rage pouring from his entire body.

"Do you see him?" Jill gasped. By the time she caught his attention and directed him where to look, the man melted into the trees again.

"He's here?" Jake asked, already in motion. "Del!" Jake called out and the two men broke into a run heading for the tree line.

Women gathered their kids close, murmuring among themselves. Clearly, something odd was going on.

"Let's gather the cardboard from the back porch and the men can find some wood. I'm sure it'll be fine," Helen told the group.

A short time later, Jake and Del returned. Jake shook his head in answer to her questioning look.

"He's gone," Jake said. "The guy must really know the woods around here." He gave his deputy a look and Del nodded.

Looked like Del would be doing some research tonight. Although they didn't find anyone, Jill said she had seen someone. So, Jake trusted her word. If Jill saw him, he had been there. Problem was, where did he go?

Both men wished they could have found him.

Fourteen

Ben waited until the evening was over but kept a close eye on Jillian and her girls. It was high time for them to have a serious chat. He knew it would be like pulling teeth, but how could he do the necessary things if he didn't know what those things were?

Jake helped his mother place her empty pie dishes in her car, assured her he would be home soon and watched as she drove down the driveway.

Jillian helped her girls bring in toys and games and directed them upstairs.

"You have exactly one hour for a video game, then it's bath time and bed."

Jake walked into the house and sat at the kitchen table. "I'm putting extra men on patrol out here," he told her. "Anything happens, anything at all, you call me."

He wasn't comfortable leaving her, but he couldn't exactly move in with her, either. Ben's here, he told himself. She'll be okay.

"I can see you're worried. I wish you'd tell me why," Jillian said.

Jake sighed. "I don't care for the thought of you and the girls in this house while some strange person is wondering around the place. I thought that was obvious."

Jill gave him a small smile. "It's nice, this worry you have, but unnecessary. Ben is here and I'm not without resources. I can and will protect the girls and myself. My dad made damn sure I knew how."

Jake almost threw out the fact that she hadn't done such a great job of protecting herself from her ex-husband. He bit his lip, but she read his mind.

"I stayed with Noah because I was stupid. I didn't believe in divorce and, like a fool, hoped he would change. So yes, I stayed with him until he almost killed me. I learned a lesson, Sheriff. No man will ever put his hands on me in anger again, much less my girls."

"Point taken." Jake got to his feet and turned to the door. "I still want you to call if anything happens."

Jill nodded and gave him a rare smile. Damn if he didn't feel ten feet tall, watching those lips turn up just a little. He'd have to think about that, too.

Jake walked into his home and was not surprised in the least to see his mother sitting in her favorite chair. Since she hadn't bothered to turn on the television, he correctly assumed she was waiting for him.

"Ma! If you're gonna start on me, I swear, I'll send you out to the barn to sleep. I know exactly what you're going to say and, frankly, I don't care to hear it!"

Helen gave him a look that was all *mother*. "Jacob Logan! I don't care how old you get, you will never be old enough to take that tone with me, and don't you forget it!"

In spite of his age and his profession, not to mention the fact he dealt with criminals every day, the sad fact was, when Helen took that tone, it could still shrivel his balls to the size of grapes.

"She's nothing but trouble, Jake. Jillian Tolivar is worth a dozen Steffi Brandts! What's it going to take for you to realize that?"

Jake rested his head in his hands, using his fingers to massage his temples where a headache was forming.

"I get it, Mom. I informed Steffi any friendship I may have felt for her was over." And, he thought, she hadn't taken that news very well, either.

"Let's get something else straight while we're at it." Jake gave his mother a hard stare. "I'm not looking to get married again. I like my life just the way it is." He raised his hand as Helen opened her mouth. "You had your say, it's my turn. My previous marriage was a disaster. Some of it was my fault as well as hers. It's over. I know you would like grand-kids. That's not going to happen, either. I'm sorry. I'm just not going to take a risk like that again."

Helen sat back, crossing her arms over her chest. Jake thought her face was carved from stone, so when it suddenly brightened, he immediately became suspicious.

"Well, son of mine… you never know what the fates have in store for you, do you…" Wisely, she kept the rest of her thoughts to herself. She had noticed the soft look in Jake's eyes whenever he glanced at Jill and her girls.

He may not realize it now, she thought, but he was definitely in trouble. How nice.

Steffi fumed all the way into town.

She headed for Mike's Diner, hoping to find someone, anyone she could vent her anger toward, but the diner had closed.

Jake didn't have any right talking to her like that! Who did he think he was, anyway? She would show him. She would show them all.

Steffi turned her car around and drove to a small bar just outside of Molton. She wondered if she'd be able to stir up a little action.

Steffi was not adverse to a one-night stand now and then, as long as word didn't filter back to town. The beauty of this particular bar was she often could find a trucker or traveler, stopping for the night.

She was thrilled when she spotted the BMW parked in the lot. Very nice wheels, she thought. She hoped the owner was just as nice. She hoped he was alone.

Fluffing her hair and checking her make-up, she doused herself in expensive perfume. She planned to make a statement and a conquest.

Noah sat at the bar, drinking Scotch. He managed to get away from his current flavor of the month. Now, in a haze, he wondered how the hell he was going to find Jill in this forsaken wilderness.

He had a score to settle with her and he would have satisfaction.

Even inebriated, he noticed the woman as she sashayed through the door. A man in a coma would notice her.

Noah liked the way her thin blue summer dress clung to her curves and that glorious hair just begged for his hands to take a trip through. He also liked her frosty eyes and had a feeling he finally had come face to face with his female counterpart.

After, he told himself. After he settled things with his bitch of an ex-wife, he would find this creature and see what he could teach her... and maybe what she had to teach.

Steffi spied him sitting at the end of the bar and casually made her way toward him. The car sitting outside had to belong to this guy, she thought.

"Is this seat taken?" Steffi gestured to the bar stool next to Noah.

"It is now, pretty lady." Noah worked to focus. He really wanted to get a good look at this vision. He wanted to see if she was that hot or just a figment of his drunken imagination.

Steffi held out her hand and, after a little fumbling, Noah captured it in his paw.

"I'm Steffi Brandt and you are?" she purred.

"Noah Tolivar."

The name stopped Steffi in her tracks. Her luck just could not be that good, could it?

"Are you, by any chance, related to Jillian Tolivar?"

Noah tried to nod, his head bobbing drunkenly.

"My ex-wife," he slurred.

"Really! How interesting!" Steffi's mind raced. She had heard some vague story about him. Something about restraining orders. She wished now she had paid closer attention.

"What brings you up here?" She snuggled closer as she signaled for a drink. "My usual," she told the bartender. He hoped he could remember what her 'usual' was.

The bartender set a frosty Grey Goose martini in front of her and she rewarded him with a cool smile. She gestured toward Noah's glass and he promptly filled it with ice and three fingers of scotch.

"I'm looking for that no good miserable bitch. She owes me and I'm gonna collect." Noah looked at her through painfully-red eyes and, mentally, Steffi rubbed her hands together.

"It just so happens I know where she lives. She bought my aunt's house for way under market price. She owes me, too."

"Looks like she owes both of us," Noah slurred, grasping his fresh drink and spilling most of it down the front of his shirt.

Steffi caught the bartender watching Noah's little mishap and was pretty sure what was coming next. Noah was about to be cut off.

"Hey. I have a great idea. I have a nice bottle of wine chilling. We can move this to my house."

Noah shook his head. "Can't. Can't drive."

Steffi shook her head. "No, you can't. We can leave your car here. I'll bring you back in the morning."

Noah shrugged. What the hell, he thought. He was almost out of money. The woman was easy on the eyes and she had stuff to drink. It was win-win.

The bartender watched as Steffi helped him out the door, shaking his head. He didn't care where they went, so long as they were out of his bar.

Jill helped the girls bathe, read them a little more of *Black Beauty* and then tucked them in.

"Tonight was fun, mom," Bree said, snuggling into her pillows. "We even made some more friends. The kids here are nice."

Jill leaned down and gave her oldest a hard kiss on her forehead. "I'm so glad, sweetie. I want you and Megan to be happy here."

"We are, Mom. Honest!" Megan's voice held the sleepy weight that told Jill her youngest would soon be nodding off. "This is a good place. Right?"

"Yes, sweetheart. This is a very good place." She kissed Megan's sweet cheek and gently drew up the blankets around her little chin.

"Sleep well, my little loves. Only good dreams allowed," Jill said as she snapped off the light.

Hugging herself, she walked into her sitting room. Tonight *had* been fun. The women were sweet and just as nice as their men. The kids made her own children feel welcome. Yes, Jill thought. This is a very good place.

Devin would have loved all of this, she thought, and tears filled her eyes. Rubbing them briskly, she headed for her sitting room, planning to do a little reading before bed.

"Kids asleep?" Ben's deep voice boomed from her doorway. Jill spun around, her hand over her pounding heart.

"Good God, Ben! You almost gave me a heart attack!" she gasped.

Ben grinned. "Now, I doubt that, little girl. Let's go down. You can make me some coffee and fill me in on everything I don't know, which seems to be quite a bit."

She made him coffee, grabbed a bottle of water for herself and made herself comfortable at the kitchen table.

She poured her heart out, starting with Noah managing to get her phone number, no matter how many times she changed it. When she reached the part of her story about the strange man appearing and disappearing from her daughters' room, he perked up.

"Seriously? He just appears and disappears?" Jill nodded. "Megan swears he 'melted' through the doors," she said.

"What? You got a ghost here?" Ben's black eyes sparkled with amusement.

"Oh Ben! You know there's no such thing."

"Nope. Gotta be some other explanation and we'll get to the bottom of it, sweetie. I don't want you to worry none."

Jill reached across the table and took his worn hand in her small one. "Ben, I'm so glad you're here. I don't know what I'd do without you."

He patted her hand. "No need to worry about that. Especially since I *am* here. Now, tell me about your plans for this place and put this other crap outta your mind."

"I'm going to breed some but, primarily, I'm going into boarding. There's a lot of horse people around here and not one decent place to board. There was one place, but the barn burned down a year ago. The owners never rebuilt but do allow their boarders to keep the horses on the land. It's rough in winter."

"Well, it would be, wouldn't it. Okay, what else? I know you, little girl. You wouldn't have bought a house this size unless you had plans for it."

Jill grinned. "You know me so well. Actually, some of the horses will be therapy horses, like I said. I'm going to use this place as a therapy camp." She sat back and waited.

Ben mulled it over before nodding. "I think it's a good plan and it could work, but what about your other business? That game thing you do."

"I'm going to continue with that, as well. Every penny I received from mom and dad's estate went into a trust for the girls. I plan on making more so money is the one thing they'll never have to worry about." She gave a slight shrug. "Besides, I like that kind of work, too."

Ben sighed. "You've bit off quite a bit but you always were a worker." His dark eyes searched her face. "I think you'll do just fine."

"I will because I have you, Ben. We always made a great team and no one knows horses like you do."

"Speaking of horses, looks like the good sheriff owns Chief now. When you gonna go down and take a look at him?"

Jill took a drink and turned her gaze out the window. "I don't know. I don't know if I can handle seeing him, knowing he belongs to someone else." Tears stood in her eyes, and Ben patted her hand.

"You should go see him, missy. He'd be hurt if you don't."

Jill gave him a small wan smile. "I'll probably go over in a day or so."

"Make sure you do," Ben told her. "Now, you get yourself to bed. We have a lot of work to get done. Can't have you sleeping on the job."

She got to her feet and walked around the table, going into the arms he held wide. "Oh, Ben, my life is such a mess."

He patted her back and then leaned back a little, pulling on one of her curls. "It's going to be okay, little girl. Just take it one day at a time."

Jill nodded and gave him a hard squeeze. "I'm just so damn glad you're here," she told him.

He hugged her hard and then released her. "Go on now, go on up to bed. Those little hellions of yours will be up before you know it."

She smiled and patted his cheek. "Night."

He watched her go up the stairs. Moving to the coffee pot, he poured himself a cup and took a chair at the table. He had a lot to think over.

Horse therapy and computer games, he thought. Don't that just beat all.

Jill treated herself to a long hot shower, letting the water pour over her body. Only after the water cooled did she turn off the taps.

She lathered herself with lavender-scented moisturizer and reached for her blue nightshirt. She wrapped a towel around her hair and strolled into her bedroom, sitting on the bed as she rubbed her hair dry.

It felt good, she thought, this talk with Ben. She felt a little lighter.

He's right, she told herself. She needed to visit Chief. She raised him from a colt and helped train him, so she'd just have to gird her loins, whatever the hell that meant, and just do it. He probably won't remember me, anyway.

Her musings were interrupted by the buzz of her cell. Seeing Trudy's number on the face, she quickly answered it.

"Trudy! Hello! How are you doing?"

Trudy's drunken voice raged over the instrument, causing Jill to cringe.

"How am I doing? My husband and baby are dead, Jill. Dead! How the hell do you think I'm doing?"

"Trudy, I'm so sorry. I wanted to talk to you today, but I couldn't stay. I couldn't stay, not with Noah there. You know that."

"No, you couldn't stay. Does your conscience bother you, Jill?"

"No Trudy. Why would it?"

"It's your fault they're dead." Trudy began to sob. "Noah explained it all to me. Whoever killed your parents are eliminating everyone around you. Am I next, Jill? How about the good judge and his damned wife? Will Marcus and Lavinia be next?"

"Trudy, please." Jill began to cry. "You don't mean these things. This isn't like you."

Trudy snorted into the phone. "How would you know if this is me, or not? Do me a favor. Stay away from me. Lose my number and stay away from Marcus and Lavinia before you get them killed, too." Trudy hung up, leaving Jill reeling from shock.

For a moment, she thought about going down and telling Ben about this but, on second thought, decided against it. She unloaded on him enough. She would deal with this at the proper time.

Jill thought her head would explode, so she swallowed a couple of Advil and burrowed into her pillow. Maybe Trudy is right, she thought, maybe this is all my fault. Tears soaked her pillow. Trudy's words raced through her mind, and she sobbed quietly.

She thought sleep would never find her, but she was wrong. After crying herself out, her eyes grew heavy and she slipped into a deep dreamless sleep.

It lasted until three in the morning.

The cigarette smoke woke her first, followed by a man's cologne mingling with the scent of cigarette.

Her eyes popped open and her heart began to race.

He stood at the foot of her bed, blue eyes blazing in a face so wan.

"Where is my birdie?" he demanded, his voice little more than a hollow echo.

Jill's mouth worked but no sound came out.

"Where is my birdie?" he demanded again, moving closer to Jill, who quaked in her bed.

"I don't know who you are talking about." Jill's voice was a terrified whisper. "I don't know what birdie is. We don't have birds, we have a dog." And, she thought, we're getting a bigger one.

Sheer rage flashed over the man's pale face. "Don't be stupid! Where is my birdie?" He was in a rage.

The bitter cold in her room penetrated through the terrified fog in Jill's brain. She shivered and noticed her breath came out in terrified little puffs.

"I told you, I don't know who or what you are talking about."

She wanted to throw the covers over her head but reached down in her guts and found her courage. She sat up in bed and reached for her cell phone, planning on calling Jake.

The man gave a small wave and sent her cell phone skidding across the room, coming to rest against a far wall.

"If you broke that," she began, "you're going to regret that." How stupid, Jill told herself. Threatening a deranged man in your bedroom.

"Find birdie!" he ordered before turning and walking out to her balcony. He turned, a deep scowl on his face. "Find my birdie!"

He turned and walked down the stairs and into the garden below.

Shaking like a leaf, Jill scrambled out of bed on legs she didn't think would hold her and ran over to her phone. She snapped it open and released a shaky sigh when the face lit up. Dialing quickly, she called the one person she knew she could and should count on.

Jake's sleepy voice became instantly awake when the words tumbled from Jill's shaky lips.

"I'll be right there. Don't go outside. Lock your terrace doors. I'll come to them after I check out the garden. Do it now, Jill. Lock your door and wait for me."

True to his word, he soon roared up the driveway, coming to rest next to the stairs leading to her room.

She watched him move through her gardens before disappearing around the side of the house. Only after what seemed an endless time to Jill, he climbed the stairs outside her verandah doors.

She whipped them open and launched herself into his arms. So ferocious was her attack, he had to take a step back or they both would have fallen down the stairway.

"No one's here. Whoever he was is gone, Jill." He stroked her hair and just held on while she sobbed out her relief.

"How did he get in here? Didn't you lock your doors?"

Jill leaned back a little and met his eyes. "That's the thing, Jake. My doors were locked." She wiped her eyes and then reached over and caught his hand and dragged him into her room, taking care to close the door behind him.

"I made sure I locked my doors, and now that I think about it, Jake, they were still locked when he left." She shook her head. "You're going to think I'm nuts but, Jake, I think I have a ghost and don't think I don't know how that sounds."

Jake led her to the sofa in her sitting room, lowered her down, and then took a seat next to her, keeping her hand in his.

Jake took a deep breath before replying and Jill gave him a hard stare.

"Don't you dare tell me there are no such things," she said. "I know there are no such things, but it's the only explanation I can think of that makes even the remotest sense of what's going on."

"There are two people we can ask." He checked his watch and reached for his phone. She watched him punch in a number and then waited. He tossed her a wink.

"Mary Lee? Yeah, sorry to call so late, but this is kind of important. Either Jill or I will explain in the morning. Mary Lee, do you know what sort of leverage Steffi used to gain control of her aunt's estate?" He listened and Jill thought his face turned a little chalky. "Okay, hon. Sorry for disturbing you. We'll talk in the morning. What? Yeah, everyone's okay. It does seem, however, that you sold Jill a haunted house. Talk to you tomorrow."

Mary Lee was still sputtering when Jake ended the call.

Jill was on pins and needles waiting for Jake to finish his call.

"Well? What did she say?" Jill all but bounced up and down with impatience. "How did Steffi gain control over her aunt?"

Jake let out a slow deep breath. He turned to Jill and took her hand in his again.

"The aunt claimed she talked with her dead husband and here's the kicker. The aunt's given name. Alberta!"

Fifteen

Jake needed some time to mull over this little tidbit he received from Mary Lee but, for now, he'd take a shower, grab some coffee, and get on into work. He'd just think about this later.

Following that particular plan of action, it made him feel better. He was better off dealing with real crime. Going down the woo woo trail was a bit disconcerting.

He also planned on having a talk with Jill before heading into work.

Jill's thoughts were traveling down the same line. She made a quick pot of coffee, waited for it to brew, grabbed a mug, and headed into her office. She would be able to get some serious work done on her expansion pack, maybe get some bugs worked out of the program before the girls would be up and around.

The thought she had a ghost in her house was unnerving, and she tried not to think about it while she worked. Her self-imposed discipline lasted just so long before the events of the day before intruded.

Trudy's call had upset her, and she planned to call Marcus or Lavinia just as soon as the clock told her it was a decent hour.

Then, there was the man in her room. She couldn't bring herself to think of him as anything other than a man. The alternative was just too weird.

Trying to concentrate on her project was probably useless, but Jill was determined to try. A movement in her doorway, though, almost made her heart stop.

"God, Ben! Next time, just shoot! You almost gave me a heart attack!"

Ben grinned. "What's got you so jumpy, little girl?"

Jill debated with herself for about half a second. She never kept anything from Ben and now would be a stupid time to start.

"If you have a minute could you sit down and talk with me? I don't want the girls to hear this."

Curious, Ben took a seat across from her desk, kicked back his long legs, and waited.

"I had a visitor last night, Ben. A very weird visitor."

She went on to explain everything that happened. Ben was not amused.

"Hell fire, little girl! I'm right downstairs! Why didn't you come get me?"

Jill gave out a long sigh. "I thought about it, but I didn't want to disturb you. Besides, I unloaded so much on you, last night; I didn't want to burden you further."

The look Ben gave her made her blush. "Little girl, we are family, aren't we? Next time, you come and get me! I don't care what time it is or what the circumstances are! You come get me! Understand?"

"I understand. I just don't want to be a pain, you know?"

Ben sighed. "Little girl, let me lay this all out for you. You're the daughter I never had. You can't ever be a burden, but you sure can be obstinate. You get that from your old man, I guess. He could be a stubborn, ornery cuss. Don't know how your ma ever kept him in line. I miss them."

This was the first time they ever discussed her dad and she felt a lump rise in her throat.

"I miss them every day. Now Devin's gone, too." Tears stood in her eyes and she willed them back.

"Yeah I know you do. Just remember, you have two beautiful girls to raise and you still have the judge and Ms. Lavinia and me. You're not as alone as you think you are."

Charlie raced into the office at that moment and around the room before heading to the kitchen and the back door.

He stood staring at it until Ben strolled over and opened it for him. The little dog bounced out the door.

Jill took a seat at the table and sipped her coffee, watching through the window as Charlie raced around, obviously on important doggie business.

Bree and Megan followed a few minutes later and wrapped their little arms around Jill's neck.

This, she thought, is home. It didn't matter where they lived, as long as the four of them were together, it would be home.

She reached out, took Ben's hand, and held it to her cheek. Her love for the older man and her girls filled her heart. She was more than content.

Ben patted her cheek, completely understanding her unspoken feelings. Megan broke the moment, demanding breakfast.

Jill got to her feet but Ben waved her back into her chair. "You girls want some scrambled eggs and toast?" he asked.

Megan bounced on her toes. "Yay! Eggs and toast! Our favorite, right Bree?"

Bree blinked at her sister. "You like anything that's food, Megan." She then turned her beautiful smile in Ben's direction. "But, if you're making it, it'll be really good."

Ben laughed. "Better go into politics, Bree. You got that silver tongue down."

Ben slapped bacon in a pan and began to scramble eggs while Jill poured out orange juice and made toast.

They were just sitting down to eat when Jake strolled in the back door.

"Sorry to disturb you." He felt at home enough to grab a mug of coffee before taking the one empty chair at the table.

"Want some?" Ben asked gesturing at the platters of food.

Jake shook his head. "No, thanks. Ate already." He sipped his coffee and slid a glance in Jill's direction. She looks tired, he thought. Tired, worried and confused.

"Did you get any sleep?" he asked and frowned when she shook her head.

"Actually, I did some work on my project and then Ben woke up and we had a chat. Now we're eating breakfast before stringing some fence." She cleared her throat a little and it struck Jake that she was a little nervous.

"I plan on going over to your place and visiting Chief and Gypsy. I'd like to see her baby." She looked straight into his eyes. "Is that okay with you?"

Jake nodded. "Yeah, of course. That's fine." About time, he thought, but kept it to himself. A wise move. Jake refrained from sharing his thoughts with Jill in the presence of the two little ones. No point in scaring the hell out of them if it wasn't necessary.

Steffi woke up to the sounds of Noah's drunken snores. Just as well. Now, in the pre-dawn light, she had things to do and she had better get to it.

She snagged Noah's keys from his pants pocket and dressed quietly. She left her apartment on quiet feet and ran to her car. Driving quickly, she headed back to the little bar where she met Noah.

She used his keys and let herself into the luxury car. It didn't take long to find something useful. His bankbook lay in the glove compartment and she quickly flipped through it.

"So," she murmured, "he's got money. Good!" That knowledge would come in handy one way or another.

She rummaged a little more and found the paperwork for his trust fund. How stupid to leave something like this just laying around, she thought.

She also found the restraining order for Molton County. More useful information, she decided. She was sure she could find a way to use this as well.

Steffi put everything back in place and emerged from the car. A little more research, she thought, and she would have an assistant, if he were willing or not.

There was still one more thing to do before heading back to her apartment. She would then wake the man and together they would decide on a course of action.

Getting rid of Jillian Tolivar, one way or another, was on Steffi's agenda, and Steffi always got what she wanted.

Zach pulled into Jill's driveway just as she and Ben finished cleaning up the breakfast dishes. The girls were dressed and playing outside. Charlie was busy bombing around the yard, having the time of his life.

Jill and Ben walked out to greet Zach and his crew. Ben grinned. If anything, Zach and his workers were punctual.

"Good morning!" Zach called out, and Jill and Ben returned his greeting. "We're gonna knock out those stalls today and finish roughing out the tack room. I want to start on the next barn next week."

Ben stood with his hands on his narrow hips. "Little girl and me plan on getting some fencing done. Hopefully, we'll be able to start boarding before the snow flies."

Zach nodded and pointed toward the loft in the first barn. "We're gonna re-enforce that floor before you start hauling in hay and such. Got some weak spots but that won't take us long to fix." Zach reached into his shirt pocket and produced a card.

"This guy has hay for sale. His prices are reasonable. You might want to give him a call."

Jill took the card and nodded. "Good thinking. So far we only have the promise of one maybe two boarders, but we're still going to need hay."

Zach made his way into the stable and, before long, the air hummed with the sounds of work in progress.

Jill and Ben grabbed their own tools and made their way into the fields.

Following Jill's guideline, it didn't take long for Ben to punch holes in the earth for poles. Pausing only once, he reached down and pulled up a handful of green.

"Good rich clover in these fields," he said. "The grass is good and rich. Lots of good grazing land here."

Jill paused and looked over. "Maybe, we should think about getting a beef steer."

Ben chuckled. "Little girl, you wouldn't be able to eat it. You'd end up naming it and the damn thing would die from old age."

Jill laughed and got back to work, stringing the first strands of her fence.

They paused at lunchtime and, after lunch, Jill tossed a roast in the oven and joined Ben back out in the field again.

Before long, she was ready to string the second strand. Ben walked over. "I think we should go ahead and mount the fencer."

The fencer would provide a low shock, keeping horses where they belonged.

Jill nodded and she ran to the house to fetch it. Entering the back porch, she was overwhelmed by the smell of cigarettes once again. The little room was freezing and Jill just knew her unwanted guest was back.

"I don't know who you are or what you want, but this is *my* house now! I'm not leaving! Either you find a way to tell me what you want or stay away!"

The pounding on the walls happened so fast and so furious, she thought the little room would cave in on itself.

Good job, Jill thought. Now you've pissed off a ghost.

Ben and Zach heard the commotion and ran over. They found Jill standing in the middle of the enclosed porch, a look of fierce determination on her face.

"That's not going to scare me, either!" she shouted over the din.

A wild wind whipped through the room. Shoes and boots flew around the room and the door leading to the kitchen slammed open and shut repeatedly.

Jill's head began to pound, but she would not give ground.

"Just keep that up and you'll be sorry! I'll find a way to get rid of you! See if I don't!"

The din began to die down and Jill took one more shot at her unseen guest.

"And, stay out of my daughters' room! This is between you and me!"

Zach pulled Ben out of the way just as a boot flew directly toward Ben's head.

"What the hell..." Zach stood slack-jawed.

"I need to speak with Mary Lee, right away!" Jill looked around the room. Shoes, boots, and coats were tossed helter skelter across the enclosed porch.

"This really pisses me off!" Jill shouted it at the top of her lungs.

Ben grinned. "Looks like you finally found your mad, little girl."

"You bet I did. What if the girls had witnessed this? Damn it!"

Ben reached over and snagged the fencer, tucking it under his arm.

"Well, they didn't, but I guess you're going to have to get to the bottom of this." He moved out the door, and his long legs quickly ate up the ground between the house and the paddock.

"I'll tell Mary Lee to call you." Zach followed Ben out of the house and turned to the stable. He wasn't sure what to think, but perhaps a chat with Jake would be in order. Damn, if he had not seen it for himself, and heard it, he wouldn't have believed it.

"I won't have this," Jill muttered as she set the room to rights. "Go throw your tantrum somewhere else! I don't know what was done to piss you off, but it's not my fault. This is my house now. Get used to it!"

She didn't know if her unwanted houseguest was listening or not and she didn't much care. It felt good to get her thoughts out there, though, just in case.

"No man is going to control me! Not now and not ever again! Better get used to that, too!"

She went into the kitchen and checked her roast, paused long enough to peel potatoes and toss some ears of corn into a pot laced with sugar water. Doing something normal, something homey, settled her, but her anger simmered just under the surface.

Ben hooked up the fencer, ran the electrical line to the stables, and grounded the whole thing. He finished stringing the second line of fencing and figured it would be safe to enter the house.

Jill retreated to her office and worked on her project for a little longer until it was time to put dinner on the table. She walked out to where Ben was busy stringing the second line of fencing.

"Could you call the girls, Ben? Dinner's ready."

Ben nodded, lifting his hand in a wave as Zach and crew left for the day.

"Bree! Megan! Chow!"

Charlie bombed through the door and took his usual place between Bree and Megan's chairs. Ben looked at Jill, an eyebrow raised.

"No, I don't encourage them to give him 'people' food. He keeps hoping, though."

Ben barked out a laugh as the girls scurried into the kitchen.

"Hands washed first," Jill reminded them. Bree dashed into the small powder room, leaving Megan to bounce on her toes.

"Bree always gets there first."

Jill walked over and held her littlest daughter up to the kitchen sink. "Just this once, right mom?"

"Yeah Megs, just this once."

After dinner, Ben sat sipping coffee. He watched the girls take their plates and place them on the counter next to the sink, and it brought a smile to his craggy face.

"Those two remind me of you at their age."

Jill nodded. "Mom taught me, so I'm teaching them."

She rinsed and loaded dishes into the dishwasher while Ben finished his coffee.

"Care to take a walk with us?" Jill asked.

"You goin' down to see Chief and Gypsy?"

Jill nodded. "It's time, don't you think?"

Ben grinned. "Past time, I'd say. Hell yeah I wanna go. I wanna see how that baby is doing."

Bree and Megan raced on ahead, Charlie bouncing along behind them. Jill picked up a stick and cut through the air with it.

Ben kept the conversation light, not wanting to bring up the happenings of the afternoon in front of the girls. So, they talked about fencing, the work on the stables and he accepted the card Jill handed him.

"Let me keep this, Jill. I'll take a ride out and check out the guy's crop. If he doesn't want an arm and a leg for substandard hay, we'll make a deal."

Jill reached over and squeezed his arm. "I don't know what I'd do without you."

"Yeah, seems like you mentioned that once before," he told her with a wide grin.

Jake's place was just coming into view. She couldn't know he had been watching for her and, having spied the girls and their little dog, came out to meet her.

As Jill walked into the yard, the quiet was split with a high-pitched whinny and thundering hooves.

"Looks like Chief caught wind of you," Ben said as the big horse charged the fence.

Jill raced forward and held out her hand, a signal to stop.

Chief ran right up to the fence and pawed the ground until Jake leaned over and opened the gate for Jillian to enter.

Horse and woman met each other halfway, and tears streamed down Jill's face as she wrapped her arms around Chief's silky neck.

Another high-pitched whinny caught her attention as Gypsy came toward her at a dead run, her foal trying desperately to keep up.

Ben felt a lump build in his throat as he watched the reunion.

"She trained both of them," he told Jake.

Jake stood silently, watching the three greet each other. The horses took turns nuzzling Jill while the two men and the foal looked on.

Bree walked over and tugged on Jake's hand. "Can you let us in there, too?" she asked. Jake looked at Ben and, when Ben nodded, he opened the gate and let the two little girls in.

Bree and Megan walked calmly toward the horses and their mom.

"Now, that's a pretty sight," Ben said as the little family and the horses became re-acquainted.

"Yeah it is and I'm beginning to wonder if I'll be losing my horses to them."

"Horses are funny creatures," Ben said. "They choose who they truly belong to."

Jake snorted. "Don't I know it," he said as he watched Jill and her girls pet and coo to the horses.

Jake turned and studied Ben with inscrutable eyes. He jerked his head and the two men walked away a few feet from the small corral.

"Gonna fill me in?" Jake asked. Surprise flitted across Ben's face. "You don't miss a thing, do you…" Ben muttered. Jake shook his head. "Nope. I wouldn't be a very good cop if I did."

Ben sighed and slid his hands into his back pockets.

"Zach call you?" he asked. Jake shook his head.

"Jillian and you both are upset and trying to look like you aren't upset, so I figure something happened. I need to know what that something is."

Ben quickly filled him in, keeping his voice low. Jake swore briefly and quietly.

"I'm going to talk with Alberta Peterson. I figure she has some of the answers we need to figure out what the hell is going on in that house."

Ben nodded. "Good idea. Fill me in if you can."

Jill and the girls were walking back toward the two men, and Ben quickly changed the subject.

"Stalls are about done and we've got a good portion of paddock fenced in. Good quality grass and clover in those fields, and that will do until we can get some hay in. We'll be mixing our own sweet feed blend, too, as soon as I can make arrangements for the ingredients," Ben told him.

"Good. This corral is too small for the three of them. The sooner they have room to stretch their legs, the better."

Ben looked around. He didn't see anything wrong with the horses' living arrangements, but kept quiet. If the man wanted to give Jillian a leg up on her boarding business, it wasn't any of his business.

"They look so good," Jill commented. "That little foal is gorgeous! What did you name her again? I forgot."

"Jillian's Gypsy Rose."

Jill's lips turned up in a small smile, but sadness shone out of her expressive eyes.

"My parents would have loved her." She looked off into the distance until she could regain her composure. Sighing, she reached out a hand for her daughters. Jake noticed how gently Bree patted her mother's hand. Megan laid her cheek against the hand she held and looked up at her mother.

Jill gave a watery laugh. "Well, girls, time to go."

At that moment, Helen emerged from her house, a pitcher of iced tea on a tray along with six tall glasses filled with ice.

"Stay and have some iced tea before you head home," she sang out.

Jill couldn't think of a graceful way to decline. Obviously, the woman had gone to some trouble and Jillian felt it would be rude not to accept her invitation.

Helen put the tray on a very attractive round picnic table and hustled back into the house, only to reappear with a plate of homemade sugar cookies.

Jill sighed and walked over to the table. She sank onto one of the cushioned chairs and signaled for her daughters to do the same. She shot them the *mother* look and they sat quietly, one on either side of her.

Helen poured the tea and handed out the cookies, then took her own seat.

"Isn't this nice!" she chirped. "I love having company and I was beginning to wonder if you'd ever make that trip up the road to visit us."

"I've been meaning to come sooner, but between getting the house situated, working on my project and then getting the stable and the paddock ready, it seemed like I ran out of day before I ran out of things to do."

Helen reached over and patted Jill's hand. "Oh, honey, you don't have to explain. I see you working so hard." She tossed a bright smile in Ben's direction. "But, now you have help and it's good to see that, too. So tell me, how are you all settling in?" Her sunny disposition encompassed them all, including Ben.

"We're settling in just fine," Jill told her. "We love the house and the stables and all are coming along great." Jill gave a small laugh. "I keep waiting for the other shoe to drop."

Neither Jake nor Ben brought up the odd happenings going on in that lovely house. They didn't want to alarm the girls, but Jake promised himself a chat with his mother as soon as their visitors left.

The four adults kept the conversation light and included the girls. Helen could hardly contain her happiness at hearing the girls were beginning to make friends.

"And, you're hosting the annual Halloween party, as well," Helen said to Jill.

"Yes, I am. Can I count on you to help me with refreshments? I thought light finger foods, but something teenagers would enjoy."

Helen beamed. "Oh, count on me, honey! You bet I'll help!"

Talk turned to the Halloween party and the fact that time was short.

"Where are you planning on holding this?" Helen asked.

Jill gave a small shrug. "I was thinking of the old barn toward the tree line. I thought I would have Zach check it out and make sure it's safe to use. We could make a sort of haunted house out of it for the teens, but I've decided we'll use the ballroom on the top floor of the house for the kid's portion. Then, to keep the teenagers out of mischief, I'm thinking of using what will be the riding arena for a kind of dance hall. I'll hire a couple of DJ's to keep the tunes rolling and hope for the best. We're going to need chaperones, though. Ben and I can't be everywhere."

"Get some of the parents to help. This is for their kids, too," Jake advised. He was all for keeping the teens off the streets, especially on Hell Night.

"I'll be there, too, and Del will volunteer as well," Jake told her, making her laugh.

"Does Del know he's volunteering?" she asked. Jake just smiled and reached for another cookie.

"We're going to have a barbecue on Friday evening. You come too," Jill told Helen. "The families of Zach's crew will be there and we can get some workers and chaperones lined up then."

"Oh, honey, I'll be there with bells on." Helen laughed. It made her happy to see Jillian beginning to settle into the community.

"Helen, thank you for the iced tea and cookies, but I've got to get these kids home and into their bath. They only have an hour after that for either television or video games."

Jill gathered up the glasses and returned them to the tray. She started to hand the plate of cookies to Bree when Helen stopped her.

"You just leave that. Jake'll help me."

"I don't mind," Jill began, but Helen stopped her. "Don't worry about it. Those girls look a little tired and we don't want to rob them of their hour. You can help me next time."

Jill surprised everyone when she leaned over and kissed the older woman's cheek. Tears welled in Helen's eyes and spilled over onto her cheeks.

Touched, she reached out and stroked Jill's cheek. "Honey, that's just the sweetest thing anyone has done to me in a long time. Now you go on. Take those sweet young girls home and get them settled."

Jill took Helen's hand and gave it a hard squeeze before reaching for her daughters. Helen watched as Jill, her daughters and Ben began the quarter mile walk back home.

"She's just the sweetest thing, Jake. So much sadness there, though."

She began to gather up the tray and the plate of cookies, but Jake's hand on her arm stopped her.

"Put those down and sit down, Ma. I want to talk to you for a bit."

Helen sat and looked at her son, big question marks in her eyes.

"What's up, Jake?"

Jake sighed. He supposed the direct approach would be best with his mother.

"What can you tell me about Alberta Peterson and what do you know about how Steffi managed to get control of Mrs. Peterson's estate."

Helen gave him a thoughtful look.

"Steffi had Alberta declared incompetent."

"How?"

"Alberta claimed to be talking to her dead husband."

Sixteen

Helen sat back and watched Jake's reaction. When he continued to stare at her, she waved a hand. "I know how that sounds, but believe me, Jake, Alberta Peterson is the least flaky person I know. She wouldn't have said something like that without good reason."

"How much do you know about her?" he asked.

Helen shrugged. "Well now, let me think for a minute." She stared off into space, gathering her thoughts.

"She and Gray married young. She was nineteen and he, barely twenty. He was called up in the draft sometime in nineteen sixty-eight and they sent him off to Vietnam after basic training. Less than a year later, he was killed."

"Obviously, they had no children," Jake said and Helen shook her head.

"No. They planned to have them after he came back from the war, but that didn't go exactly as planned. So, she took some of the life insurance money, paid off the house, and then opened up her flower shop. That place was really something. It was innovative. Alberta had a knack with candies as well as flowers. She grew most of her stock right in her own gardens and even had a greenhouse to keep herself stocked right on through winter. Besides flowers, she offered candy of all sorts, including the best fudge I ever tasted. She did so well, she expanded again and was able to offer Christmas trees at a reasonable price. So, she kept on investing and expanding until she was quite the wealthy woman. She never stopped working, though, until she became too old to keep on going. A young couple took over her business, but it was never the same. After a couple of years, they lost everything. They sold the building the Flower Pot was housed in and just left. It almost broke Alberta's heart."

Jake mulled the information in his mind.

"You worked for her," he said and Helen nodded.

"Yes, I did. Kept house for her, but only for a short time."

"Where does Steffi come in?" Jake asked. He felt he should be taking notes but figured he would end up answering more questions than getting answers, and he needed answers before speaking with Mrs. Peterson.

"Somehow, she managed to get control of Alberta's finances and, finally, of Alberta herself."

Jake chewed on that for awhile.

Sighing heavily, he got to his feet and walked over to the corral, reached in and petted Chief's velvety nose.

Turning to his mother who waited patiently, he walked back over and sat down again.

"She's living at Graceful Pines, isn't she?"

Helen frowned at her son. "Yes! And if anyone does not belong in a nursing home, it's Alberta Peterson!"

"One last question. Who pays her bills? Even with Medicare, Graceful Pines is pretty pricey."

Helen nodded. "Steffi is paying, but rumor has it she's almost out of money. I don't know what will happen to poor Alberta if that's true."

Jake picked up the tray and gestured with his chin. "I've got this, you bring in the cookies. I've got a phone call to make."

"What's this all about, Jake?" Helen wanted to know. To her irritation, he just shook his head.

"Can't talk about that now." He moved off ahead of her and walked into their comfortable kitchen.

He didn't like where his thoughts were taking him, but if his suspicions turned out to be true, there would be hell to pay.

Jake flipped open his phone and punched in a number.

"Del, I know you're on second shift these next two weeks, but I need to see you first thing in the morning, in my office."

If anyone could investigate thoroughly and with a cool head, that person would be Del.

Jill helped the girls bathe. "You girls can have either an hour of television or a video game, then it's reading time and bed."

Megan wrapped her chubby arms around Jill's neck and snuggled in. "I'm kinda tired, mom." She looked over at their little dog, laying in the middle of the bathroom floor. "I think Charlie's tired, too. We were busy exploring."

"You don't want your hour?" Jill asked and Megan shook her head.

Bree joined her sister and laid her head on Jill's free shoulder. "Can we just have our story and have two hours of television tomorrow night?"

Jill breathed in their sweetness and cuddled them both close to her. "Sure you can."

She waited until the girls snuggled their heads onto their pillows before bringing out *Black Beauty*.

Both girls were sleeping before she finished the chapter. Moving quietly, she put the book back on the shelf and drew the blankets up around their little shoulders.

Her heart filled with so much love, she didn't know why it didn't burst. Sighing quietly, she stroked Charlie, now snoozing on Megan's bed before going to her own sitting room.

Too restless for television, but not wanting to go down to her study, she felt at loose ends.

She spent an hour arranging her room and then grabbed a nightshirt. Maybe, a shower would do it, she thought.

Jill decided to make her evening shower an event. She lit some scented candles and, as the lavender fragrance filled her bathroom, she searched until she found a body wash of the same scent.

Getting out of the shower, she lathered cream on her face, arms, legs, and body.

Feeling relaxed, she cleaned up her bathroom before returning to her bedroom. Her mind still churned, but not at the frantic pace of before.

Climbing into her comfy bed with the fluffy white duvet, she grabbed her notebook and made out her to-do list.

Unable to speak with Mary Lee, Jill made that the first thing on her list after working on her program.

She would send Ben on the hunt for hay and give him the authorization to arrange regular shipments. Then, there was the matter of feed. She decided to leave that in Ben's capable hands, as well.

Which brought her to another thought. Ben would have as much time and energy invested as she herself would. Why not make him a full partner? It made perfect sense.

She would have to call Uncle Marcus and ask him to draw up the necessary contracts. Thinking about her decision, she decided she felt good about it. She felt very good.

Jill slept for a few hours until the now-familiar odor of cigarette smoke woke her.

She opened her eyes and saw him standing at the foot of her bed, confusion and anger pouring out of his cold blue eyes.

Fear coiled in her belly like an icy snake as her eyes met his.

"I want my birdie!" he said in his weird, hollow voice.

"I don't know who that is for sure. Is 'Birdie' your wife?"

He stood looking at her with hate-filled eyes.

"I want Birdie! Find her!" he demanded again before melting away.

Jill swung her legs over the side of the bed and made a mad dash into her girls' room, terrified she would find the specter hovering around her daughters.

Relief turned her legs to jelly. The girls slept on peacefully and, with the exception of Charlie, they were alone.

She carefully pulled the blankets up around their shoulders and ran a loving hand over their heads. She would do anything to make sure they were safe.

Unsure what to do, Jill made her way back to her bedroom and flicked on the lamp next to her bed.

She supposed she should call Ben and Jake, but couldn't see the point. Her ghostly intruder was gone, end of story.

Restless again, she headed down to the kitchen. If nothing else, she could grab a bottle of water, slug it down with a couple of Advil and just maybe she could fall back asleep.

With a half-laugh, she ran her hands through her hair. Of all the houses she looked at, leave it to her to buy a haunted one.

Jill went back to sleep, prepared to toss and turn until the sun came up but, as soon as she nestled into her pillows, she was out for the night.

Waking at five, she felt refreshed. Her sleep had been deep and dreamless. Surprising, considering her late night visitor.

"Now that I'm thinking about it," she said to the empty room, "I'd appreciate it if you didn't just pop in and pop out! We're going to find out what happened to your Birdie but, for heaven's sake, I need to sleep." She felt ridiculous talking to an empty room but, then again, it was entirely possible the room wasn't empty, at all.

"If you would like to communicate with me, please do so at a decent hour."

She had no way of knowing if her unwanted houseguest heard her, but the little talk made her feel better.

She dressed for the workday, but added a touch of gloss before heading for the kitchen.

The smells of sausage and coffee drifted up to her room and her stomach growled.

Nice to know nothing puts off my appetite, she thought as she headed down to the kitchen, not even ghosts. And doesn't that just say it all.

"Sit down here and get some fuel." Ben pointed at a plate laden down with all of her favorites. He poured her a mug of coffee and a glass of juice.

"Eat and make sure you drink that orange juice down. I swear, little girl, you don't eat enough to keep a gnat alive."

"What's your plan for today?" Ben asked.

Jill shrugged a shoulder. "I plan on debugging my program for a couple of hours and then finish stringing that fence. The sooner we get that done, the sooner we can start taking in boarders."

Ben shook his head. "I'm beginning to think you've bitten off more than you can chew but ain't gonna harp on it. You'll just dig in and take on more projects."

Jill grinned at him, thinking as long as she had Ben, she'd be okay. She loved him with her whole heart. As long as she had Ben, she'd have family.

The girls and Charlie wandered down and sleepily took their seats while Charlie ran to the door, looking over his shoulder as if to say, "Well?"

Jill opened the door and watched the little dog bomb out the door while Ben heaped food on two plates and placed them in front of Bree and Megan.

He poured them each a glass of juice. "You girls drink that all down," he told them.

"You're awfully quiet," Jill mentioned as she ruffled Bree's hair. "Something bothering you?"

"That man was in our room again, mom. We don't care except he smells funny."

Ben shot Jill a questioning look. "Later," she mouthed and he nodded.

Jill gave her girls a hug before re-taking her seat. "I'll take care of that, sweetie. Don't you worry."

"Maybe, we should get a bird," Megan said. "Maybe, that will make him happy."

Jill sipped her coffee and remained silent. If she were correct, it would take more than buying a bird to make that particular specter happy.

After breakfast, the girls ran up to get dressed. They had the whole day to explore.

Jake sat in his office, going over reports. Del poked his head in. "Boss? Gotta minute?"

Jake leaned back in his chair and waved Del in. "What's on your mind?"

Del took a chair opposite Jake and kicked out his legs. "Jim Barnett is nearing retirement. I was wondering if you have someone to fill his place."

Jake shook his head. "Got some apps but none I'd be interested in. Why?"

"My brother just got out of the Army. Was deployed twice and came back relatively sane. He was an MP, so he's got skills."

Jake nodded. He thought back to the day Devin was killed and how Del's brother stepped up.

"Have him come in and talk to me and we'll see. I'll be looking for someone part-time once the snow flies and the snowmobilers head up this way. Then we'll see."

"Fair enough." Del got to his feet. "We had a busy weekend." He pointed to the pile of reports stacked on Jake's desk.

"Yeah, I see that. Ben Richards' barn burned down."

"What? Did he sneak out there to smoke again?"

Del shook his head. "He swore he gave them up for good this last time out. He didn't smell of cigarette smoke, either."

"Looks like there were several small fires," Jake pointed out and Del nodded.

"Weird. Waiting on the fire chief to make a determination, but I'm thinking they were set."

Jake looked thoughtful as he sorted through the reports. Most dealt with small fires. Not a lot of damage, but a nuisance just the same.

"Keep an eye out, Del, and pass that on to the other deputies. Have your brother come in and talk to me later today."

"Will do." Del walked out of the office, whistling a soft tune and almost bumped into Steffi Brandt as she surged into the office.

"Steffi. What can I do for you?" Jake moved the reports out of view and got to his feet. "I've only got a couple of minutes to give you."

"Why, Jake. What can you do for me? I thought that was obvious," she said with a sultry laugh. Jake sighed.

"I'm on my way out, so if there's something official, just tell me."

Jake couldn't explain it, but he felt embarrassed by her innuendo. It made him feel dirty. He didn't know how he could make it plainer to her. Now, in his books, she overstepped the friendship bounds after her behavior at Jill's home over the weekend.

"No. I just wondered if you had enough of playing family man and wanted a little adult company."

He chaffed at her cavalier reference to Jill and her kids. When he had time, he would have to think about the why of that.

"If you think that's what I'm doing, Steffi, I'm not going to try to change your mind. Let me just say this; she's my neighbor, we have similar interests, her kids fascinate me and she's been through hell and back. The fact that she pulled herself up by her bootstraps is a big plus. Can't be any plainer than that."

Steffi pushed that beautiful spill of auburn hair off her shoulders as a pout crossed her gorgeous face.

Jake sighed. Steffi absolutely did not take rejection well, and that is exactly what he had done. He wondered what her next move would be. He couldn't know she had already taken the first steps in the getting even game.

She left in a huff.

Jake worked most of the morning and then took off at noon.

"I'm on the radio, but I've got some things to take care of. Call me if you need me," he told one of his deputies. "I shouldn't be gone more than an hour or so.

"Okay. Should be a quiet day. We should enjoy them because once the snow flies, we'll be jumping around here like hot peppers."

Jake grinned and waved as he headed out the door. His first stop, he decided, is the nursing home and hopefully a chat with Alberta Peterson.

The home was small and, after stopping at reception, he found her in short order.

He rapped lightly on the door jam.

"Mrs. Peterson. May I come in?"

He took in the fine white hair and the impossibly young face. Her figure, still trim, bent gracefully as she tried to gain her feet.

"Please, stay seated," Jake advised.

Sharp black eyes took in his uniform and traveled up to his face.

"You're a big one," she commented.

"Yes, ma'am. Do you mind if I ask you a couple of questions?"

She gestured gracefully to a chair across from the one she occupied.

"You're the new sheriff, correct?" she asked. Jake nodded.

"I don't know how I can possibly help you, Sheriff, but ask away."

Jake took his time as he studied her. She didn't have the vacant look of one suffering from dementia. Actually, she looked pretty damn sharp. The one thing he *did* see was utter and complete boredom.

"Ms. Peterson, how did Steffi manage to gain control of your estate? Do you know?"

"I was honest."

"How so?"

The old woman's eyes sharpened as she honed in on his face.

"I confided something to her and she used it against me." Alberta Peterson sighed and looked out her window again.

"Would that something happen to be the fact that you've not only seen your late husband, but also talked with him?"

Alberta's head snapped around. She leaned back in her chair and now, it was time to study this young man.

She liked that his eyes, so calm and clear, met her own. His craggy face composed. There was no hint of derision as he looked into her eyes.

"Before I answer, tell me of the young woman who purchased my house."

"Okay, fair enough." Sometimes you have to give a little to get a lot, he thought.

"She's divorced with two appealing kids. Been through the wringer with an abusive ex-husband. She's in the middle of building stalls to utilize the outbuildings. Her plan is to raise, train and board horses. More, she's going to run a riding academy and use the horses as therapy."

Roberta hung on his every word. "She can afford to do all this?"

Jake nodded. "Yes, ma'am. She can."

Roberta said nothing, but Jake could see the war within her. Just look at the wheels turn, he thought.

He knew she was wondering how much she could trust.

"Ms. Peterson, I've seen and heard things in that house. You can trust me, and I'm going to see if I can't help you."

"How? How can you possibly help me?"

"All I can say is we're investigating, but I need to know what sort of lever Steffi used against you."

Alberta folded her hands in her lap and lowered her head. Once she trusted but did she dare trust again? This young man appeared to want to help, but to what end?

"You have the right of it," she began and then faltered.

Jake leaned forward and took of her small hands in his large one.

"I know this is difficult, but please trust me."

Alberta sighed. Having made up her mind, she let the words out in a rush. Better to get it over with, she decided. "Yes, I not only saw Gray, but I would talk with him."

Tears stood in her eyes and with sheer will, she pushed them back. She was not a weepy old woman. She would tell him what he wanted to know and see where the chips would fall. What else could happen, she thought.

She studied Jake's face. Odd, she thought, he doesn't seem surprised.

"Mrs. Peterson, I'm going to share something with you. I believe that not only has Jillian Toliver seen him, she talked to him as well. Her girls as well. I also believe I've interacted with him."

Alberta sat back in her chair, never taking her eyes from Jake's face.

If he's playing a game with me, she thought, she couldn't see the point of it. She had nothing more to lose.

"I'm not sure how I'm supposed to respond to that," she said.

"I'm not sure how I'm supposed to respond to it, either, but there it is."

"I'd very much like to meet this young woman." She would decide for herself just the sort of person Ms. Toliver is.

"I can arrange that." Jake blew out a deep breath. "I'll stop and have a chat with her on my way home from work." Jake was about to step over an abyss, but he could see no other way. He would simply have to trust his instincts. They never failed him before.

"Ms. Peterson, I'm going to ask you not to say anything to Steffi about this. Let's keep it between ourselves for the time being."

Alberta let loose with a very unladylike snort. "If you think you can keep a secret in a place like this, Sheriff, you are sadly mistaken. Steffi will know about this visit twenty minutes after you leave here."

"And if she questions you?" Jake wanted to know. Alberta shook her head. "I'll simply tell her I don't have any idea what she's talking about. She thinks I'm crazy, anyway, so let her sit and stew."

Jake took her hand and pressed it to his lips. "Ms. Roberta, I think you and I are going to get along just fine."

Jake got to his feet and headed for the door. Alberta stopped him.

"Sheriff, you be careful. My niece is insidious. She'll try to destroy you if she catches wind of what I believe you're about to do."

Jake smiled, but it was a cold smile. One that sent a shiver up her spine.

"She can try, Ms. Alberta."

Jake mulled over his visit. The old woman definitely had all her faculties. Which made him wonder what kind of help Steffi had. No way did she pull this off by herself.

He also wondered what Del found.

Walking into his office, he wasn't surprised to see Del sitting at his desk.

"You look like hell. Didn't get any sleep, did you," Jake said.

"No sir, I sure didn't. I wanted to get a jump on this. Found out quite a bit and I'm not through digging, yet." Del sipped from the mug sitting nearby.

"You're not going to like this," Del added.

"Let's see what you've got." Jake reached for the pile of papers Del held in his hand.

"Giving you a brief summary, Boss, Steffi Brandt came into a pile of money after her parents died. She blew through that like a force ten hurricane. About the time she was dead broke, she came into another heavy infusion of money. That coincides with the take-over of her aunt's assets. She blew through that money, as well. She was in dire straits when Ms. Tolivar bought that house. Now, she's almost broke again, so I figure she's going to either be looking for a wealthy husband, which is where you come in, or she's got something else simmering on the back burner."

"Interesting, Del, but she had to have had help. Got any leads on that?"

Del nodded. "Oh, yeah. She had help. She landed herself a shady lawyer from down in Milwaukee. Since it doesn't look like she paid any sort of fees, we can figure she found other ways to pay him off. Between the two of them, they wrapped the old lady good and tight."

"It's a dirty deal, Del. We're gonna have to see what we can do about all of this."

Jake mulled it over, looking at the problem from different directions. Jill bought the house on good faith, and Mary Lee had listed it on the same, but one fact remained. An old woman had been robbed of her rights.

Anger simmered just under his skin. Any respect he held for Steffi Brandt was gone. He could see her for what she was. A money grubbing gold-digger of the worse sort.

He rubbed the back of his neck and his thoughts bounced around in his head. He would let Marcus Brentwood know what they had found, and he still had friends on the job in Milwaukee. They would wrap up the crooked lawyer tighter than a Christmas goose.

He also needed to talk to Jill and Mary Lee. Let them know what was going on.

Reaching for his phone, he thought he could kill two birds with one damn rock.

He quickly punched in numbers and waited for Jill to answer her phone.

Seventeen

Jill and Ben worked side by side breaking only for lunch before hitting the work again. They were almost finished stringing fencing when Jill's phone went off.

"Jill?" Jill's heart skipped a beat.

"Hi, Aunt Vinia. How are you and Uncle Marc?"

"Holding our own. We thought we'd take a ride up over the weekend. We need an infusion of you and those girls."

"Of course. Come whenever you like." Jill's mind began to race. She would have to stop working and get their rooms ready, but that wouldn't be a problem. The problem would be Trudy. What if they decided to bring her with them? What would she do?

As if reading her mind, Lavinia continued talking.

"We know about the phone call from Trudy. She won't be coming with us. As the matter of fact, we haven't seen nor heard from her since the funeral."

"She's welcome to come, Aunt Vinia. I just don't know where she got the idea Devin and I were ever romantically involved. It was never like that."

"Oh, child, I know that. Noah had a great deal of influence over her, but we'll discuss that when we get there."

They quickly made plans. Lavinia and Marcus would arrive on Thursday evening and stay until Sunday evening.

Jill ended one call and another came through.

"Afternoon, Jill." Jake's voice boomed over the phone. "We need to talk. I'm going to stop over right after work if you don't mind."

"No, I don't mind." Jill didn't like the tone of the call. She noticed an underlying edge to the sheriff's voice. She guessed, correctly, that he was angry and wondered what she had done to make him so.

"Fine. I'll see you around five."

They ended their call and she spun around to see Ben watching her.

"First call was Lavinia. She and Marcus are coming up for the weekend. Second call was Jake Logan. He said we need to talk, but he sounded pissed."

Ben shrugged. "It'll be good to see the judge and his wife and if Logan is pissed off about something, speculation won't help. Let's finish this fence and then break for the day."

Jill nodded and bent her back into the work again. She supposed Jake will tell her what is on his mind soon enough, but she couldn't rid herself of the little nugget of fear.

They worked until the sound of a vehicle coming up the drive interrupted them. Glancing up, she was surprised to see the sheriff's cruiser pulling up to her back door.

She took a quick peek at her watch and saw it was after five. Time just flies by, she thought. She wished she had taken the time to clean up a little and that irritated her.

"Where are the girls?" Jake asked as he emerged from his vehicle.

"They went over to play with Mary Lee's boys. Why?"

"Why what?"

A frown line appeared between Jill's eyebrows. "Why did you want to know where my kids are? Should I consult with you every time they want to go play with their friends?"

Jake's lips twitched. He just loved that irritated look on her face. It wiped away the sadness that usually rested there.

"I need to talk to you," he glanced at Ben, "to both of you."

"Do I need to sit down?" Sarcasm dripped from her voice like honey.

She didn't know why she was so irritated. She just was and didn't care to think about the reasons for that irritation.

"No, I don't think it's necessary. It's also not necessary to worry your kids, is it?"

The little worm of fear Jill carried in her gut since his phone call grew a little bigger.

"Actually, I'd like to sit down. We have a lot to cover before the girls come home."

"I don't think I like the sound of that," Ben grumbled.

Jake shrugged. "Let's go in the house and do that sit down thing. Okay?"

Jill led the way into the kitchen and busied herself with making coffee. She didn't think she was going to like what the sheriff had to say.

They sat around Jill's kitchen table and listened as Jake laid out his cards.

"I'm pretty sure Steffi seized control through illegal means."

"You mean fraud." Jill's tone was flat. "Where does that leave the girls and me? Are we going to lose this house and all the work we put into this place?" Jill clenched her hands in her lap to stop them from trembling.

"We're going to wait until Mary Lee gets here. She's dropping off your girls, right? So we wait. Knowing Mary Lee, she has all her I's dotted and T's crossed, but we'll have to see." Jake reached over and gave her hands a reassuring squeeze. "Don't borrow trouble until you have to."

Ben shook his head. "It's what the little girl here does best. If she wasn't worried about something, she wouldn't be breathing."

Jill frowned at Ben before turning her attention to Jake. "I bought this house in good faith! Mary Lee is an honest person, so the problem would seem to be the seller." She glared at Jake. "I want to know what you think she's going to attempt. You know the woman, I don't."

Jake raised his hand. "Don't shoot me. It's not my fault I know her. I know a lot of people." Jill was not amused. "In my opinion, I believe Steffi will try to shake you down. She'll try to weasel more money out of you, and I believe she'll use your fondness for Mary Lee and Zach to do that. If she does, you call me."

Ben slid a glance at Jill's face and suppressed a grin. Time to get the conversation back to the so-called ghost.

"So, Sheriff, you telling us this place is haunted?" Ben asked.

Jake nodded. "Yes, I believe it is. We've all sensed, heard, or seen something with the possible exception of you," he told Ben. "I figure it won't be long before the resident spook makes himself known to you as well."

Ben grinned. "Bring it."

Jill sighed. Male bravado rears its head, she thought.

Jake spotted Mary Lee's car pull into the drive and park behind his cruiser. He jerked his head.

"Mary Lee's here. We need to talk to her. She needs to know what's going on."

Bree and Megan led the way. They were full of chatter, taking turns telling their mother about their day. Jill listened as calmly as she could. She didn't want to frighten the kids.

"How about a snack?" Jill asked after the girls chatter settled down.

"Can we have melons? I love melons!" Megan said. Jill got to her feet and grabbed the watermelon and cantaloupe from the fridge, placing slices on paper plates then helped the kids get it outside.

Mary Lee glanced from Jake to Ben to Jill. "What's up?"

Jake sighed. He knew he could trust Mary Lee. He also knew her reaction would be far from pleasant.

"I'm investigating Steffi Brandt." He sat back and waited for a reaction. Mary Lee merely nodded, which surprised Jake.

"I heard you went out to see Alberta Peterson," she said. "Small town. Word gets around."

Jake cursed softly under his breath. He should have remembered that.

"I suppose it won't be long before Steffi gets wind of it. I'll deal with that if and when," Jake said. "The main problem is it's our belief she's going to try to shake Jill down for more money using you and Zach as leverage."

"She came to me earlier," Mary Lee said. "Foolish me, I thought I was clear enough but, now, it seems she's blathering all over town. Wonderful! Just wonderful!"

Many Lee brooded for a short time, then shrugged. "People will believe whatever they want. I'm not going to worry about it. I'm just not!" Then, she got to her feet and headed out the door. "Zach needs to be in on this conversation," she said as she bounded out.

Jill rubbed a finger against her temple while Ben drummed his fingers on the table. Jake sat deep in thought.

They are more concerned with the problems Steffi will bring, he thought, than the fact they have a resident ghost. He thought that an interesting facet.

Mary Lee returned with Zach in tow. Both looked worried.

"Any point in going on with the work?" Zach asked. Jill nodded.

"Oh, yes. I bought this property; everything on my end is legal.

Everything on Mary Lee's end is legal. Judge Brentwood and Lavinia are coming up this weekend and I'll have him go over everything, but yes, we will continue on with the work."

"I'll get copies of everything to you for Judge Brentwood to peruse," Mary Lee said. "Jill, I'm so sorry to get you in the middle of this mess. It was never my intention."

Jill reached over and squeezed Mary Lee's hands. "Oh, Mary Lee. I know that! We'll get through this just fine. No one here did anything wrong. The problem is that gold-digging little bitch! She's the problem!" Jill stormed.

Jake didn't even try to hide his smile.

"Maybe, we should get the bitch out here and confront her," Zach tossed in.

Jake shook his head. "Not a good idea. I'm trying to keep a low profile on this but, Molton being what it is, that's going to be next to impossible, but we're going to try."

"I go along with Zach," Ben said. "Get her out here and let her know we all know what she did." He shook his head in disgust. "Robbing an old lady that way. It's wrong."

Upstairs a door slammed, causing them all to jump.

"Must be the wind," Jill murmured and Jake shook his head.

"We all know what it was. No point in pretending it's anything else."

Zach huffed out a half-laugh. "Seriously, Jake! You're gonna sit there and tell me you believe in ghosts?"

"Yes, I am and if you had talked to Alberta Peterson, you'd believe it, too," Jake said with some heat.

"Okay, let's just take ten and then get off the woo-woo trail and get back on track," Ben offered.

"What exactly is back on track?" Jill asked.

Ben looked over at her and his eyes crinkled into a smile.

"Let's figure out just how to nail the bitch and make sure she doesn't cause anymore problems." He looked around the table. "Suggestions anyone?"

Steffi Brandt breezed into the nursing home, looking cool and confident. She made one stop at her apartment to make sure her houseguest was still in place and to leave him an offering.

Noah's snores filled the room, telling her he was still in the process of sleeping it off.

Steffi left a bottle of Cutty on the table where he'd be sure to see it, changed her clothes, and headed out for her weekly visit to see her aunt. She was almost to her aunt's small room when a perky voice called her name.

The aide bounced up, irritating Steffi beyond belief. Everything about the girl irritated Steffi.

"Your aunt had a visitor yesterday. It was so nice to see her have visitors and now you're here, today. She's going to love that!"

Steffi frowned. "Who was the visitor?"

The girl shrugged. "I was off yesterday, but I heard the nurses talking about it and how the visit seemed to perk her up."

The last thing Steffi wanted was her aunt feeling perky.

Steffi studied the young woman standing in front of her. She hated the young face, just getting the first bloom of womanhood that she herself would soon see fade. The girl positively vibrated with energy and that irritated Steffi as well.

"Heather, isn't it?" Steffi asked and the girl practically preened.

Heather took in the cool pale green dress and the glinting gold in Steffi's ears, around her throat and at her wrists. She wanted to be just like Steffi when she matured a little more and figured out how to get those things for herself.

"Yep!" Heather grinned.

"Heather, I want you to find out who this visitor was and please inform the nurses I want to see them before I leave."

"You bet!" Heather rushed off, eager to please.

Steffi walked into her aunt's room. The old cow doesn't look perky, she thought. Better make sure, though.

Steffi took a chair next to Alberta and made light conversation. As usual, Alberta gazed out the window and said nothing.

Going in for the kill, Steffi took Alberta's hand. "I hear you had a guest," she said and waited for a reaction. There was none.

"Aunt Alberta! Who came to see you?" Steffi asked again with more force. Alberta remained silent, just gazing out the window.

The woman's silence grated on Steffi's nerves.

Steffi got to her feet. She would be damned if all her hard work went to hell because of some do-gooder. She would find out who this mystery guest was and put an end to future visits, as well.

"I have to leave, Aunt Alberta. I'll be back next week."

Alberta continued to stare out the window.

As Steffi walked out the door, Alberta turned her head and watched her with burning eyes. Alberta didn't know how she would make her niece pay for the wrongs done, but pay she would. Alberta took a vow on it as she whispered Gray's name.

Steffi paused at the nurse's desk on her way out the door.

"I understand my aunt had a visitor yesterday. Who was it?"

The nurse on duty merely shrugged. She didn't much like Steffi Brandt.

"I couldn't say. I wasn't here."

"In future my aunt will not receive visitors except family. I don't want her upset."

Sure, the nurse thought, can't have the poor old dear remember she's still alive. Wisely, she kept her thoughts to herself.

"I'll just make a note of it on her chart," the nurse said and Steffi nodded. "See to it that you do."

Steffi breezed out the door, confident she had successfully isolated her aunt once again. Sadly for Steffi, the nurse forgot to add that little tidbit to Alberta's chart.

Still, the thought that someone had visited nagged at Steffi all the way home. She would have to be careful now.

Money was getting tight, but she was prepared to move on plan B. All she needed was someone to do the deed and someone else to pin it on.

Alive, Alberta was worth next to nothing, but dead? The old lady was worth a cool quarter of a million. Maybe, it was time to collect. She would have to think about it and plan accordingly.

Arriving home, she discovered her houseguest was just beginning to stir. She took the time to study him.

Maybe, she thought, at one time he had been good looking, but hard drinking was taking a toll. Bags under those cold blue eyes gave testament to his love affair with the booze. Flab around his once trim waist also proved he was letting himself go.

In spite of the obvious evidence hard drinking was taking a toll, he still looked strong as an ox. Steffi decided she could use that.

There was also no doubt in her mind this man could be and probably was dangerous. So much the better.

"What the hell you lookin' at?" Noah slurred. Steffi could almost see the headache pounding behind those blurry blue eyes.

Without a word, she picked up the bottle of Cutty and poured him a hefty drink.

"Hair of the dog?" she purred. Noah snatched the drink out of her hand and allowed himself a large swallow.

In Noah's world, the scotch beat coffee, easily. "Thanks." He took another smaller sip and sat down.

"I'll get you some towels so you can shower. You don't have any luggage with you, so you'll have to make those clothes work." Steffi told him.

"You could wash 'em for me," Noah said.

Steffi laughed and shook her head. "I don't do my own laundry, I sure as hell am not going to do yours," she told him.

In the shower, Noah let the hot water flow over him. He felt like death warmed over, but the drink helped.

Now that he was thinking clearly, he wondered what the woman's agenda was. He vaguely remembered picking her up in that bar, but where the hell was his car? He didn't remember driving anywhere.

He let the water run cool, then reached for a towel she had provided. It didn't please him when the shakes set in. That made him vulnerable and Noah didn't like feeling vulnerable.

Emerging from the bathroom, he found her sitting in the same place he left her.

"Where the hell's my car?" he growled as he poured himself another stiff one.

"We left it at the bar. We can go get it anytime you're ready."

"Yeah? Let's do that now. I don't like not having my car handy."

Steffi smiled slyly. "If I were you, I'd use the extra toothbrush I have in the bathroom and leave the drink behind. The cops in this area are real pricks."

Noah stopped and looked at her. "Why are you being so helpful?" he wanted to know, and Steffi shrugged, pushing that spill of auburn hair off her shoulders.

"We can be of mutual assistance. I'm assuming you want to find your ex-wife. I want you to find her."

"Why?"

"Simple. She's in my way and she stole my aunt's house. Bought it for way less than its worth. She needs to pay me more. This could be a win-win for both of us."

Noah didn't buy it. One thing he knew was Jillian was honest. Too honest, but that would be her problem.

Probably has something to do with a man, he thought, taking a good hard look at his benefactress. The woman had looks, but she also looked hard and used up, while Jill, in spite of what he had done to her, still looked fresh.

Not his deal, though. He'd just hang out and see what develops. If he can shake a few thousand out of Jillian, so much the better.

"Yeah? She owes me, too," Noah mumbled and Steffi's ears pricked up.

Oh yes, he is going to be very useful, she thought. Noah decided the same thing about Steffi. She would be very useful.

"If you're ready, let's get your car and park it here. We'll take a little ride and I'll show you where she's living," Steffi told him. "After that, we can send out for food and discuss how we can be of mutual assistance.

"Works for me." Noah searched his pockets. "One little problem here. Can't seem to find my keys.

Steffi picked them up from the end table and dangled them in front of him.

"Okay, let's go." He gave a half-laugh. "We're on a mission."

She drove him to his car and entering it, he sensed something not quite right. Someone had been in his vehicle and he just knew who that someone would be.

He followed her back to her apartment and parked in the space she pointed out. Together, they walked back to her apartment and once inside, he grabbed her arm and spun her around.

"You were in my car." His cold blue eyes bored into Steffi's and she felt a small thrill of fear race up her spine.

She decided to play it straight for the time being.

"So what if I was? I didn't steal anything."

"I don't like anyone in my car," he gave her a little shake. "What were you doing in my car?"

"Looking around. I don't often bring strange men home with me. I wanted to know who I was dealing with."

Noah didn't believe her for a minute but he gave her the lie.

"You're my ticket to finding Jill and her brats, but don't push your luck, lady."

Steffi smiled.

"My name's Steffi Brandt and you would do well to remember that. We're partners, Noah. Like it or not, we are partners and if you play fair with me, you'll have all your heart desires."

She saw his clenched fist and angled her head, staring straight into his eyes.

"Hit me, Noah, and you will regret it."

Noah released her after giving her upper arm a hard pinch. She thought she was in charge. Steffi wasn't in charge and she was about to make a deal with a devil.

Eighteen

Noah made his way to his car until Steffi's voice stopped him. "We can't take your car, Noah."

Noah's head snapped around. He glared at the woman, his eyes glittering with anger. "Why the hell not?"

Steffi shook her head. Really, men can be so dense. "Oh, I don't know. Maybe because your ex-wife will recognize the car. Unless I miss my guess, you aren't supposed to be here. Add in the fact that you've been drinking and the cops here take a dim view of that sort of thing, it's wiser to take my car."

Steffi opened the passenger door and held it open. "We're going to have to be careful," she advised. "It's best if no one sees you." She waited until Noah caved and climbed into the passenger seat. "Slouch down so no one sees you," she told him and waited until Noah did as he was told.

She walked around to the driver's side and slipped in behind the wheel. "I've been thinking. We should drive down and pick up some clothes for you. You'll be staying with me until our mission is accomplished. No point in you going about looking like a bum."

She started to ease the car out of her parking spot, unprepared for the stinging blow across her face.

"Don't tell me what to do. Don't ever tell me what to do," Noah growled.

Steffi slammed the car into park and turned to face him. "If you ever hit me again, you'll find out just how many problems I can make for you. I'm not your wife nor am I your girlfriend. You'd be wise to remember that."

Noah sat and stared at her. Never before had a woman ever taken that tone with him. Unsure how to react, he said nothing, studying her through narrowed eyes.

He knew how to bide his time, and he wouldn't forget every little slight this bitch dished out. For now, he would let it ride. He needed her help to exact his revenge and he could be very, very patient.

Noah held his tongue while Steffi put her vehicle in reverse and eased it out of her parking space.

"Now, after we do a little sightseeing, we'll head down to the city and get your stuff." Steffi slid a glance at the glowering man next to her. "You'll be here for awhile, so it might be best if you tie up any loose ends."

"I don't have to stay here. I don't see a reason to stay here."

Steffi raised a polished shoulder as if to discount his words.

"Don't be stupid. Of course you have to stay here. We have to plan. You don't just go into something like a little pay-back without a plan. That's how you get caught."

Her words smacked him in the face. She was right. The one time he let his emotions run him, he paid a high price. He was still paying it.

"Okay, fine. I'll stay in the area. That's all you get." He looked at her and realized he didn't even know her name.

"Who the hell are you, again?"

Steffi gave a tinkling laugh. "Steffi Brandt, and I'm your new best friend."

Steffi pointed her car out of town, pointing out Mary Lee and Zach's home.

"That bitch helped your ex-wife cheat me and now they're all the very best of pals."

Noah filed the information away for future use. In his mind, Mary Lee helped Jillian escape him. She would pay for that.

Steffi made the turn off and Noah paid close attention, mentally marking off landmarks. He'd need the information when he paid a call on Jill. And he'd be alone.

As they came over the rise, Noah sat a little straighter in his seat.

"This is her place?" He was astounded and furious.

"Yep. This is her place," Steffi told him. "Nice hey?"

"Are you freakin' kidding me? It looks like something out of *Gone with the Wind* for God's sake. What the hell's she gonna do with a place this big?"

Steffi shrugged. "I don't know. I heard something about horses and a camp or something. I'm not that interested."

She glanced at her passenger and thought he was about to stroke out. His face was purple and a very interesting vein throbbed in his forehead.

"Calm down, Tonto. You're gonna give yourself a heart attack or bust a brain vessel," she told him. "Relax. Think about how sweet it's going to be when we take all of this away from her."

Oh yeah, Noah thought. I'm gonna take all this away from her. All of this and so much more.

"All I wanted was a house on a beach in sunny old Mexico and she told me no. Said we couldn't afford it and then she gets Shanghai La! That bitch!" he stormed.

"I said calm down. We'll take it back and she'll pay us a lot of money to boot. You can still get your beach house."

"Any chance of getting closer to the house?" he asked. Steffi nodded. "Yeah, but we'll wait until evening. We can go in through the gardens."

It could be a way in, he thought. He'd get his hands on Jillian and that would be to his benefit. He could then shake himself loose of his unwanted partner.

He clenched his fist on his knee and rode the anger. Maybe, he couldn't smack this one around, either. Not now anyway, but times change. He'd get a shot at this one, too. He'd make them pay. He'd make them all pay.

Steffi spied Jake's cruiser in Jillian's drive and seethed. That trouble maker and her girls stood between Steffi and everything she wanted.

"How much you want to bet that isn't an official call," she gestured toward the cruiser.

Noah's reaction interested her. He was practically smoking in his seat. She wondered if she hadn't pushed him too far.

"Let's head down to the city, get your stuff and get back here before anyone has wind you're in the vicinity," she told him. "This is a small town. Word spreads fast."

"Yeah, okay. Whatever. I want to come out here tonight, though." No drinking for this afternoon, Noah thought. He'd need a clear head.

Steffi turned her car around. Neither of them were aware that unseen eyes watched them as they sped down Ransom Road.

"You know, Labor Day is coming up," Jake mentioned.

Jill nodded. "Yes, I know. Kids will start school that Tuesday after. I don't know where the time is going."

Ben grinned. "You're busy. When a body's busy, time flies. That's just how it is, little girl."

Jake cleared his throat. "Well, the reason I brought it up is, there's a big party in town. Rides, food, and a street dance. It's actually a pretty good time."

Jill cocked her head, wondering where he was going with this. She had so much to do around the property. She didn't have time for parties and carnivals and such.

As if reading her mind, Jake grinned. "I thought we could take the girls. It'll be fun for them and a nice break for you."

"Are you asking us to go out on a date?"

Jake didn't know if he should be amused or insulted at the look on her face.

"Not a date, exactly. Just something fun to do."

Ben turned a laugh into a cough and mumbled something about seeing a horse about a person. He left the kitchen quickly, leaving Jillian to flounder on her own.

Jake jerked his head toward the door. "Walk me out to my car. Couple of things I want to run by you." Jill got to her feet and followed him.

Jake waited until they were out of earshot of anyone in the house.

"I'd like you to meet Alberta Peterson. If you can get someone to watch the girls for an hour or so, we could do this tomorrow." He slid a glance in Jill's direction. "By now, Steffi knows Alberta had a visitor and will take steps to make sure she doesn't have more. They can't stop me and they can't stop my secretary."

Realization dawned on Jill and she gave him a cool smile. "No, they can't. I'm sure Ben will watch the girls while we're gone. I'll dress accordingly."

Jake barked out a laugh. "Don't forget a notebook."

He started to climb into his cruiser and Jill walked toward the house. His voice stopped her. "What about Labor Day?"

She turned slowly, that cool smile still in place. "Sure. We'd love to go. You're right. It should be fun." She turned and walked into the house.

Noah and Steffi made the trip to the city in record time. "Get in and get out," she told him. "We can't afford to be seen together."

"Shut up!" Noah growled. "Just shut up! I'll get my shit and be back, but don't nag at me." Looking at Steffi, he thought what a pleasure it would be to just punch her face in. He didn't like pushy women.

He'd be teaching her a lesson soon.

In his condo, he grabbed some clothes, shaving gear, and other personal care items and tossed them into a duffel bag. Looking around, his lips tightened.

Jillian had left almost everything they had behind. Not good enough for her, he thought. Nothing was ever good enough for the little bitch. That was fine. It would just add to the payback.

He yanked open Steffi's car door and tossed his stuff in the back seat. He climbed in next to her and glared into her eyes.

"That fast enough for you?"

Steffi thought fast. This animosity between them could be their undoing. They had to put up with each other until they came up with a plan and then implemented it.

"Look," she began in a gentle voice. "We've started off on the wrong foot. I can be bossy. I know that. I'm not your enemy, Noah. I am your friend. Let's call a truce until this is over. After that, we each can go back to our own lives."

He didn't trust her. Not for one damned minute. She was up to something, but he'd go along. For now. If she crossed him, she would pay. They'd all pay.

"Okay. I can go along with that. Just don't cross me, Steffi. You'd be very sorry."

She realized that was as close as he would get to accepting her half-assed apology.

"We need a plan. One that will deflect from both of us."

Noah nodded. "Yes we do and I have an idea on that. Be quiet. I'm going to lay a little ground work."

"Such as?" Steffi asked. Noah grinned.

He dragged out his cell phone and punched in a number.

"Hey, Trudy. How are you doing? Huh. Really? Sorry about that, I was sort of out of touch," he said in a silky voice. He paused while he listened to the woman on the other end. Steffi wished he would put it on speaker phone.

"Listen, Trudy, the reason I'm calling is because I wanted to make sure you're okay. I know it's rough. You know what we talked about? Yeah, well it seems you're right on target, hon. They look just like him. I don't know how I ever missed that before." He forced a break in his voice as if deeply hurt. "Trudy, I'm going to be sort of out of touch for awhile, but I thought you should know something. The day of Devin's funeral? Yeah, Jillian had a big party out at her place. How do I know? I have it on excellent authority. A woman who happened to be there told me. How about that? You're burying your husband and she's out partying."

Now, Steffi could hear the other woman's sobs. Trudy was screaming over the phone. Steffi couldn't make out what the woman was saying, but her anguish came through loud and clear. Steffi didn't even bother to hide a smile.

Noah ended the call, promising to keep in touch when he could. He glanced at Steffi and saw a huge smile on her face.

She looked at him and tipped her head a little.

"Oh, you're good. You're very good. I'm also guessing you have convinced her that Jillian's brats were fathered by the dearly departed. Nice job."

Noah grunted. "The seeds were always there. She always thought there was more between Jillian and Devin than either of them would admit. I just helped make those seeds grow."

"What's in it for you?" Steffi asked.

Noah shrugged. "Trudy's gonna come into a pile of money. I'll get her in line, marry her, and help her spend it. She's drunk all the time now, so this will be a piece of cake."

"And if she doesn't fall in line?" Steffi asked. Noah grinned. "She will. She's cut all ties to her own family. I'm all she has left."

Steffi shook her head. "Someday, you're going to have to tell me how you managed that."

Noah's grin bloomed into a smile. "Not on your life, lady. That's my secret."

As she drove, she noticed Noah was beginning to shake. It had been awhile since his last drink and looked like he needed one, badly.

"I thought once we get back to my place we could have a few cocktails and begin planning," she mentioned, casually.

Noah wiped his mouth with the back of his hand. He nodded once. "Yeah, that would be good."

He rested his head on the back of the car seat and let his mind drift. He liked to plan. It was good to look at all the angles, make sure nothing could go wrong. Once before he let his anger lead and it had been a disaster. That wouldn't happen again.

Trudy stood in the middle of what was once her home, feeling Devin's betrayal. Noah had been right all this time, she thought.

Fact is, her own jealousy allowed her to buy into Noah's lies. Now, she would act on that jealousy.

In Trudy's mind, her marriage had been a sham, and she was grieving for a husband who never truly loved her.

She let herself picture Jillian and Devin together, making love, laughing at her, and making those two little girls together.

There will be retribution, Trudy vowed. And then, she went mad.

Marcus and Lavinia pulled into Jillian's driveway just as she and her family were sitting down to dinner.

Everyone streamed out of the house to greet them. Jillian was wrapped in a long, hard hug from Lavinia.

"I couldn't wait to get here. I needed an infusion of you and the girls," Lavinia said. "I just needed to be here."

Jill hugged the woman back and then reached for Marcus, including him in the embrace.

He looks so old, Jill thought. They both do. Tears gathered in her eyes as she stared at the couple she loved so much.

"Let's not stand out here. We'll bring your stuff in. We were just sitting down to eat. There's plenty. After dinner, we'll take your stuff up to your room."

Lavinia nodded and Marcus looked around. "You've been busy," he commented. Pointing at the fenced-off areas, he shook his head. "Really busy."

Ben nodded. "We're ready to start taking in boarders. Zach gave us the name of a guy. His hay is aces, and it's getting delivered in the morning." Ben pointed at the stable. "Zach re-enforced the flooring up top, so we're ready to rock."

"It's all coming together," Lavinia said. She walked with Jillian toward the house, their arms around each other's waists.

Jill only nodded.

The little group feasted on stuffed pork tenderloin, scallop potatoes and lemon and herb green beans. For dessert, they enjoyed strawberry shortcake with real whip cream.

"That was an excellent meal, Jill." Marcus leaned back in his chair. "I feel like I need to open my belt." He gave Jill a wan smile.

"Come on. I'll show you the stable and you can walk off that meal," Ben said.

"I'll just help Jill with the dishes," Lavinia began but Jill cut her off.

"You go on with the men and keep them out of trouble. I've got this."

Jill would have chewed off her tongue before she admitted the truth. Seeing Marcus and Lavinia, usually so vibrant, wan and sad knocked her feet out from under her. She wished to God she knew how to comfort them. Little did she know, they were comforted by her presence along with the gay chatter of her girls. Jillian and her daughters gave them that just by being themselves.

A shout from the backyard had Jill running to the kitchen window. Ben, grinning widely, pointed up the road and Jill raced out of the house.

Jake rode up the road on Chief with Gypsy and her filly following behind on lead ropes.

The magnificent stallion caught her scent on the breeze and tossed his head and gave out an ear-splitting whinny. He fought for his head, trying to get the upper hand on his rider.

Jill watched with pride as the big beautiful bastard side-stepped up the road, hooves flashing in the late afternoon sunlight. Chief's proud head tossed as he pranced toward her.

Jake kept control of his horse using knees and gentle hand, all the while keeping a close watch on Gypsy and her baby.

Marcus and Lavinia came to stand next to Jill, their faces split in wide smiles.

"Jillian, that's the stallion you trained, isn't it?" Lavinia asked.

Jill nodded. "He's gorgeous, isn't he?" she said to Vinia.

Horses and rider came up the drive and came to a stop in front of the small group.

"I heard you were ready for boarders, so I thought we'd come up and get our pick of the finished stalls," Jake told her.

"Let's get them settled for the night," Ben suggested. "I'll come down and get a couple of bales from you. Ours won't be delivered until tomorrow morning."

Jake swung down from the saddle and handed the reins to Jill. He watched, a foolish smile on his face as horse and woman nuzzled each other.

"Careful," Marcus said, "You may lose him."

Jake nodded. "I wonder if he was ever mine," Jake said.

Jill led the stallion toward the stable while Jake, leading Gypsy and her baby, brought up the rear.

"Gypsy's Rose has been weaned, but maybe she'd like to be close to Gypsy until she is accustomed to being here," Jake suggested.

Jill agreed. "We'll put them in the birthing stall for now. Just until Rose gets her hooves back under her." Jill sighed as Chief nickered and pushed his great head onto Jill's shoulder.

Megan and Bree dashed into the house, Charlie hot on their heels and emerged quickly, holding a couple of apples.

"Can we give these to the horses, mom?" Bree asked. "You said they like apples and grampa use to let us give them some."

Ben took out his pocket knife and cut the fruit into pieces. "Mind you only give the baby one piece. She isn't use to that and it could make her sick if you give her too many."

Bree and Megan nodded. "We'll be careful, Ben. We promise," Megan said and headed toward the horses now situated in their new stalls.

"I appreciate this, Jake. I know they're not mine anymore and that's fine. They went to a good home, but having them here helps me more than you know," Jill said.

Jake ran a gentle hand over her hair and down to her shoulder. "I do know, Jill." He pulled one of her curls and gestured with his head. "C'mon, let's get them settled for the night."

The sound of a diesel coming up the drive had them all stopping to check who it was. Helen was driving Jake's big Dodge, and piled in the back were several huge bales of hay.

"Jake and I figured this would keep you until you get your own delivered," she sang out, a wide smile on her face.

"I'll deduct the cost of these bales from the boarding fee," Jill told him.

Jake shook his head. "Consider them a stable warming gift," he said. Jill's face took on the countenance of a thunderstorm. He held up a hand. "Okay, fine. Deduct away. Damn, woman, you can get mad faster than any five people I know."

Jill's face flushed. "This part has to be separate," she told him. "Business is business and that's how it has to be."

"Okay. Fair enough," he said. She peered up into his face. "I know why you're doing this, Jake. I'm not stupid. I've seen your stable. There's nothing wrong with it, but just starting out, I'll board your horse. I can use the revenue. The stable has to make its own money or this will fail, so I appreciate you boarding these three here."

He grinned. "I hear a But in there somewhere."

Jill nodded. "But, I'm not going to take charity, either. This can all work, but we're building something from the ground up."

"I can buy that. So, like I said, deduct away... and I expect a receipt from you for each month's rent." He turned and walked away, smiling. He didn't know why her independence pleased him, but it did.

Something was building inside of him and he wasn't sure if he liked that either, but it was building and there wasn't much he could do about it. One thing he was sure of, though. He was crazy about those two girls, and he was pretty sure he was crazy about their mother. Or, maybe he was just plain crazy… no matter what, he'd need to think it all over.

And damn if he wasn't actually looking forward to the Labor Day festivities. He'd have to think about that, too.

Nineteen

*Tr*udy paced. Something had to be done. Something *would* be done. It would be done by her. No one would believe her if she told that Devin was unfaithful. Devin's family had such hate for poor Noah.

And, she wondered, where was Noah? Why wasn't he here with her?

After the accident, he never left her side. Oh, her brothers and parents objected. They detested Noah. No one understood him like she did. They were kindred spirits. Hadn't he told her that very thing time and again? Now, when she needed him again, here at her side, he was gone.

"That's okay," she whispered. "I know what has to be done. I'll take care of it. Noah will be proud."

She dressed in black. She left her television on. The neighbors would swear she had been home. They'd heard her, after all.

Trudy slipped out the door and made her way around her apartment and into the garage. She backed out of her space and drove quietly up the ramp. Squealing tires would be detrimental at this point.

Free of the garage, she pointed her car north. She wouldn't wait to make

Jillian pay. She wanted revenge now!

She arrived in Molton just before sundown and hid herself until the time was right. She'd make that bitch sorry she ever lived.

The Brentwoods, Jill, Ben and Jake sat in Jill's living room. Most of them sipped coffee, except Lavinia. She opted for tea.

"It's good to be back up here. Those girls are just what I needed right now," Lavinia said.

"How's Trudy doing?" Jill asked. "I wish I could talk to her, but I don't think she's going to accept my calls."

Marcus shook his head. "She's in bad shape, Jill. She's drinking quite a bit, and her family is at their wit's end." He sighed and leaned his head against the back of the chair he was sitting in.

"We've tried talking to her, but Noah's done quite a job on that girl's head. I think we've lost her."

Jill's eyes filled with tears. "Noah is very good at making bad situations worse. What could he possibly have told her to make her turn on me?"

Marcus and Lavinia exchanged glances. Jill caught it and leaned forward.

"What? What's going on?"

Lavinia took a long deep breath. "Jill, Noah has convinced her Devin was unfaithful." They exchanged looks again. "He convinced her he was unfaithful with you. From what I've gathered from her family, the girls are not Noah's but Devin's kids."

Jillian's face turned the color of bone. "You can't be serious. I thought we had put that behind us."

Ben make a pithy comment under his breath. "Little girl, some people just can't be made to see sense. She's going to think what she wants to think. You can't fix stupid! And, if she believes one word Noah has to say, then she's brick stupid." He got to his feet. "I need more coffee." He sauntered out of the room.

"He's right, you know," Lavinia said, taking Jill's hand and giving it a squeeze. "She's going to believe what she wants."

Marcus cleared his throat. "There's more, Jillian. It was Trudy who kept giving Noah your phone numbers. She was in constant contact with him. She even told him about this place."

Jill felt absolute betrayal. She had loved Trudy like a sister. Now, this. How much more was life going to toss in her lap for her to deal with, she wondered. When was it going to end?

"Has anyone seen or heard from him lately?" Jake asked. Marcus and

Vinia shook their heads. "No and that worries me," Marcus answered. "It worries me a great deal. Noah isn't the type to just give up."

Jake got to his feet without saying a word. He pulled his phone from his pocket and headed for the back porch. He intended to put extra patrols on Jill's house until they found that son-of-a-bitch. He wasn't going to get close to her or the girls.

Trudy parked her car on an old, little-used logging road and waited.

Timing would be everything. She couldn't make her move until everyone was asleep. Sound asleep.

She spent the evening torturing herself with images of Devin and Jillian, and those images drove her deeper into her madness.

"They must burn," she muttered to herself. "They all have to burn."

It became her refrain as she let herself out of her car and into the inky blackness. She moved around to the trunk and removed two cans of gasoline. She checked her pockets. Yes, the matches she had the forethought to grab were still in her pockets. She was ready.

"Burn, baby, burn," she said and then cackled.

It was late. She glanced at her watch and noted it was after midnight.

"Burn, baby, burn. They all have to burn." She chanted her refrain as she made her way into the heavily-wooded land.

Trudy was confident she would find her way to Jill's home.

The fire god will show me the way, she thought.

Briars caught at her clothing as she ventured deeper into the woods. One caught her ankle, sending her sprawling into a blackberry patch.

She lost her cans of gasoline and spent vital time searching until she had them both.

The vines caught at her hair, merrily digging into her scalp and face. Blood flowed from the wounds, giving her a macabre mask of blood and dirt.

Still, she moved on. Her eyes, hollow with grief and madness, searched the darkness, looking for shapes of buildings. She saw nothing as she stumbled along.

Finally, finally she saw the outline of a barn. She heard the sounds of horses moving about in their stalls and a soft wicker now and then.

Insane triumph gleamed in her dead eyes. Finally, finally this was *her* time. She would show everyone what happened if they tried to take what belonged to her.

Trudy hurried toward the house on silent feet. She splashed the gasoline around the doors and windows. "Let them try to get out now," she whispered.

A giggle escaped her lips and she put a finger to them. "Shh!" She must be careful now. If they tried to get out now, they would succeed. Quiet. Quiet.

She lit a match and tossed it into the pool of gasoline and watched as the fire slowly built.

Good enough, she decided, and turned her attention to the barn.

She poured the fuel around the stable and set that on fire as well.

She reveled in the terrified screams of the horses. Her revenge was almost complete.

As the flames grew higher, she danced in the firelight.

The overpowering smell of cigarettes yanked Jill out of a sound sleep. Looking over, she saw the form of a man standing on her balcony. He slowly beckoned her and then pointed.

Jill ran to the door and threw it open. The man still stood there, pointing, and she followed the direction his finger indicated and a terrified gasp leapt from her lips.

A red glow came from the direction of Jake's house. Fire! Oh my God! Jake's place is on fire!

The pounding began, rousing her household. It seemed to come from every wall and door. The house seemed to shake from the force of the blows.

Jill threw some clothes on and raced for the stairs. She met Marcus and Lavinia in the hall.

"Jake's place is on fire!" she gasped as she ran down the stairs. Marcus and Lavinia followed.

Ben was just emerging from his room. "What the hell is going on?" he bellowed over the insane booming going on all around them.

"Jake's place is on fire!" she called out and then skidded to a stop. "Oh my God, the girls!" She turned to run back up to get them. She couldn't possibly leave them alone.

"Go!" Lavinia ordered. "Just go! I'll stay with them."

"Call the fire department!" Marcus called out to his wife.

"I'm already on it. Just go! Get them out."

Marcus jumped into Ben's truck just before he gunned the engine and raced down the driveway. Jill dashed to the stables, grabbed Chief, and together they raced across the fields, jumping fences and arriving at Jake's just as Ben and Marcus pulled in.

Jill's heart was in her throat, terrified at what she might find.

Ben raced for the house and saw Jake trying to help his mother. The doorway was engulfed in flame and Helen appeared to be unconscious.

Ben plunged through the flames, scooped Helen up in his arms and dashed back out again.

Marcus stood with his arms around a struggling figure as Jake ran out the door.

Jillian leaped off Chief's back and, after telling him to stand and stay, dashed to the stables. She grabbed lead lines and hurried to the stalls, murmuring to them, gently.

The four horses inside were panicked. If she didn't get the upper hand quickly, they would hurt themselves.

She clipped lead lines to halters and began to lead the terrified animals out of their stalls. They balked, giving out high-pitched whinnies. In spite of the flames licking at the walls, Jill kept talking to them, trying to calm them.

Jake rushed in, grabbed a couple of the lines and pointed to the door where the flames hadn't yet taken a good hold.

"Let's get them out through there," he said. Jill nodded and together they managed to get the four remaining horses out of the stable before it caught in an inferno.

Fire trucks screamed up the road but, try as they might, the frame house and stables were lost to hungry, hungry flames.

Ben stayed with Helen, talking to her until she began to come around. She struggled to sit up, and he put a strong arm around her and supported her.

Her dry sobs tugged at everyone who heard them. Jake walked over and crouched down in front of her. "It's okay, mom. We'll rebuild. We're alive. The horses are a little smokey, but they're okay. We'll rebuild."

"How? How did this happen?" Helen clutched Jake's hand and looked up into his eyes.

Jake pointed to where Trudy now sat quietly on the ground. As reality set in, she was defeated. She had set fire to the wrong place.

Jill took the lead lines from Jake and knelt down in front of Helen.

"You'll rebuild, Helen. The important thing is you and Jake are safe. You're both alive! Everything else is just… well… it's just details."

Helen clasped Jill's hand and brushed tears from her cheeks with the other. She nodded. "You're right, Jill. I know you're right. It's just that we've lost everything. All those memories."

"Mom. We haven't lost our memories. We've lost things. Things can be replaced." He glanced over to where Trudy sat in total defeat. Marcus stood over her, keeping guard. Helen looked at her, as well.

"Why?" she asked, and Jake shrugged.

"Who knows." Something in his tone made Helen's eyes snap to his face and then to Jill's.

"Yes you do, Jake. So do you. She got the wrong place, didn't she?" Seeing her answer in Jake's eyes, she clasped Jill's hand and squeezed it. Jill thought the older woman was about to snap her fingers in two.

"You and those girls could have been caught in the fire. You wouldn't have been able to get out in time. You all…" She left the rest unsaid.

"Well, it wasn't us and we're all safe. You and Jake will be staying with me. God knows I have plenty of room. Tomorrow, we'll get you and Jake some clothes." She glanced up at Jake. "And I'm not taking no for an answer."

Jill stood and then leaned down to help Helen stand. "Do you need a doctor?" Jill asked and Helen shook her head.

"I fainted out of fear, I think. I'm fine. Really, I'm fine."

"Okay, then. I'm going to take these horses home and get them settled and fed. We have just enough room for all of them." Jill's mind raced. "You'll ride back with Ben. You take a nice hot shower, or soak in the tub, whichever appeals to you."

She turned to Jake. "I imagine you're going to be awhile, untangling this mess." She looked over at Trudy and stared into the wide, vacant eyes. "Trudy may have done this, but it's not her fault, and I know exactly who is. Be gentle with her, Jake. She's wounded."

Jake nodded but his reply died on his lips as Del came roaring up. His deputy surged from his car and ran over to the little group.

"I'm sorry, Boss. I was clear on the other side of the county when I heard. I got here as fast as I could."

Jake patted Del's shoulder. "Nothing to apologize for." He pointed to Trudy and lowered his voice. "Cuff and stuff her, Del. Be gentle with her, but get her out of here. I'll be in when I can and fill you in." He looked at the smoldering ruins of what had been his home and felt anger and grief fighting to take hold. Ruthlessly, he crushed both.

"She set the fire, but she's sick, Del. She's real sick. We're gonna have to get a judge out of bed and get the paperwork going on this but, in the meantime, take gentle care of her. She's not responsible for her actions."

Del walked over and gently helped Trudy to her feet. She didn't fight him while he put the cuffs on her, nor did she fight him as he led her to his cruiser.

The fight began when she spied Jill. If Trudy could have killed Jillian right where she stood, it would have made her night, but Del gently restrained her and got her into the backseat of his car.

Jill watched, grief shining in her eyes. She would mourn the loss of the woman she once considered a sister for the rest of her life but, for now, she had work to do.

"Little girl? You ready to head out of here? Those horses need tending and so does Helen," Ben said.

Jill nodded. "Yeah, let's get everyone home and get them settled. I'll deal with anything else that might come along when it becomes necessary."

She swung up on Chief's back and reached for the lead lines she had tossed to Ben. Jake noticed the stallion stood calmly and wondered again if that horse had ever been his.

"I'm going to put them in their own stalls," she told Ben. "They're still skittish. If we try to put them together, it could be a disaster."

"You do that. As soon as Helen's ready, I'll be along and give you a hand with feeding and water. Some nice fresh hay might help them settle a little. I'll want to look them over and make sure none were injured. Might be smart to have the vet come out in the morning and look them over. Make sure they didn't breathe in too much smoke and such."

Ben stalked back over to Helen and gently nudged her toward his truck as Jake made his way to Jill.

"I'll get them settled, Jake. Don't worry about them or your mom. We'll take care of her, too. Lavinia is there. Taking care of people is what she does best. Your horses and mother are in good hands."

He patted her leg. "I know that. I just wanted to say thank you."

Jill grinned down at him. Looking at his dirty face and rumpled hair, she felt something stir inside her. He looked a little like a little boy who was lost. She found it endearing.

"No thanks are necessary, Jake. We're neighbors. More than neighbors, we're friends. This is what friends do. Remember?"

In spite of the harrowing events, he found it in him to grin up at her as she tossed his own words back at her.

"Jake? What's going to happen to Trudy?" she asked.

Jake shrugged. "It's going to depend on the judge. For now, Del's got her in a cell and will make sure she's as comfortable as we can make her. Other than that, I don't know."

"You know who's responsible for her breakdown, don't you?" Jill asked.

"Yeah, I do. But, Jill, you have to understand. The seeds were probably planted long ago. He just helped make them grow and, when Devin was killed, it all grew out of control like a weed."

Jill sighed as she met his eyes. She saw compassion there and knew he would see to it Trudy would be treated well while under his care.

"Well, I'm gonna take these babies and put them to bed." She tossed him a reckless smile. "No charge."

In spite of the horrors of the evening, Jake found it in himself to laugh. God, she was good for him. Then his thoughts turned to Trudy.

Jake scrubbed his hands over his face. Part of him knew this wasn't truly Trudy's fault. The woman was sick, but part of him wanted to beat the living hell out of her. He didn't like that part, but he was human and he was looking at the ruin of his home. More, his mother could have died. That didn't sit well with him.

His thoughts turned back to Jill. He needed to think of something calming before facing Trudy.

He didn't think he had ever seen anything more beautiful; more heroic than seeing her take that last fence separating her property with his, bareback.

She and Chief were perfection in motion. Then to see her dash into the burning stables to rescue those horses, talking to them, trying to calm them, and risking her own life. She just knocked him out.

She stirred something in him and he decided he just would be better off to roll with it. No point in fighting the inevitable.

Jill's thoughts traveled similar lines. She had to admit to herself as she rode home, the thought of Jake trapped in the burning house terrified her.

Maybe he got to her, she thought and grinned. Okay, he got to her. She liked his sense of authority and responsibility. She liked the way he was around her girls. She loved his humor. Yeah, he definitely got to her. Now, what in the hell was she going to do about him?

"I'll have to decide that later," she whispered to Chief. "For now, let's get these boys and girls settled for the night. You're going to have to help me with that, Chief. I'm depending on you to help calm them."

As if to agree, Chief's magnificent head bobbed up and down.

From the road, she could see Lavinia standing on the balcony. Worry emanated from her body and, even at a distance, Jill could tell the woman was on pins and needles.

The waiting was almost killing Lavinia, but she couldn't leave the girls alone, and she would only be in the way, anyway, so she stayed put. Waiting was not one of Lavinia's finer skills.

Jill road up the driveway and Lavinia dashed down the exterior stairs and raced over to Jill. She reached up and took the lead lines, holding the four horses in place until Jill dismounted.

"The girls never woke up. All that pounding and they never woke up." Lavinia looked toward the house. "What the hell was that?"

"Let's get these babies to bed. Ben, Helen and Uncle Marcus will be here shortly. We'll need to get her settled and then I'll explain what I can."

Lavinia touched Jill's arm. "Just tell me one thing. Is everyone okay?" She sighed with relief at Jill's nod.

"Everyone's fine and, look, here they come now. Jake will be a while. He's got a mess to untangle but Helen's here."

Lavinia watched Ben gently help Helen out of his truck. She rushed over and encompassed Helen in a monstrous hug.

"We're going to go in and you're going to have a nice soak in a hot tub. I have a nightshirt that will fit you and an extra robe. We'll take care of you, hon." Lavinia kept her voice soft and soothing. "Come with me, Helen. You're going to be fine."

She led the other woman into Jill's house, sending a sad look over her shoulder at Jill. Jill nodded. Lavinia would take care of Helen until the woman got her feet under her again.

Ben strode in and took two of the mares, leading one into a roomy stall and then doing the same with the other.

Jill did the same with the remaining two and began loading hay into a cart.

"Hold up, little girl. We should wait on the hay until the vet looks them over. I'm just going to check their outsides, make sure no one has any major burns," Ben said. "We'll give them water and give the vet a call in the morning."

Chief paced the stable, moving from stall to stall, nickering to each of his new stablemates.

"Looks like Chief is doing a better job of calming them down than we are." Jill pointed with her chin to where Chief was "talking" to one of the more skittish mares."

Ben grinned. "He always did have a way with the ladies," he said.

"Yes, he did." Jill walked over to Chief and leaned her head against his silky neck, stroking the other side. The great horse leaned his head toward her as if in a hug.

"Oh, Chief. You are such a good boy," she whispered. Turning to Ben, she grinned. "Did you see? Did you see him? He did everything I asked." Ben grinned at her and jerked one of her curls. "He always did, honey. He always did."

The sound of a big diesel engine roaring up the drive alerted them to a visitor.

"You stay here, little girl. I'll see who the hell this is." When Ben used a particular tone, Jillian listened.

When Ben returned, he was accompanied by the same large animal vet Jillian planned to use.

"Jake called me and told me what happened out at his place. I thought I better take a ride out here and check on them, make sure they didn't inhale anything nasty," Doctor Reagan said as she moved toward her patients. Ben followed behind her, ready to offer assistance.

Jill liked the way the vet took her time, examining each horse carefully, talking to them and reassuring them.

"They're in good shape." She patted one of the mares on the rump as she moved to exit the stall. "That in itself is a miracle."

Ben pointed at Jill. "If little girl there hadn't charged in, the outcome could have been tragic."

Doctor Reagan looked at Jill and grinned. "I knew I liked you, Jillian. It's going to be a pleasure working with you."

Jill's face flushed. Doctor Reagan didn't hand out compliments like cupcakes.

"Go ahead and give them a little feed. No more than a handful and a few flakes of hay. See how they are in the morning. If they seem okay, go ahead and give them a full feeding. If anything seems off, give me a call." She looked around the stable. "You have a great place here, Jillian. Well, I'm off. Gonna see about getting a few more hours of sleep. I'll swing by in the afternoon, just to make sure all is as it should be." She patted Jill's shoulder as she headed out of the stables.

"I think I like her," Ben said as he led Chief to his stall.

They stayed with the horses until Ben felt they had settled down enough to leave them.

"We'll keep a night light going and some soft music. That'll help 'em, too."

Together, they prepared the stable for nighttime and then headed toward the house.

"I'd sure like to know about that pounding," Ben said.

Jill nodded. "If you're not too tired, I'll make some coffee and tell you what happened."

"Too tired? Little girl, I'm all ears! Let's go!"

Twenty

*L*avinia ran hot water and tossed in lavender bath beads while Helen sat on a small stool and watched.

It was painful to see her pale face and tear-reddened eyes, but Lavinia knew just what to do.

"You're going to get into this tub and have a good soak. If you feel like bawling, this is the place to do it. I'm going to see which rooms Jill wants you and Jake in. Would you like me to bring your tea up here?"

Helen reached up and clasped Lavinia's hand. "Thank you so much. I know it's silly. It's just a house, after all, and Ben told me Jill was able to get the horses out in time."

Lavinia patted her hand. "Yes, it is just a house. It's *your* house and you have every right to grieve the loss of it. Now, here's the nightshirt and robe. Tomorrow, we'll see about finding you something you can wear and we'll go shopping." Lavinia ran her fingers through her short, straight hair. "I imagine Jake is going to need clothes as well." She shrugged. "I'm sure you have his sizes in your head, so we'll take care of him, too."

Helen just stared until Lavinia became aware of the other woman's steady gaze.

"What?" Lavinia asked, afraid she had overstepped some sort of boundaries.

Helen sighed and reached for Lavinia's hand. "You're good for me, Vinia. Your common sense is putting things in perspective. So, we'll go shopping and I'll call the insurance company if Jake hasn't done that already and I'll concentrate on rebuilding."

Helen wondered if Lavinia knew who had set the fire. Lavinia's next words answered that.

"Marcus told me it was Trudy. I'm so sorry, Helen. She's so sick, but that doesn't excuse what she's done."

"No, it doesn't, but you have nothing to apologize for. This isn't your fault. I'm not sure just who is at fault, but I know it isn't you and Marcus. Maybe, her family. I don't know. I can't seem to blame her, either. It just is what it is."

Lavinia let out a long deep breath. She turned to Helen, tears standing in her eyes. With almost savage willpower, Lavinia squelched them.

"You soak. I'm going to be just downstairs. Do you want your tea up here? I can bring it up for you."

Helen shook her head. "It may sound silly, but I think I need people around me. I'll come down, but thank you."

Leaving Helen to soak, Lavinia made her way to the staircase and headed down them, lost in thought.

Lavinia entered the kitchen and walked to the stove. She reached up into a cabinet and brought down the tea kettle, filled it and placed it on the burner to boil.

She measured out tea leaves and waited for the water to heat. She had decided to make Helen lemon balm. It was soothing and Helen badly needed soothing.

While she waited, she stared out the kitchen window towards Jake's house. The glow was gone. Only darkness remained.

How had she missed just how out of control Trudy was, she wondered. Granted, they hadn't seen her since Devin's funeral but, still, she should have known. Why hadn't *her* family alerted them to how bad Trudy was?

This sort of thinking could lead the way to madness. She didn't have any answers and Lavinia liked having answers.

Keeping busy, she moved to the coffee maker. No one would get much sleep tonight, and coffee could be just the thing.

She set out platters of cookies as well as makings for sandwiches. Food brings comfort, she decided. So, she would offer comfort.

Marcus walked up behind her and wrapped his arms around her, pulling her close. With a deep sigh, he rested his cheek on the top of her head. He wished they could stay just this way for the rest of their natural lives.

"I've talked with Trudy's parents. They're driving up here right away. According to her dad, there was no contact between them since Devin's funeral. Noah ran interference, keeping Trudy isolated."

"I rather thought that might be the case, Marcus. But, we both know there was something not quite right about Trudy right from the get-go."

Marcus sighed deeply before kissing the top of Lavinia's head and then moving to take a chair at the kitchen table. He took a cookie and broke it in half.

"I always thought, Vinia, that it was because we preferred Jillian and we hadn't given Trudy a fair shot. Maybe, we're partially to blame here."

Lavinia whirled and faced her husband. "Don't! Don't even go there, Marcus! I felt guilty, too. We have nothing to feel guilty over!" She put her hand on his shoulder. "It's no secret we always hoped he and Jill would get together. It wasn't meant to be. So, I refuse to feel guilt over something we had no part of. As Helen so succinctly put it, 'It just is what it is.' We're going to go with that!"

Jill and Ben made their way to the kitchen. Seeing Marcus and Lavinia together made them pause.

"Should we keep going?" Jill asked.

Lavinia shook her head. "You should sit down. I'm making tea for Helen. Do you want that or coffee? Both are close to being done."

"Coffee!" Ben and Jill said in unison as they sank into chairs. Ben reached for a cookie. Jill thought she'd be sick if she tried to eat anything.

"Any word from Jake?" Ben wanted to know.

Lavinia shook her head. "No, I imagine it will be some time before we hear from him." She ran her hands through her hair and sighed. "What a mess."

They sat silently until headlights slashed the darkness. Helen dashed to the window and peered out, hoping it was Jake.

"I'm not sure who this is. I can't make out the vehicle in the dark," she said. Ben got to his feet and headed outside. In a few minutes, he ushered in Mary Lee, Zach, and two very sleepy boys.

"We just heard," Mary Lee gushed. "It's all over town by now. My God! Is everyone all right?" She hurried over and put her arms around Helen.

"We're fine, Mary Lee. Jake is in his office trying to sort this all out.

The horses are safe, here, thanks to Jill and Ben." Helen rubbed Mary Lee's arm. "Could you loosen up a little? You're strangling me, hon," she added.

"Oh! Sorry!" Mary Lee released her.

At home in Jill's kitchen, she snagged two mugs and filled one and handed it to Zach before filling the second.

Sam and Cody sat in a quiet corner, drooping a little.

"Mary Lee. Let's take the boys upstairs and stick them in a bed. God knows there's enough of them," Jill suggested. "We can put them in the rooms next to the girls. Let them sleep and I'll bring them home after breakfast," Jill said.

"Great idea but I can come back in the morning and get them."

Mary Lee shepherded her boys up the stairs and saw them tucked securely into beds before coming back down and joining the group in the kitchen.

"How did you hear so soon?" Helen asked.

Mary Lee grinned at her. "Are you kidding me? This is Molton. Folks are burning up the airwaves! This is big news."

"How did it happen?" Zach asked. He looked pale and shaken. His eyes traveled from one to another until Helen finally answered him.

"It appears that a very sick young woman set fire to our place."

"That sick woman was our daughter-in-law." Lavinia's voice was flat. "I'm still trying to get my head around that." She gave a small smile as Helen reached over and patted her hand.

"Jake's in his office. God only knows when he'll be back." Helen sighed. "He's going to need his rest, but he'll do the job until it's done."

Ben finished his coffee and got to his feet. He rinsed out his cup before turning to the group. "I'm heading off to bed." He gave Helen a pointed look. "You should get some rest, too," he told her.

Helen seemed composed. Ben had been watching for cracks in her veneer, but she seemed to be dealing.

"I will, Ben. Thank you again."

Ben turned to Jill. "I'm going to turn those horses out in the morning. They need to get out of those stalls for the day." He slid a glance at Helen. "Any of those mares in season?" Helen shook her head.

"In that case, we'll put Chief in the front pasture and the rest in the back one. We'll leave the middle one empty in case we need to move Gypsy and her Rose out of general population," Ben said. "You okay with that?" he asked Jill. She agreed.

"Maybe, we should think about fencing off a few more acres," Jill suggested but Ben shook his head.

"For now, we have plenty of pasture. We'll see what we need come Spring."

"Ben? What woke you?" Jill asked.

He grinned. "Tell you in the morning although I'm pretty sure you know." He gave a small wave and headed into his room, closing the door behind him.

Helen got to her feet and rinsed out her cup. "I can't keep my eyes open another second. I'll say goodnight and thank you all again."

Jill watched her ascend the large, formal stairway before turning to Lavinia and Marcus. She could see the questions in their eyes.

"It appears we have a ghost in residence," she said.

"What? You can't be serious!" Lavinia refused to accept that. Marcus studied Jill's face. His mind was a little more open.

"Why don't you tell us what makes you think your house is haunted," he suggested.

Jill sighed and leaned back in her chair.

She told them about everything that had happened since the last time they had visited.

"Then, tonight, the smell of cigarettes was so powerful it woke me from a deep sleep. He was standing on my balcony, beckoning in that slow and creepy way you read about. He pointed toward Jake's house. I could see the glow from the fire and ran back into my room to grab some clothes. That's when the pounding started. It must have woke you," Jill said.

Lavinia's first instinct was to dismiss such an outrageous claim, but she could read the truth in Jill's eyes.

"Really? You're sure about this?"

"Quite sure, Aunt Vinia. I've seen him and so have the girls."

"I was here when he pitched a hissy fit," Zach chimed in. "Saw it but had a hard time believing it, but it's true."

"I thought it was your water pipes or something," Lavinia's said quietly. "A ghost! Aren't you terrified?"

"I was in the beginning. Jake had planned on taking me to meet Roberta Peterson today, but I doubt that will happen." She rubbed her face. "It appears her niece managed to get her hands on Mrs. Peterson's estate through fraudulent means. Jake's looking into that as well."

"Well, I just don't know what to think of all this," Lavinia said.

"Why think about it, Vinia? Just go with it for now," Marcus told her.

"If it makes it a little easier to swallow, Aunt Vinia, Jake believes it as well."

Lavinia sat back in her chair. She knew Jill. She knew the younger woman would saw off her tongue before telling a lie and if Jake and Jillian believed it, who was she to argue.

Vinia gave an elegant shrug. "I'm not going to dwell on it, but you have to admit this is something rather hard to digest."

Lights again cut through the darkness, bringing Jill to the kitchen window once again. "It's Jake!" she announced.

He's so tired, she thought as he came into the kitchen. He's so pale and just exhausted.

"Mom?" he asked as he sank into a chair. Jill poured him a mug of coffee and set it in front of him.

"She's upstairs. We're going to put you in the rooms next to her. We thought you would want to be close."

Jake nodded, too tired to answer.

He sipped and waited for the hit of caffeine. He was tired to the bone, but there were things that needed to be said. He just had to find the energy.

Jill's heart broke for him as she watched him fight fatigue. She placed her hands on his shoulders and he reached up, took one of her hands and placed it against his cheek. The coolness of it felt so good against his hot face.

"Thanks. God, thanks!" he murmured. "I don't know what we would have done without you and Ben."

"We were happy to help."

"Mom's sleeping?" He took another sip of coffee and let it and the gentle woman standing next to him warm him.

"Aunt Lavinia took care of her. She was in very good hands," Jill told him.

"Oh, all I did was draw her a hot bath and make her tea." Lavinia looked straight into Jake's eyes. "That's a strong woman, Jake. I wish I had half of her strength."

Jake met Lavinia's eyes. "I'd say you're no slouch in the strength department," he said. He thought she would need to be just a little stronger, yet.

Lavinia pinked a little and smiled. "Yes, well, I think I'm going to head off to bed. You coming?" she asked Marcus.

"I'll be up in a minute," Marcus said and she patted his cheek before turning to Jill.

"I sincerely hope this ghost of yours doesn't peek at me while I'm getting into bed." Jill snorted in response and Mary Lee looked from woman to woman, trying to decide if they were joking.

"I'll explain it all later, Mary Lee. For now, let's just say that Roberta

Peterson isn't crazy." Jill told her and left it at that, adding to Mary Lee's confusion.

"Just one thing, Jake," Lavinia said. "What's going to happen to Trudy? She's not well, you know."

Jake sighed. "That's going to be up to her family and the judge." He scrubbed his face with both hands. "I do have a little pull in the county and I'm going to suggest she be placed in a facility and get the help she needs."

Lavinia reached over and squeezed his hand.

Jake stretched out his long legs and sipped his coffee, watching Jill over the rim of his mug. "We all know she had help going over the edge and we all know just who helped her."

Everyone nodded. "Her family?" Marcus asked.

"On their way up. She's going to be a guest of our fine facilities until tomorrow, Friday. Monday is Labor Day and all, but the judge agreed the sooner we can get her help, the better."

Jill worried her thumbnail. "I wonder if I should offer to let them stay here," she said. Marcus shook his head.

"No, Jillian. Much as I like them and feel for them, she is their problem and mine and Lavinia's. Don't let your soft heart get in the way. Remember, it could have been this house burned to the ground with you and the girls trapped inside. I don't know if I can forgive her for that."

Jill let out a gusty sigh. "Nothing more to be done tonight, then. Let's all get some rest. Come on, Jake. I'll show you to your rooms. Take your coffee with you."

She started up the wide staircase. "Tomorrow, your mother and Lavinia are going shopping. You're all going to need clothes and stuff. I'm going to take care of the expenses for now, Jake, and you're not going to argue with me."

Jake kept quiet. He didn't think he had the energy to argue with her.

"I'll keep track and you can pay me back whenever."

"Fine. That's fine but I have my credit cards. God knows you've done plenty."

Jill looked at him and raised an elegant eyebrow. "Can your mother sign on your account?"

"Okay, point taken. Obviously, I can't work in these clothes and it's going to take a little time to get me a uniform, but we'll figure it out as we go."

Marcus came out into the hallway, holding a pale blue shirt and jeans.

"We're not exactly the same size, but these are long on me. Maybe they'll work on you and the shirt is way too large."

Jake took the garments and looked at them doubtfully.

"Just try them on in the morning," Marcus suggested.

Jake nodded.

Jill fussed at Jake until he entered his rooms. She kept at him until he stripped and tossed his smokey clothes into a pile.

She quickly scooped up the clothing, ran downstairs and tossed them into the washer. She decided to dry them in the morning. At least he'd have something clean to wear if Marcus's clothes didn't fit him.

As she entered his room, he emerged from the shower, a towel wrapped around his waist.

She kept her back to him until she heard his soft sigh as he drew the crisp, white sheets to his chest.

"I know you have things to do tomorrow," she told him, "But, I want you to sleep in a little. Coffee will be on when you want it."

"Jillian," he began and she shook her head.

"Just get some sleep. Don't worry about anything. Somehow, it'll all work out."

She left his coffee mug next to the bed and then gently brushed his damp hair off his forehead.

"Sleep now. We'll talk in the morning," she told him.

He was out before she closed his door.

Noah and Steffi had a busy night.

After feasting on take-out, they brain-stormed until the sirens interrupted them.

"Must be something big," Steffi said, walking to the window and peering out. "Fire engines from the neighboring town just rolled past."

Noah shrugged. "Who cares. Sit down. We need to figure out a way to get to Jillian and get our hands on some serious money."

"You can always use the kids for leverage," Steffi reminded him. "Threaten to take the kids unless she pays." Steffi stretched out her long legs and watched Noah take drink after drink.

"I can't do that. She's got Brentwood in her pocket. Seems like she's got the county cop in there as well."

Steffi stiffened at that. She didn't like the little jab. She was very much aware of the fact that Jillian became a successful rival for Jake's affection. A blind man would have seen it.

She forced herself to relax but before she could frame a retort, more fire trucks screamed past.

"Let's see what this is all about," she suggested.

Noah shrugged. If it would get him out of her apartment, he was game for anything.

"We'll take my car," she said as she snagged her keys. "Keep low. It wouldn't do for anyone to see you."

"Yeah, yeah, yeah. Quit nagging." Noah had about all he could stand of the bossy bitch. He glanced over at her as they climbed into her car. It would give him a great deal of pleasure to smack her around. Maybe teach her a lesson or two. Well, he thought, the day will come and very, very soon.

"It looks like they're all heading for Ransom Road!" Steffi pointed. "Wouldn't it be a hoot if they were heading for your ex-wife's house?"

"Not really. If she loses everything, so do we," Noah noted. He wasn't too drunk and his greedy mind was functioning just fine.

"Hmm… hadn't thought of that." Still, her pulse raced at the thought of her competition homeless. She could still get more money out of her, maybe enough so the little twit couldn't re-build. Talk about killing two birds with one stone.

They followed the emergency vehicles right up Ransom Road until they were abreast of Jillian's home. Steffi moved to get out of the car.

"Don't get out!" Noah ordered and pointed. "It's not her house. It appears to be a house up the road."

Steffi gasped. The only house up there was Jake's.

Steffi debated with herself. She was dying to see what was going on, but didn't want to compromise her plans, either. Someone, she was sure, would notice the man beside her and, eventually, Jake would hear about it. That would raise more questions.

Steffi pulled off the road into a small clearing. She couldn't see Jake's house, but she could see who was coming and going.

Before long, she made out a rider on horseback, leading several horses behind. She knew it was Jillian even before Noah spat out curses.

"Shh. Be quiet. We don't want anyone to know we're here. You start bellowing, you'll give us away," she told him.

Pushed to his limit, Noah reached over and pinched her upper arm hard enough to bruise.

"I told you! Never tell me what to do!"

Steffi rubbed her arm and gave him glare for glare. "And I told you not to raise a hand to me. Do it again, Noah! I can make trouble for you like you would never believe."

She was beginning to regret making a deal with the man. His drinking was bad enough, but he was unpredictable. She didn't like men she couldn't predict.

A truck coming slowly up the road caught their attention. They watched as it turned onto Jill's property. Wanting to see who was driving, Noah put his finger to his lips and then motioned for her to follow him.

"We'll stay low and in the shadows," he whispered. Steffi nodded. She wanted to see who was in the truck as well.

They moved carefully, staying in the shadows cast by the large pines until they had a clear shot.

Steffi sneered, watching Ben help Helen from the truck.

"Who is that?" Her whisper was so low, Noah had to strain to hear her.

"Ben Lightfoot. He worked for Jill's father."

As they watched, another couple emerged from the house.

"Who's that?" Steffi asked.

Noah strained to see where she was pointing and felt his rage build. "Fuck! That's the Brentwoods. What the hell are they doing here?"

Afraid Noah's anger would give them away, she jerked her head for him to follow.

Moving carefully, they walked back to her car and got in. Steffi moved to start her vehicle when Noah put a hand on hers and motioned with his head.

"Wait. Another vehicle coming."

They watched as Del drove past. Noah let out another pithy remark as he recognized the woman in the back seat of Del's cruiser.

"That's Trudy Brentwood. What the hell? What did the silly bitch do?"

Steffi smothered a snort. "It would appear, dear Noah, your friend Trudy burned down Jake's house."

Steffi started her car and carefully pulled out onto the road and headed back to town.

Tonight, she thought certainly has been eventful. She wondered how she could use it.

She drove slowly, keeping her distance behind Del's car. She couldn't chance Del seeing her.

Neither Steffi nor Noah were aware that a pair of eyes watched as they emerged from their hidden spot. He watched as she progressed up the road.

Twenty-One

Jake woke to sunlight streaming into his room. He slept well and that surprised him.

He made his way to the bathroom and found a toothbrush, toothpaste and floss laid out, along with a razor and comb.

Emerging from the bathroom, he saw his clothes freshly laundered and folded neatly on a chair.

Jake shook his head. He knew who was responsible for his clean clothes. He wondered if the woman ever slept.

Heading down toward the kitchen, he glanced at his watch and then looked again. He felt like he had slept for days. In reality, it was just a little past six.

Jake made his way to the kitchen where the scent of fresh coffee and frying sausage greeted him. Ben stood at the counter, scrambling eggs.

"Morning! Where's Jill?" he asked. Ben jerked his head toward the stables and Jake walked over to the window. Jill was working with Chief and it didn't surprise him in the least that Chief was cooperating.

"He never worked like that for me," Jake commented as he watched Jill put the big horse through his paces. Ben grinned.

"Girl always did have a way with the critters," he informed Jake. "Sides, she raised him up from a colt. They do have a connection."

"Yeah, I can see that." Jake poured a mug of coffee and took a seat. "Anything I can do to help?"

"Nah. I got this handled," Ben told him as he poured the eggs into another pan.

The sound of pounding feet and excited barks alerted the two men that Jill's girls and Charlie were awake and raring to go.

Bree and Megan skidded to a halt, jolted by the sight of Jake sitting at their breakfast table.

The girls had become accustomed to the big lawman hanging around, just not this early.

Charlie didn't give a snap. He needed to get outside and he stood at the back door, staring holes in it until Bree walked over and opened the door. He bombed outside, his happy barks alerting anyone who cared that he was out and about.

Ben made to move to the refrigerator, but Jake stopped him.

He looked at the girls with a twinkle in his eyes.

"Orange juice, grapefruit juice or coffee?" he asked. Bree giggled.

"We can't have coffee, Mr. Logan. We're too young."

Jake shook his head. "Never too young for coffee," he told her.

Bree giggled again and, this time, Megan joined in.

"You give those girls coffee and their mother's gonna skin ya," Ben said from his position at the stove.

"Yeah? She'd have to catch me first," Jake said.

"Mom could catch you," Megan told him. He grinned at her.

"Yeah? How? She couldn't catch a flea with those short little legs of hers."

"Easy!" Megan said with a grin, "She'd just ride Chief."

Bree became quiet and studied the big man pouring orange juice into her glass.

"How come you're here so early?" she asked.

Jake glanced at her, prepared to give her a smart ass answer until he saw the fear beginning to grow in her eyes.

"Why do you think I'm here, Bree?"

"Is my dad here? Is that why you're here? To protect us?"

Jake's heart broke. He knelt down on one knee next to her and took her small hand in his large one.

"No, Bree. That's not why I'm here. Our house burned down last night. Your mom and Ben were nice enough to come help. My mom's here, too."

Megan scooted off her chair and put her arms around his neck.

"Who's going to take care of your horses? Won't they be lonely?" Megan asked.

Jake gave her a gentle squeeze. She's such a little thing, he thought. They both are with hearts as large as their mother's.

"Our horses are here," he told them. "You should have seen your mom. She and Chief sailed over fences to get to my place. It was awesome."

Bree nodded. "Mom's a really good rider. I want to be just like her."

"You both are going to be good riders," Ben offered from his position at the stove. "Both of you have good seats and gentle hands. You get that from mom."

"Mom said she's going to get us ponies, but we don't want ponies. We want regular horses. Ponies are for babies," Megan said.

Jake grinned at her.

"Maybe, we can get her to change her mind," he whispered as Jill came in.

The first thing she saw was her girls with their arms around Jake's neck. The next thing was the gentle way he was holding them.

Something moved in her heart, but she didn't have the time think about it.

Marcus, Lavinia and Helen came into the kitchen together. Jill noted Helen's outfit. Obviously, Lavinia had found something that not only worked on Helen, but it worked quite well.

"You both look beautiful this morning," Jill told them.

Lavinia sported a pair of white capris, topped with a soft red blouse, and carried a blazer in a brighter shade over her arm. Gems twinkled at her ears, fingers and wrist.

Helen wore a khaki culotte topped with a draped black shell. Both women wore mules in a neutral shade and both carried small purses.

"My purse is gone, so are my credit cards are toast, as well," Helen said turning to her son. "Can you take a few hours off and go shopping with me?"

Jake shook his head.

"No, but I'll give you my cards. There shouldn't be a problem," he told her.

"What time is court?" Marcus asked Jake.

He looked very dapper in khaki pants topped with a light blue shirt.

"She's on the docket for nine this morning. The clerk did some juggling, but we were able to get her in first thing."

Marcus nodded. "Lavinia and I will be there. I'm assuming her family are here by now, although they haven't called us as yet."

"They're not thinking clearly, I'm sure," Lavinia said as she poured coffee for everyone.

Ben dished up sausage, eggs, and toast and took a seat himself.

Nothing like having family, he thought as Mary Lee's boys dashed into the room.

"We're starving!" Sam announced and Ben chuckled.

"Sit yourselves down! Breakfast is ready."

"Got a load of hay coming in today. What are your plans?" Ben asked Jill.

"I'll help with storing it. We're going to have to see what Zach has planned for today. Things are moving a little faster than we anticipated."

"Don't forget, we have a date to see Alberta Peterson," Jake reminded her.

"Oh! I thought, under the circumstances, you would want to forget about that."

"Why? I have to meet with the insurance guy in about an hour and be in court by nine, but after that, I'm a free bird." Jake glanced over at Ben. "After our visit with Alberta, I'll be on hand to help with storing that hay."

Ben nodded. Another pair of hands wouldn't hurt.

"What about tonight?" Jake asked.

Jill looked at him, puzzled. "What about it?" she asked.

"This is Friday. Remember?"

For a moment, she was at a loss, and then it hit her. The barbecue! "Oh my God! We'll have to cancel it!"

Now it was Jake's turn to be puzzled. "Why?" he asked.

"Well, with everything going on, we can't do a barbecue or any kind of party tonight. I'll call Mary Lee and have her pass the word that it's canceled."

"Don't! Don't cancel on our account," Helen chimed in. "Life doesn't stop because of a hiccup, and that's what this is. A damn hiccup. We don't know why she did what she did, but don't cancel because of it."

"Okay, then," Jake said. "We don't cancel. I'll tell Del to pick up beer, soda, and bottled water. We can handle the meat part of it on our way back from visiting Alberta."

He's such a take-charge kind of guy, Jill thought. It's kind of nice.

"After shopping, I'll whip up some desserts. I have some in mind that aren't difficult."

Lavinia, listening, caught the fever. "I'll whip up some potato and tuna salads," she offered and Jill grinned at her.

Jill whipped out her phone and punched in a number. "Mary Lee? Hi! Listen, we're going to need some extra grills. Tonight's on." She listened and grinned. "Yeah, as Helen put it, life doesn't stop because of a hiccup. Spread the word about the grills, okay? I'll be in and out most of the day, but I have my phone with me just in case."

"School starts on Tuesday," Helen reminded them. "Knowing you, the girls are outfitted very well, but what about supplies?"

Jill sat back. She had managed to get the girls' fall wardrobe taken care of but forgot about school supplies.

"Damn. I clean forgot!" she said.

"Not a problem. I'll take these two little beauties with me. Just give me a list of what they need and we'll take care of it today."

Jill bolted from the kitchen into her office and snatched up the sheet of paper she received from the school the day she registered her daughters.

She came back in and handed it to Helen while Ben chuckled.

"Now, we've established that Jill is becoming forgetful, can we continue to plan the day? Daylight's wasting," Ben said.

"Can we help with the hay, today?" Sam asked. "We hate shopping."

Ben ruffled his hair. "Sure thing! We can always use two strong guys."

A truck, rumbling up the drive, caught his attention. "Speaking of which, that's the feed guy. I'd better get to it," he said and surged to his feet. He looked at the mess in the kitchen and grinned. "I cooked," he said as he headed out the door.

Jake got to his feet, rinsed out his mug and made to follow Ben. "I've got the insurance guy and then have to get to court," he said as he strode out the door.

Lavinia, Jill, and Helen looked at each other and then at Marcus.

"I've got a thing," he said as he too bailed. The three women shook their heads.

"You girls go up and get dressed and brush your teeth. Helen's going to want to get on the road pretty quick," Jill said.

Bree and Megan picked up their plates to put in the sink and, seeing it was full, looked at their mom.

"Just leave those," Jill said and then sighed deeply.

Getting to her feet, she began to make some sort of sense to the mess.

"I'll give you a hand," Lavinia offered as Helen began to stack.

"You ladies don't have to help me. I've got the most time since I won't have to begin to get ready for a couple of hours. I should be able to wade through the mess in that time," she told them, but Lavinia shook her head.

"That would qualify as cruel and unusual punishment," she said.

It took the three of them practically no time to get the kitchen in order.

Jill dashed up the stairs, intending to get a shower in and figure out just what a "secretary" would wear on a hot summer day. She settled on a cool linen dress and decided to keep jewelry to a minimum.

She slipped on a pair of white sandals that were attractive, but practical. She added a large white bag and tossed in a small notebook, pen and bottle of water.

Checking herself in the mirror, she decided she was ready for her first meeting with Alberta Gray.

Entering her sitting room, movement near the wide French doors startled her. She gasped and Jake turned toward her, grinning.

"Sorry. I'm sorry. I didn't mean to startle you," he said with a laugh.

"God, Jake! Next time just shoot me." She held a hand to her chest, trying to calm her racing heart.

Taking her hand, he led her to a small settee.

"I wanted a minute alone with you, Jill." He cleared his throat.

He's nervous, Jill thought.

"I wanted to thank you for last night. If you hadn't acted so quickly, those horses would have panicked." He played with her fingers, unable to meet her eyes.

"You don't have to thank me," she began, but he put a finger to her lips.

"Let me finish," he said. "You saved those horses and came to our rescue as well." She shrugged, and he tugged gently on one of her curls. "Just be quiet for a minute, woman. This is hard enough for me." He frowned at her when she opened her mouth to make a retort. Obediently, she closed them again, tilting her head and wondering where he was going with all of this.

"I know it's what neighbors do." He seemed to be able to read her mind. "But not all neighbors. You took in my horses, my mother and me." He cleared his throat again and then took a deep breath.

"I'm going to owe you for the rest of my life, but there's more, Jill. There's so much more. Something's started between you and I. I don't know what it is, but I think I like it."

Jill grinned at him. "I know what you mean. I feel something more than sheer friendship for you, too. So, let's do this. Let's just enjoy the moment and see where it leads us. No pressure on either of us."

He gave her a lopsided grin, and she felt it go straight to her heart. Well damn, she thought. Not what I was looking for, but here it is.

"Good idea. You ready to meet Alberta?" He gently drew her to her feet and brushed her lips with his. She felt a tingle course through her, and she didn't mind that, either.

"Ready," she told him and together they headed out the door.

"I never asked you how things went this morning," she said.

Jake shrugged one massive shoulder. "Actually, pretty much as we expected. Trudy's family was there as well as the Brentwoods. All parties agreed she needed help more than incarceration. She's being remanded to a mental health hospital in Milwaukee for evaluation and treatment. After that, we'll see."

"How was Trudy, Jake?"

Again he shrugged. "Unaware of what was going on around her. Her family and the Brentwoods answered most of the questions. Ma and I had decided this morning that if asked, we would not press charges so long as she received help." He met her eyes. "The thing is, Jill… all she did was sit in her chair and rock. Her eyes were absolutely blank, and her face was slack. You can't fake that."

Jill studied him. "What aren't you telling me?" she asked.

He sighed heavily. "She had no reaction until your name was mentioned, then she went ballistic. It took two guards, Del and another, to get her back in her chair."

Tears burned behind her eyes, and she fought them back. "We know who's to blame for that. Noah did quite a number on her and when she was the most vulnerable. I'm not going to hold her hatred toward me against her, as long as she's going to get help. Maybe, someday, she'll see Noah's lies for what they are."

They entered the kitchen and found Marcus sitting at the table, sipping from bottle of water.

He looks so tired, Jill thought, so broken. Leading with her heart, she went to him and wrapped her arms around him, hugging him tight.

He rubbed her arms and sighed. "It was difficult, Jillian. Seeing Trudy in her state was difficult. I know how much Devin loved her, and I'm glad he's not here to see her like this."

"Jake told me a little. I'm so sorry, Uncle Marc. I have no words for just how sorry I am."

Marcus sighed. "Not your fault, child. Her brothers and father got me on the side. They sent you a message." Marcus sighed again.

"What's the message, Uncle Marc?" she prodded.

"They said to tell you they know you are in no way to blame for any of this, and they are thankful you and the girls weren't hurt, or worse." Marcus peered up at Jill and gave her a small smile. "They know who is to blame and, if they ever find him, there will be hell to pay."

Jill hugged Marcus and then released him.

"We're off to see Alberta Peterson. We'll be back as soon as we can. I don't know what this will accomplish, but Jake thinks it's important, so I'm going. Maybe, we can get a better handle on the situation here."

"Go on. I'm okay. I'm just tired. I will be interested in hearing what she has to say."

"Me, too," Jill said and followed Jake out the door.

The assisted living center didn't give off the depressing aura most nursing homes transmit. The grounds were well taken care of and the gardens, even this late in the season, were lovely. The building itself looked more like a villa with covered porticoes and deep patios off every unit.

Jake touched her arm and pointed with his chin to a stately woman sitting quietly, an unread book in her lap.

"Is that her?" Jill asked.

Jake nodded once as he took Jill's arm and led her over to Roberta.

"Ms. Gray. How's it goin'?" Jake asked.

Roberta seemed to come out of her reverie and looked up at the large law man.

"I'm just fine, Sheriff. How about you?"

"Just dandy, ma'am. This is Jillian Tolivar. She's the lady I told you about."

Roberta studied Jill and, with a gracious wave of her hand, motioned for the couple to take chairs across from her.

They made small talk, commenting on the weather and the oncoming Fall and Winter seasons.

The pert young aide who irritated Steffi bounced up.

"I'm sorry, but our orders are family visiting only. Ms. Brandt doesn't want her aunt to be over-taxed."

Jake snapped out his badge and flashed it as her. "That doesn't pertain to someone doing his job."

The aide turned red and hustled back to the interior of the building. Alberta watched her go with a snide smile on her face.

"She's no doubt going to phone my niece and inform her you're here. We better get down to it and quickly."

Jake and Jillian took turns asking questions, first dealing with Steffi's managing to take over Alberta's estate and then questions pertaining to the resident ghost.

"Gray did smoke, and he always wore the same cologne. He never varied in either. Tell me quickly what you saw."

Jill described her ghost right down to the insignia on his lapels. Roberta nodded, and her face became wistful.

"I'd so like to see him again," she said. "I know one day we'll be together, but I'd still like to see him."

Jill reached over and gently squeezed the delicate hand. "Maybe, we can arrange that," she suggested.

Roberta shook her head. "My niece will see to it that I never leave this place."

Jake spied the young aide hustling back over, accompanied by a rather large and all business-type nurse.

The nurse, in her starched white uniform reminded Jake of a ship in full sail and he grinned.

"I'm sorry. As per family orders, Mrs. Peterson is not allowed visitors," the nurse said and Jake got to his feet and flashed his badge.

"I'm conducting an investigation. We felt Mrs. Peterson would be more comfortable answering questions if she was in a familiar setting. Next time, we can always take her down to the station if you like."

The nurse, accustomed to having her orders obeyed, huffed and puffed but made no come-back. Turning on her heel, she sailed away.

"I think you've tried their patience long enough, Sheriff," Alberta said. "You know, by now, someone has called Steffi."

Jake shrugged, irritation riding his face. "Let them call. She can't stop me from doing my duty, Mrs. Peterson. If she tries, I'll have her arrested for interfering with an investigation. Let her get her big city lawyer up here. I'd like to have a chat with him, as well."

Alberta got to her feet and surprised Jill and Jake with tight hugs.

"Perhaps, next time, you could take me in for questioning," she said with a secret smile. "You could take me into my old house and question me there."

Jill gave her a wide grin. "That's a wonderful idea!"

Jake nodded. "It could work so long as they don't insist on one of these care-givers going along."

Roberta cocked her head to the side and looked Jake up and down. "Sheriff, if you can't put the fear of God into someone, you're in the wrong business." She patted his arm and walked inside.

"Well, Sheriff Logan. Gonna put your money where your mouth is?" Jill asked, and he grinned at her.

"You bet but, in the meantime, let's get back to your place. We've got that barbecue to get ready for, and I want to see if ma's back from her shopping expedition."

Her home was a hive of industry, inside and out, Jill noticed.

Zach and his crew were busy in the second stable while Ben carted hay into the first.

"Let me see what I can change into before I give you a hand," Jake called to Ben. Ben waved a hand before picking up another bale.

"We're going to have to get a belt going to move that hay, unless we move it by hand," Jill mentioned.

Jake agreed. "I'll toss that at Zach when I see him, if you like."

"Yes, please do. I'd better get inside and see about the girls."

Walking into the house, Jill was bombarded with more sounds of work in progress.

Bree and Megan charged up to her, brand-new backpacks in hand, both clamoring at her to look at everything.

"Okay. One at a time, please!" Jill said in a calm voice.

It took a little time to check out the packs and everything inside of them. Jake shook his head at her almost serene expression. He supposed someone who had been through all the things she survived would be able to handle most anything.

It touched him when the girls insisted he check out their purchases as well. Nothing would do but that he inspect every single item, just as their mother had.

"Okay, girls. Take those upstairs, put them next to your desks and change into play clothes," Jill ordered, and Jake watched them run off.

"I'm hooked on those two. Just so you know that," he told Jill before heading for the stairs. He suspected Helen would be up in her room, putting her purchases away. He wondered if his mother broke the bank.

In the kitchen, Lavinia and Marcus were busy mixing, boiling and washing up. Soon, Helen would need the kitchen for her desserts and Lavinia wanted her to have a clean kitchen to start with.

Jill was about to change clothes when she became aware of a change in the atmosphere around her. The room was insanely cold and the smell of cigarettes surrounded her.

"I know you're here. You may as well show yourself," she said. Her voice was amazingly calm.

Turning, she saw him standing in the doorway between her sitting room and her bedroom.

He's angry, she thought. He's terribly, terribly angry.

Looking into those blazing blue eyes sent fear racing up her spine on spiked hooves.

"I know you're angry, Gray. You need to know I had nothing to do with what happened to your wife. The sheriff and I are going to do what we can to fix things."

Disbelief blazed from his eyes. He raised a hand, but before he could pitch a tantrum, Jill spoke up again.

"Don't do that! My children are here, and I won't have you scaring them half to death!"

Perhaps it was her tone or perhaps it was the fact she had children, she could never know, but he lowered his hand and just glared at her.

"We talked with Alberta today. We're going to figure out a way to bring her here. I promise you. We'll fix it! We'll get your Birdie here!"

Jill's legs turned to jelly and she sank to the side of her bed before they gave out altogether. Jake found her just sitting, her entire body trembling. He rushed in and knelt in front of her.

"Jillian? Jill, honey! What's happened?" He took one of her cold, trembling hands and rubbed it, trying to bring some warmth into it.

"He was here, Jake. Gray Peterson was here. He's so angry. We have to do something."

"I know, honey. We will. We are. Did he hurt you?"

Jill shook her head. "No. Just scared the living hell out of me."

Little by little, Jill came back to herself and some of the fear left her. Looking at Jake, she grinned.

"I see your mom took care of getting you some clothes," she said, and he grinned.

"Are you kidding me? It's my mother we're talking about. She bought me enough clothes for every occasion. Even dress clothes and informed me she's ordered me a suit which I'll have to go in and get measured for." Jake shook his head. "I knew it was a mistake letting her go with my credit cards."

A small laugh escaped Jill's lips. "At least she thought to get you rough clothes as well." Jill pointed at the t-shirt and jeans he now wore.

"Yeah. I'm grateful for small miracles." He looked at her face and was pleased to see her color coming back. She had been bone white.

"I'm heading outside to give Ben a hand. I guess the feed guy was here as well. Came early but Ben handled it just fine. He's a good guy there, Jillian. It's easy to see why your dad depended on him."

"Ben? Ben's the best!"

"Well, we'd better get going. Company will be here before we know it," he advised, and Jill nodded.

"I'm just going to change into more comfy clothes and I'll be down to lend a hand."

"Take your time. More than enough hands around here as it is."

Jill shook her head. As fearful as she had been, it had been a comfort and relief when Jake walked through her door.

When she had time, she would have to think about that. For now, though, she had guests coming and work to do.

She made it as far as her doorway when a thought hit her.

"I would really appreciate it if you showed yourself in other parts of the house," she told her unseen guest. "It's rather unnerving to have you in my bedroom, especially when I'm changing clothes."

She may have imagined it, but she could have swore she heard faint laughter.

Bombing into the kitchen, she saw Helen hard at work, whipping up cupcakes and cheesecakes.

"These look yummy," she said, pointing at the cupcakes Helen and Lavinia were frosting.

Helen smiled. "Of course they are. Lavinia and I whipped them up."

"Salads are all done and cooling in the fridge," Lavinia informed her.

Jill nodded before opening the fridge for the things she needed.

She pulled out watermelon, cantaloupe, strawberries, blueberries, raspberries, lemon juice and sugar. She found a can of mandarin oranges and opened that, draining the juice before she began chopping, peeling and hulling.

She began to loading everything into a large bowl, drizzling the lemon juice over the fruit and adding a little sugar.

Jill smiled as Marcus worked making hamburger patties.

"Those look good, Uncle Marc," she said, and he grunted.

"These women said all I'm good for is making these damn patties." He washed his hands after patting the last of them into shape.

Getting out another platter, he mounded hot dogs and brauts, and then covered them before putting the meat back in the fridge.

"How did your meeting go with Alberta?" Helen asked, and Jill shook her head.

"There isn't a thing wrong with her thought process," Jill said. "She's sharp. She should have been left in her own home for as long as she wanted to be here." Jill sighed. "I feel so guilty. This is her home. She *should* be here, but then I wouldn't have this place."

"It's a puzzle, isn't it," Helen said and patted Jill's shoulder. "Things will work out as they're meant to be. Wait and see," she advised.

Jill looked at the older woman and sighed deeply.

"The truth is I can't give up this place now. I don't know what to do."

"Like I said, don't fret. Things do have a way of working out."

Lavinia glanced out the window at the sound of vehicles coming up the drive.

"In the meantime, why don't you relax and enjoy tonight. We heard the impromptu party last week was a complete success. This one will be as well and, frankly, I'm looking forward to it."

Jillian covered her fruit salad and stuck that into the fridge to cool down a little more.

"Okay. For now, we're not going to think about Steffi Brandt, ghosts, and illegal dealings. We're going to have a party and, dammit, we're all going to enjoy ourselves," Jill decreed.

Everyone agreed with her as they streamed out of the house to greet the newly arrived guests.

Twenty-Two

Steffi strolled into the living room and noted that Noah had finished off one bottle of booze, but he was working on a second. She wondered where he got that second bottle, then decided it really was none of her business.

"Guess who's a houseguest of your ex-wife," she said without preamble.

Noah looked up and tried to focus his bleary eyes on the woman standing in front of him.

"Who?" he managed to croak out.

"Our illustrious sheriff and his mother. Seems like dear little Jillian opened her home to them after their own place burned to the ground."

"Yeah? How did you find this out?" Noah was definitely slurring his words and Steffi doubted he'd remember this conversation come morning.

"People talk. Everyone in town thinks it's so wonderful that she opened her home to them. Made me vomit in my mouth a little."

"Why do you care?" Noah wanted to know, and Steffi thought maybe he wasn't as drunk as she thought.

Steffi shrugged. "I don't care who she sleeps with."

Except Steffi did care. She cared a great deal. Jillian was scoring all kinds of points with the people in town, especially now that word had spread about her wild ride and selflessness in getting Jake's horses out of the burning barn.

Why, Jill was practically Joan of Arc to the people in this town while they hardly spoke to her and it rankled. Jill's a newcomer, she thought. I've been here all my life and I'm ignored. Well, I'll show them. I'll show them all.

Steffi chose to set the burr a little farther under Noah's saddle. "I really don't care, but you should."

"Why is that?" Noah asked before taking another hefty sip.

"If she hooks up with Jake, it's going to be that much harder to get your hands on your daughters. After all, that is your plan, is it not?"

"My plan is none of your business," Noah told her. He shot a warning glance at her, but Steffi chose to ignore it. She had the upper hand, after all.

"Don't be stupid, Noah. You need those girls if you're going to get your hands on some real money."

Noah shrugged. "When I figure out just what to do, you'll be the second person to know my plans." He wheezed out a laugh. Sometimes, he just cracked himself up.

Steffi shook her head. If left up to him, they'd both end up in a great deal of trouble and nothing to show for it.

"Listen to me and try to comprehend what I'm saying, Noah. Tomorrow is a big town party. Everyone attends. People even come from neighboring towns. There'll be rides, food, a street dance. Everything you'd expect from a hick town like this. We'll go, but we'll keep our distance. We can make our move on Sunday. Grab your kids and take off. We'll keep them until Jill forks over a healthy amount from her bank account. It's fool-proof. While they're partying with the hicks, you and I can scope out her house, figure out which rooms she stashed the kids in, go in through the verandah doors and back out again without her knowing."

"Why can't we just take the brats tomorrow?" Noah asked.

Steffi shook her head and sighed. The moron just didn't get it. Maybe, it was a mistake to hook up with him, but it was too late to change that now.

"Because there'll be a big cop presence there. It's too risky."

Steffi thought her plan was fool-proof. Noah thought it was a waste of time.

He took a sip of Scotch and studied her over the rim of his glass. She was a looker, if one discounted her shrewd eyes and lips that seemed to be in a perpetual pout.

This is a woman accustomed to having her own way. Noah's female counterpart. Noah didn't like her and he didn't trust her. They would do things her way for the time being, but very soon, she'd learn he is not a man to be trifled with.

Saturday dawned warm, the sun shining in a perfect blue sky.

Jillian laid out the clothes she wanted to girls to wear before diving into her own closet to find something suitable.

What does one wear, she wondered, to a town party.

Jake sauntered into her room, since her door was open and, turning, she looked him up and down.

Dressed in jeans, a white t-shirt and sneakers, she didn't think he could dress more casually.

"I take it comfort clothes is the order for today," she said, and he grinned.

"It's going to be warm. All those people, the sun on the cement. Oh yeah, it's going to be warm. It's also going to be fun," he told her. "Dress in something cool and comfortable," he advised as he turned and headed toward the stairs.

"Cool and comfortable," she murmured. "That's not real helpful."

She settled on a pair of denim walking shorts and a floaty light blue top. Slipping her feet into blue deck shoes, she added a touch of lip gloss and a dab of mascara and quickly ran a comb through her short curls. Checking the overall finished product, she decided she looked pretty damn good.

She bounded down the stairs and, letting her good mood lead her, she bounced into the kitchen.

Ben sat at the table, sipping coffee and chatting with Helen and the Brentwoods.

He glanced around to Jill and grinned. "Lookin' pretty good, little girl," he said with a wink. Jill felt the heat rise in her face and walked over to ruffle Ben's hair.

The girls sat eating their breakfast and Jillian joined them, helping herself to pancakes, a fruit salad and orange juice. Jake poured her a mug of freshly-brewed coffee.

"How are the horses doing?" Jill asked and Ben leaned back in his chair, stretching his long legs out in front of him.

"They've settled in just fine," he told her. "Thought we might have some problems this morning with Chief when we turned 'em out. One of the mares is coming in season, but he settled down and decided to behave himself."

"If he catches her, it's not a problem. I'd rather he didn't mount her, but if it happens, it happens," Jake said.

"That can be dangerous," Ben reminded him and Jake nodded.

"I know that, but not as dangerous if we come between young love. Anyway, we'll see how it plays out."

Jill cleared her throat to catch the men's attention and then rolled her eyes toward the girls who were avidly listening. Ben and Jake both smiled and Helen changed the subject.

"Today will be fun. We've been going to this get-together for years, and it's never boring. The street dance is especially fun."

"Do you dance?" Ben asked her and she blushed just a little.

"As the matter of fact, yes I do."

"Good. We'll have to see what you've got," Ben said with a charming smile.

The women cleaned the kitchen in record time and Jill turned as Jake walked in with a large cooler. She watched as he tossed in a bag of ice and began to fill the container with bottled water.

"It's going to be hot, and I'm pretty sure you won't want the girls sucking soda all day," he said.

"Good thinking. I'm ashamed I didn't think of it."

"You can't help it if you're scatterbrained," he said as he hoisted the cooler to his shoulder.

Bree and Megan ran up, saving him from a scathing retort

"Mom! Are we ready to go?" Bree and Megan bounced on their toes. "We're all ready! Are we going?"

"Yes! We're going. Run out and get into our truck."

"Helen and Ben are going to ride with us," Lavinia announced as she bounced into the kitchen.

She looked stunning in white capris, a white linen top and strappy white sandals.

"I packed some sunscreen in my bag," she told Jill and grinned. "I know you rarely burn, but the girls might."

Jill turned to Bree. "Run and grab Charlie's leash. We can't let him run free or he might get lost." Bree nodded and ran off, coming back with the little dog in tow.

"I think we're ready," Helen announced. She looked stunning in a breezy, pale green summer dress and matching slides.

"You know something?" Jill looked around at the group in her kitchen. They were more than friends. They were family. She did have a family after all. "I think today is exactly what we all need. A nice break from worry and work." She gave then all a brilliant smile. "Let's go! Carny food awaits!"

It was a party. A wonderful neighborhood party. Jill loved it as people would stop to talk to her, welcome her to the town and ask about her plans.

Usually shy at large gatherings, Jill enjoyed meeting everyone and answering their questions. She belonged, she realized. Finally, she found her place.

She wanted to sit down and just giggle.

"I told you this was fun! Didn't I tell you that?" Mary Lee said as she plopped down next to Jill.

"Yes, yes you did. I'm glad we came." Jill chin-pointed toward her girls, who were currently watching Ben at the shooting gallery, urging him on. Each held a large stuffed animals under an arm.

The town park looked festive with flags waving and small white lights entwined in the trees. At dusk, those lights would be switched on, giving the park a romantic look and feel.

Food and game vendors lined the perimeter, leaving the center of the park clear for seating in the shade.

Barriers separated the dancing area from the rest of the fun. These were draped in bunting and fragrant blooms.

Jake stood off to the side and watched the crowd. He felt a little uneasy but nothing he could put his finger on.

Mary Lee signaled with her head toward him. "What's up with the cop?" she asked. Jill shrugged.

As if sensing they were talking about him, Jake grinned and made his way to where they were seated.

"Gonna sit here all day?" he asked Jill. He grinned when she shook her head.

"Nope. Just taking a break." She looked around and let out a happy sigh. "Oh, Jake! This is wonderful! I'm glad you talked me into coming!"

He took her hand and drew her to her feet. "Yeah? Let's see what else I can talk you into."

Mary Lee stood up, laughing. "On that note, I think I'll scare up my husband and sons. I'm absolutely dying for a Corn Dog!"

They danced to a slow, dreamy tune. For once, Jillian just enjoyed the feeling of being in a man's arms, swaying to a soft ballad. No fear, just plain enjoyment.

Watching from the crowd, Steffi sneered. Watching Jill and Jake dance together so effortlessly almost made her ill.

Jealousy raged through her bloodstream until she felt white hot anger surge through her body.

Glancing up at Noah, she saw his clamped lips were white. The sight of the rigid anger on his face gave her pause. She wondered if it was a mistake. Maybe, she shouldn't have hooked up with him, after all.

After the dance, Steffi and Noah kept a discreet distance as they followed Jill and Jake.

Watching Jake take the girls, *his* girls, on ride after ride increased Noah's anger tenfold.

"Let's get out of here," Steffi suggested.

Noah gave a tight shake of his head.

"No! I want to see!"

Steffi sighed. "See what? Obviously, you've been replaced. Now, let's *go*! This is the perfect time to scope out her house and figure out which rooms belong to your kids. We can move on them tonight."

They started to leave when Noah froze. Steffi turned in the direction he was looking and grasped his arm.

Megan was on her own.

Twenty-Three

Noah made his move. Striding quickly, his long legs ate up the distance between his daughter and himself. All he would have to do is reach out and nab the little brat.

He was congratulating himself when he came to a dead stop. The hair on the back of his neck bristled, and he felt a cold dread in the pit of his stomach.

Cautious now, he looked around and spied Ben Lightfoot watching him.

Noah stepped back, almost tripping over Steffi. She grabbed his arm and pulled him back into the crowd.

"Who is that man?" she gasped. Noah wiped the sweat beading on his forehead. He could feel it trickle down his spine while fear rode on spiked talons up his back.

"Ben Lightfoot. He worked for the bitch's old man."

"We better go. He'll tell Jake we're here and then all of our planning will go up in smoke."

They began to make their way to the parking area when Steffi's cell hummed. She listened to the caller, her lips pinched tight.

"You go to the car. I have something to take care of before we leave." She spun on her heel and made a bee-line for Jake.

"I understand you and a secretary paid a call on my aunt," she said, poking him in the shoulder. "She's not to have visitors. If you want to see her, you come ask me. Otherwise, leave her alone."

Jake looked down at her, his eyes glittering angrily.

"Can't do it, Steffi. I was there on official business. I don't need your permission."

"We'll just see about that," she muttered as she stalked away. First thing Tuesday, after the Labor Day holiday, she'd be calling her lawyer.

She turned to look back and shot eye daggers, but they were wasted. She saw, with more than a little alarm, Ben Lightfoot say something to Jake and the big man's head jerked up. Ben had Jake's total attention.

"I'm not sure, but there may have been a man about to swoop up little Megan, there," Ben whispered.

Jake felt fear coil in his gut.

Would you know him if you saw him again?" Jake wanted to know.

Ben shook his head. "I can't be sure. He was wearing sunglasses and such. Looked pretty much like a lot of the men around here."

Jake turned on his heel and stalked off in search of Del. If there was a creep prowling around, he wanted his officers to be on the alert.

Ben sauntered over to where his party sat under a massive oak tree. Charlie raised his head, gave a thump with his tail and went back to snoozing.

"Where did Jake go?" Helen asked.

Ben shrugged. "Had to see to his guys, I guess." He plopped down on a blanket next to Helen and grinned at her.

"You know, for an old broad, you still have all the moves."

Helen raised an elegant eyebrow and gave him the once over. "You're not so bad yourself."

Ben laughed, got to his feet and took her hand, drawing her up next to him.

"Ready for another round?" He began to lead her away from the group.

Jill grinned.

"That's nice to see," she said to the Brentwoods. "It would be nice if something developed between those two. They look so right together."

Lavinia reached over and gently swatted Jill on the back of her head. "Don't you be matchmaking, missy!" she warned.

"No! I'm not! It's just… Helen's alone and Ben's alone and it would be nice if they each had somebody."

Megan and Bree arriving at that moment saved anyone from saying anything more.

"Mom!" Megan grabbed Jill's hand and tugged. "We're starving!"

Jill got to her feet and took Bree's hand and began to lead them toward the food tents.

"Hold up. I'm starving, too," Jake called out. Walking over, he took each little girl's hand.

"Well, wait for us! We're starving, too!" Marcus said as he and Lavinia joined them.

Lavinia smiled a slow, sweet smile. She wondered if Jillian and Jake realized just what a stunning couple they made.

She thought Jill's petite frame and Jake's broad-shouldered build complimented each other. Wisely, she held her tongue. Lavinia decided it would be fun to sit back and watch the fun. Grinning at Marcus, she took his hand and walked with him into the food tent.

"I not only want a Corn Dog, but that pulled barbeque pork looks divine, too. Oh, and don't forget the potato salad!"

Sitting down, she looked around. Yes, she decided, this event was just what the doctor ordered. She was so glad they came.

Steffi drove down Ransom Road toward Jill's home, her mind racing.

Jake's words swirled around in her brain. He visited his aunt on 'official business'. It had to do with her. Granted, her lawyer said it was fool-proof, but he could be wrong.

Jake had to have gotten wind of her schemes and knew she had defrauded dear old Aunty Roberta. What other reason was there for any conversation with her aunt and the sheriff.

Fear nestled in her gut. She was afraid time was running out. Maybe, she should just cut her losses and get the hell out of Molton, out of Wisconsin and maybe out of the country all together.

There was still enough in the account to get her away from all of this unpleasantness and give her a fresh start.

She slid a glance toward Noah, who sat beside her, stewing in his own angry juices.

She considered and then discarded the notion she could get some money out of him. He's too unpredictable, she decided. She would take him here and, once they were back in her condo, she'd tell him he was on his own.

With any kind of luck, she would be out of the country by the end of the coming week.

As for dear old Aunty, well, she'd have to leave that nice cushy home and probably end up in a county home somewhere.

It didn't matter. The woman was old anyway and past her usefulness. The day belonged to the young, and Steffi decided she was definitely young.

Steffi concentrated on her plans and left Noah alone.

Noah, for his part, stewed in the white heat of his anger. Jillian had escaped him and with her went all of her money.

The two brats she birthed had escaped him and, with them, all hope of ever getting his hands on Jill's money.

Seeing the big lawman with his family really pissed him off. If Jillian and her hick cop got together, the man would have all that money at his disposal.

Bottom line, Noah was out and there wasn't a blessed thing he could do about it. Or so they thought. He'd just see about that. He'd damn well see.

His attention turned to the woman driving. She's bossy and demeaning. He didn't like women telling him what to do. He liked to be in charge and, tonight, Steffi would find out just what that meant. He was done taking orders from her. After tonight, he'd be back in charge if she liked it or not.

Steffi pulled into the drive and parked. "We'll walk up from here," she told him. "I'll leave the car here so we can get away quickly."

Noah shrugged. "Sure and if they come home early, they're going to see your car sitting here, but I'm sure they won't notice."

Steffi narrowed her eyes at him, started her car and backed into a small clearing across the road.

"There! Satisfied?" she asked. Noah didn't answer her. She'd get her answer later when he had her cornered; when she couldn't run. Where there'd be no witnesses.

Moving together, each lost in their own thoughts, they began the climb, using the outside stairs. Steffi took the lead and pointed. "This would be the master suite." Noah peered in and recognized some of Jillian's personal items. "She'd keep the brats close to her," he said.

Steffi checked the next set of doors. The occupants were obviously mature. "No kids stuff in here." She moved to the next set of doors, peered in and turned away, cursing. "This is Jake's new abode."

"Found it," Noah sang out as he tried the door. It swung open and he stepped in.

Hands on his hips, he looked around, a deep frown on his face.

"Look at all the loot those brats have. She cuts me off with nothing and spends wads of dough on those two worthless little brats!"

Noah continued to grumble as Steffi came up behind him and, at that moment, all hell broke loose.

The wind came up, fast and wicked, plastering them both against a wall.

The specter came at them, his face contorted with rage, his eyes bulging with hate.

"What the hell?" Noah called out, trying to force his way away from the wall. The thing in front of him raised claw-like hands and forced him back.

Steffi, tears of fright coursing down her cheeks, tried to make it to the open door. She was almost there when it slammed shut, trapping her.

They couldn't breathe. The fierce wind seemed to suck the breath out of them, and their bodies were racked by the icy texture of it. Toys flew around the room, slamming into the two intruders and the smell of cigarette smoke overwhelmed them.

Noah forced his head to the side, trying to see Steffi. He could just make out her wide, terrified eyes as they met his through the swirling and flying toys and dust.

"We've got to get out of here," Steffi called out, fighting the wind. "We've got to move!"

"Yeah? How? I'm open to suggestions." The last thing Noah wanted was to be caught in this house. He'd go back to jail and he didn't like jail.

"I have an idea." Steffi bit her lip, thinking fast.

"Uncle Gray! I know it's you. You blame me for taking Aunt Alberta away! I had to! Now the woman living here stole the house from me! Be angry, but not at me! I'll get the house back and I'll bring Aunt Alberta back! I promise!"

The wind died down and Steffi and Noah were able to move. They dashed toward the door, yanked it open and fled outside.

"What the hell was that?" Noah asked again.

Steffi shook her head. "I think we just met my dearly departed Uncle Gray and, if he believed me, we have an ally."

"You're saying that was a ghost?" Noah scoffed and Steffi met him head-on.

"You were there, Noah! What the hell did you think it was? We may be able to kill two birds with one stone. Gray can work against your ex-wife, we can work against your ex-wife and we both get what we want. Money, honey. Enough money to last us a lifetime."

"You think it believed you?" Noah asked and Steffi gave him a cold grin.

"Of course it did. Gray released us, didn't he? Really, Noah, you are so stupid."

As they walked back to her car, they didn't realize they were being followed.

The ride back to town was quiet and tense. They didn't speak of their experience. They didn't speak, at all.

Steffi led the way into her condo. She poured both of them a stiff drink and sank into an overstuffed chair. She was still trying to wrap her mind around the experience and wondering just how they could use it.

How does one convince a ghost, an angry ghost, to help them rip off the interloper in his home?

She decided to give it a rest. Just let her mind relax and wait. The answer would come to her. It always did.

She slid a glance at Noah and sneered. Deep in thought, he absentmindedly sipped his drink.

He saw it. He experienced it. He saw that thing come out of nowhere. He couldn't believe it. He doubted there was enough Scotch in the whole world to drown out that terrifying experience, but damn if he wasn't going to try.

Noah drank, and he drank heavily. He drank more than he had ever drank before.

It was unfortunate that Steffi chose that particular time to start in on him.

"Go ahead!" She shot him a disgusted look. "Drink until you puke! Then you better get your head together because we're gonna move on those girls tomorrow night!"

"Shut up!" Noah growled. His bloodshot eyes sparkled with ire. "Just shut your mouth!"

"Don't tell me to shut up, you worthless drunk. All I hear from you is how she cheated you! Well guess what, fool! I've been cheated, too."

Noah stood. He had finished one bottle of Cutty's and was starting on the second. He weaved his way over to her and stood over her, daring her to utter another word.

"Get away from me, Noah! You don't scare me! You don't scare anyone except that mealy-mouthed ex-wife of yours and even she managed to beat you!"

Steffi laughed in his face and Noah reared back, swung his open hand and caught her on the side of her face.

Her hand came up and she got to her feet. "I warned you, asshole! I told you to never lay a hand on me, again!" Steffi brought her hand back and let him have it with everything she had in her.

Noah's head reeled and then he saw red. His hands came up to wrap themselves around her throat, and the last thing he heard before everything went black was the woman screaming.

Twenty-Four

*J*ake and Jill's phones both went off at the same time. As they flipped their phones, Marcus came running up with his phone extended.

Jill noticed the usually unflappable Marcus Brentwood was shaken right down to his feet. He almost threw his phone into Jake's free hand.

Jill answered her own phone, and Jake watched as her face went bone white.

"We have your girls." The whisper was so low she couldn't catch all the words at first.

"What?"

The voice came again. "We have your girls. Better get home fast and leave the cop behind."

"You're lying!" Jill said.

"Am I? Then, listen."

Jill's heart sank as she heard a loud slap and Bree's scream.

"I'm coming. Don't hurt them! Please don't hurt them!"

"Jill?" Marcus reached for her as she clicked off her phone. She shook her head. Her face was ashen.

"He has my kids, Uncle Marc! Noah has my kids!" She spun away and ran on legs filled with jelly. A vein throbbed in her throat, and her breath clogged her lungs.

Jake, his phone clamped to one ear, Marcus's phone clamped to his other, tried to stop her.

He listened intently to the caller on his phone then began to bark orders.

"Secure the crime scene. Cuff the suspect! No one goes in. Put your brother, Dan, and Bill Whitman in charge and get your ass over here! Meet me on Main Street. I don't have my vehicle! We have a situation out at the Tolivar place!"

He clicked off his phone and concentrated on the caller on the other phone.

"You're sure?" he asked. He was running toward the street, Marcus hot on his heels.

"Jake! Noah has Jill's girls!" The old man's breath was coming in gasps. Terror rode his back with spiked hooves.

He grabbed Jake's arm and gave it a shake. "Did you hear what I said? Noah has the girls!"

Jake clicked off the phone and handed it back to Marcus as his long legs ate up the ground through the crowd, making his way to Main Street.

He could see the light bars of Del's car flashing red and blue, and he lengthened his stride.

"It's not Noah," he told Marcus. "We've got him in custody. Steffi Brandt is dead, and he was found standing over her body with a blood-covered pipe wrench in his hand. We know who's responsible for everything, Judge, and it's not Noah!"

Lavinia and Helen rushed to Marcus. Lavinia grabbed her husband's arm and shook it to get his attention.

"What's going on? What's happening?"

Marcus scrubbed his face before turning to his wife.

"He has the girls and it appears Steffi Brandt has been murdered. They found Noah standing over her body. To top it all off, Jill's girls have been taken."

"If not Noah, then who?" Lavinia gave her husband's arm a shake. "Who?"

"If the city cops are correct, only one person is responsible for all of it. Devin's death. The fire that killed Jill's parents. Even the Brandt woman's death. He's responsible for all of it."

"Who?" Lavinia asked, and his answer brought her to her knees.

Jill raced home, one prayer on her lips. "Please, God, don't let him hurt my babies."

She repeated the litany over again until she skidded into her drive.

Racing up the outside stairs, she ran along the verandah, intent on reaching her children.

The smell of cigarette smoke overwhelmed her as she came up against a wall of sheer ice. She couldn't get through it and she couldn't get around it.

Panic swamped her as she sobbed. She batted at the invisible wall, desperately trying to get in.

He materialized in front of her, shook his head and pointed. He led her downstairs and around to her back door. The door she was so sure she had locked swung open.

He stood in front of her, put his fingers to his lips and motioned her in.

She followed the shimmery figure to the main stairway and, at his insistence, began to climb the wide stairs as quietly as possible.

If it struck Jill as odd that she was gaining the assistance of a ghost, she knew she couldn't dwell on that now. Not with her babies at risk.

She made it as far as the first landing when she saw the flesh and blood man standing between herself and her babies. She would have been relieved, but she saw the gun he held in one hand and the rope in the other.

"Ben? What are you doing?"

He would have laughed at the bewilderment on her face, but this was serious business and he didn't think he had much time.

"Come on up here, Jillian. Don't try to run. If you run, I'll kill them."

"What? Why?" Jill shook her head, trying to clear the fog of terror that nestled in her brain.

"Why? God! Noah's right about you! You are stupid." He motioned with the gun for her to advance. She took two more steps on leaden feet.

"Why are you doing this?" Keep his eyes on you, she told herself. Keep him talking until someone came home.

"Why? Seriously?" he sighed and motioned again. She took two more steps, then stopped.

"Did you kill my parents, too?" She had to know.

"Well, of course. Did you really think that drunk you married could have pulled it off?" Ben snorted in disgust.

"Why?" she asked again, stopping on the stairs.

"Why? The money, little girl. Your dad had all that money. He should have made me a partner. I worked myself to the bone for him!" Bitterness spilled out of every pore. "But would he take my hints seriously? No. Everything he did was for you and your girls. God! I hated hearing your name. You all made me sick. So, I cut your parents out just like you'd cut out a cancer. Now you and your brats are in my way, again. Time to cut you out, too."

He's crazy, Jill thought. Crazy and dangerous. If ever she needed to use her brain, it was now.

"What about Devin? What did he do to you?" she spat out.

"Oh, Devin. Well, he knew something was fishy. He gave me an odd look at the reading of the will. I couldn't take any chances, you see. He had to die. Pity that nutso wife of his didn't die, too. The nice thing is, Noah fed her enough lies to keep her off-kilter and made sure she'd lose her mind. She's out of the way for now but, sooner or later, I'll get around to her. I plan on getting rid of the nosy judge and his interfering wife, too. Just to be safe."

Jill opened her mouth, but Ben cut her off. "No more questions, little girl. Get your ass up here! *Now!*"

Slowly, Jill ascended the stairway. There would be no help coming. She and her daughters would die.

Bree and Megan felt icy fingers on their little wrists, pulling on the ropes that bound them. As if by magic, the ropes fell away, as did the ones tied around their tiny ankles.

Free, they stood up and looked around. Bad Ben was no longer in the room with them. They should run, but where should they run to?

The door in their sitting room swung open to the outside and they could see the Cigarette Man, a name Bree secretly gave him, standing on the verandah, beckoning to them.

They quickly followed him as he led them down the outside stairs and into the field. He pointed to the old barn. *Run* echoed through their minds, and they took off as fast as their little legs could go.

They followed his faint form to the old barn. He pointed at a panel and a small door swung open.

"Stay here," he told them in his odd, echoing and hollow voice. "Just stay here."

"Are you going to help mom?" Megan asked, clutching Bree's hand. Tears stained her cheeks.

He looked at Bree, saw the bruise on her face, and his distinctive blue eyes flashed.

He looked at the two little figures, now huddled in the hiding place he built all those years ago, and his features softened.

He smiled and then he was gone.

Ben followed Jillian into the girls' sitting room. The *empty* sitting room. The ropes he used lying limply on the floor.

"Where are they?" She watched as Ben stormed around the room. His face burned an ugly purple, and his eyes bulged.

A vein throbbed in his forehead, and Jill hoped he would have a stroke.

"Where the hell are they?" Ben was screaming, and Jill folded her arms in satisfaction. Somehow, her babies were free.

A movement to the right of the house caught her eye and she saw the girls running to the old barn. They would be safe.

Before that penetrated the fog in her brain, she caught sight of Jake and Del sneaking up to the house.

Ben was out of control, and this was her one chance to get the hell out of here.

Spinning on her heel, she raced through the door and down the hall to the back staircase. If she could make it down those stairs, she could run out the kitchen door.

A shot rang out, and Jillian felt the bullet whiz past her ear. She poured on the speed and kept on going.

"Get back here, you little bitch!" Ben was hot on her heels.

Another shot rang out, this time grazing her shoulder, and Jill kept on running.

Down the stairs she ran and, with a burst of speed, almost made it to the back door, when a third bullet embedded itself in the door.

"Next shot won't miss, Jillian," he called out and she sensed, rather than heard, him pull the hammer back.

She stopped and looked at him, expecting Ben to be right behind her. He stood at the top of the stairs, sure of himself and sure that she would obey him.

"Drop the gun, Lightfoot!" Jake burst in through the kitchen door, his own weapon drawn.

Jillian's legs wanted to give way, but seeing the sick hatred burning in Ben's eyes, she wouldn't give him the satisfaction.

"I said drop it!" Jake called out again. In answer, Ben raised his gun, drew a bead on Jillian and squeezed the trigger.

At that moment, Del flew toward him, his weapon drawn as well. Del's heart sank. He'd never be able to take this madman before he got off his next shot.

Everything happened in a flurry of movement.

Jake yanked Jillian behind him, prepared to take the bullet meant for her.

Del dived at Ben, hoping he could bring Ben down before he did anymore damage. Del missed, swearing as he hit the hardwood floor.

The attempt, although heroic, was unnecessary.

A shadowy figure rose up behind Ben.

"What the hell?" Ben gasped and the next moment, he was clawing at air as the shadow man sent him flying all the way down the steep staircase.

Jake pushed Jillian out of the back door before walking over to where Ben lay, face down. He reached out and felt for a pulse. There was none.

"He's dead, Del. Better get the coroner out here and get a team going."

Jake went in search of Jillian. He found her huddled next to the backdoor.

"Where are the girls, Jill?"

She looked at him with haunted eyes and shook her head. "I think they're in the old barn. That's where they were headed, I think."

Jake glanced around as the Brentwood's vehicle roared up to the house. Helen, Lavinia and Marcus piled out and dashed to Jill's side.

"Stay with her. I'm going to find Bree and Megan," Jake told them.

"What the hell went on out here, Jill?" Lavinia asked as she bundled Jill into a tight hug.

"Ben was going to kill me and the girls," Jill said through shaking lips. "He was all about the money." She looked over at Marcus. "He killed my parents and Devin. It's always been about money for him."

Lavinia held her as the sobs took over.

Jake walked into the old barn and looked around. He checked the upper floor but couldn't find them.

A noise on the floor below him had a cold feeling in the pit of his stomach.

The vision pointed at a panel, smiled and disappeared, once again.

Jake pressed the panel and it swung open, revealing Bree and Megan huddled together. He could have cried with relief as he reached in for those two precious babies.

"C'mon sweeties. Let's go find your mom." He boosted them both up into his powerful arms and headed back toward the house.

Jill saw him coming, her two precious babies in those strong arms.

Bree and Megan spied her and wiggled down. "Mom!" Megan called out and the sound was music to her ears.

She stepped away from Lavinia and then was running toward her girls, a prayer of thanksgiving on her lips.

Hugging them close to her, she rained kisses on their sweet little faces, then turned to Jake and gave him a hard hug.

"Thank you, Jake! Thank you!"

She turned back to her girls and, taking them each by the hand, she led them over to where Marcus, Lavinia and Helen waited.

"You can't go back in the house. Not until my people are done with it. Maybe, call Mary Lee and head over there," Jake said. "I can't stay. We have a homicide, and I'm needed to straighten out the mess."

Jake leaned down and gently brushed his lips against Jill's. "I'll be back," he promised.

"We'll go stay at the motel in town," Lavinia informed him. "That's where you'll find us."

It was in the wee hours of the morning that Jake knocked on Jillian's motel room door. She answered quickly, before Charlie could raise the alarm.

He looks so tired, she thought.

"Sorry it's so late. I can come by later if you want. Fact is, I should have just taken a room for myself and not bothered you at all. I don't know what I was thinking."

Jill handed him a key. "No need. We got one for you, too," she told him. He nodded. "Thanks. God, thanks."

"What's happened?" she asked and he waved his hand.

"Just let me rest for a little bit and then we'll get the others up. I only want to explain this once."

He was asleep as soon as his head hit the pillow.

Unsure what to do, Jill crawled in next to the girls sleeping on the other bed and allowed herself to drift off.

Pounding on her motel room door brought Jill to wide awake. She opened the door to see Del standing there, dangling her house keys.

"We're done now if you all want to go home," he said. He looked over her shoulder and grinned. "Hey, Boss," he said as Jake lumbered over. "Just telling Ms. Tolivar her house is open and she can go home."

Jake nodded and ran a hand through his hair. "Sounds good, Del. I'll be in a little later."

Jill looked into Jake's eyes, a million questions in her own.

"Let's get everyone together. I'll explain once I get some coffee in me," he said.

Sitting in Jill's kitchen, the kids headed up into their sitting room after breakfast. It amazed Jill how fast her kids were bouncing back from their experience.

"It seems like the whole world has gone crazy." Helen remarked, waiting for Jake to get his thoughts in order.

"That's a fact," Jake agreed. "I'll start with the easiest part of this, first." He sipped his coffee, took a deep breath and dived in.

"First, Steffi Brandt was murdered yesterday. Someone called in about a disturbance at her condo. When Del got there, she was dead, beaten with a pipe wrench. A man was with her. That man happened to be Noah Tolivar."

Jill's face paled, and she brought a shaking hand to her forehead.

"Hold on, Jill. There's more," Jake said.

Jill nodded but she felt sick.

"He's gonna sit for a while for breaking the No Contact Order. He admitted he was stalking you and the girls, so he's on his way back to the city, but he didn't kill Steffi."

"Ben?" Lavinia asked. Jake nodded and drew in a deep breath.

"Seems that old Ben lost his mind somewhere along the line. He felt he was entitled to Jill's family's estate. He murdered her parents to get to the money and planned to get rid of Jill and her girls. We got this from a Catherine Hydel. She's Ben's sister and here's where it gets complicated, so bear with me."

Jake sipped more coffee, buying a little time to get his thoughts in order.

"The detectives in the city still had no idea who killed Jill's folks and Ben thought he would get away with it. One thing about killers, though. They can't seem to be able to keep their mouths shut. So, he confides in his sister. On second thought, he decided that wasn't such a hot idea, so he breaks into her house and starts to strangle her. Her husband comes home unexpectedly, gets Ben away from her, knocks him out and calls the cops.

Ben's booked and because of certain laws on the books down in Kentucky, they take a DNA sample." Jake slid a glance at Jill. "When you couldn't reach him, he was a guest of the Louisville cops. Through a screw-up, he's released and makes a bee-line back to Wisconsin. His work wasn't finished, you see. Anyway, moving along. Devin is run off the road with tragic consequences, but ol' Ben, he gets sloppy. The cops found the truck he boosted to run them off the road. There was trace evidence and once they got a profile, entered it into CODIS. That's a data base with felon's DNA results." Jake sipped more coffee and kicked out his long legs.

"They got a hit and the DNA came back to Ben. That's when the city cops called me. By that time, he killed Steffi, snatched your girls and made his famous phone call to get you out here, alone. Only, he never took Del into consideration. Del looked at the scene, and it was too easy. Noah standing there with the pipe wrench in his hand, Steffi dead and all the rest. But Del, who is worth ten times what I'm paying him, starts nosing around and demands the wrench be finger printed. Sure enough, Noah's prints are on the damn thing, but so are Ben's. Del also found Ben's prints on the window he jimmied to get into her condo. And you know the rest."

Everyone was quiet for a moment.

"All for money," Jill said.

"What's going to happen to Alberta Peterson?" Helen asked.

Jake shrugged. "Steffi went through her money like a force five hurricane. There's nothing left, so she'll probably have to go into a county home."

"Will she," Jill said. She got to her feet. "I've got work to do."

Once Jake, Marcus and the two women caught on to what Jill was about, they joined in. In less than two hours, Jill had her house re-organized. Ben's things were removed. "I never want to see anything remotely connected with him," she announced. Everyone agreed with her.

Jill dressed carefully and went in search of Jake.

"I have an errand in town. Will you come with me?"

"Sure! As it happens, I'm taking the next couple of days off."

Alberta Gray sat in her chair, gazing out her window.

"Hello, Ms. Gray," Jill called out softly. "How are you doing this morning?"

Alberta shrugged. "They came and told me about Steffi. I wish I could say I had some good memories of her, but I don't. She was always greedy and spoiled, and I knew it. I'm ashamed I confided in her at all, but I thought she had changed. She didn't."

Alberta peered up at Jake. "Have you come to evict me?" she asked.

Jake shook his head. "No, ma'am."

Alberta gazed out the window again. "You might as well do so. I'm told I'm broke. I have nowhere else to go, and I can't stay here."

Jill sat down and took the elderly lady's hand. "Yes you do have somewhere else to go. You're coming home with me, where you belong."

Alberta's head snapped around, and she met Jill eye to eye.

"You can't be serious! You don't even know me! Why would you take a complete stranger into your home."

Jill rubbed the frail hand she held. "Because it's your home, too. Because it's the right thing to do. And you know what else? We won't be strangers for long. Helen tells me you make the best candy. I need your help. We're hosting the school Halloween party out at the place. You can make your candy, Helen and Lavinia will be whipping up their special treats, and I need all the chaperones I can get. I also have two girls who are going to love you to pieces."

Neither mentioned the ghost of Gray Peterson, but he was very much on their minds.

Jake offered his arm.

"Ladies? Shall we go?"

"What about my things?" Alberta asked. Lavinia and Helen swooped in and began packing. Alberta laughed, reached out and patted Jill's shoulder.

"Looks like you've got this all planned out," she said. Jill hugged the slight woman and smiled.

"Yes, yes I do."

About the Author

House On Ransom Road is Karen Salamone-Jourdan's third book, following Gabriel's Gate and Redemption.

A product of early Catholic education, and then, the Milwaukee Public school system, she found the joys of reading at an early age.

Since retiring, she has used the time to follow her first love; writing.

She is the mother of two and resides in Ripon, Wisconsin with her cat, SweetPea.

Stay tuned for many more works!